TWO PENNILESS PRINCESSES

By Charlotte M. Yonge

CHAPTER 1. DUNBAR

"Twas on a night, an evening bright
  When the dew began to fa',
Lady Margaret was walking up and down,
  Looking over her castle wa'.'

The battlements of a castle were, in disturbed times, the only recreation-ground of the ladies and play-place of the young people. Dunbar Castle, standing on steep rocks above the North Sea, was not only inaccessible on that side, but from its donjon tower commanded a magnificent view, both of the expanse of waves, taking purple tints from the shadows of the clouds, with here and there a sail fleeting before the wind, and of the rugged headlands of the coast, point beyond point, the nearer distinct, and showing the green summits, and below, the tossing waves breaking white against the dark rocks, and the distance becoming more and more hazy, in spite of the bright sun which made a broken path of glory along the tossing, white-crested waters.

The wind was a keen north-east breeze, and might have been thought too severe by any but the 'hardy, bold, and wild' children who were merrily playing on the top of the donjon tower, round the staff whence fluttered the double treasured banner with 'the ruddy lion ramped in gold' denoting the presence of the King.

Three little boys, almost babies, and a little girl not much older, were presided over by a small elder sister, who held the youngest in her lap, and tried to amuse him with caresses and rhymes, so as to prevent his interference with the castle-building of the others, with their small hoard of pebbles and mussel and cockle shells.

Another maiden, the wind tossing her long chestnut-locks, uncovered, but tied with the Scottish snood, sat on the battlement, gazing far out over the waters, with eyes of the same tint as the hair. Even the sea-breeze failed to give more than a slight touch of colour to her somewhat freckled complexion; and the limbs that rested in a careless attitude on the stone bench were long and languid, though with years and favourable circumstances there might be a development of beauty and dignity. Her lips were crooning at intervals a mournful old Scottish tune, sometimes only humming, sometimes uttering its melancholy burthen, and she now and then touched a small harp that stood by her side on the seat.

She did not turn round when a step approached, till a hand was laid on her shoulder, when she started, and looked up into the face of another girl, on a smaller scale, with a complexion of the lily-and-rose kind, fair hair under her hood, with a hawk upon her wrist, and blue eyes dancing at the surprise of her sister.

'Eleanor in a creel, as usual!' she cried.

'I thought it was only one of the bairns,' was the answer.

'They might coup over the walls for aught thou seest,' returned the new-comer. 'If it were not for little Mary what would become of the poor weans?'

'What will become of any of us?' said Eleanor. 'I was gazing out over the sea and wishing we could drift away upon it to some land of rest.'

'The Glenuskie folk are going to try another land,' said Jean. 'I was in the bailey-court even now playing at ball with Jamie when in comes a lay-brother, with a letter from Sir Patrick to say that he is coming the night to crave permission from Jamie to go with his wife to France. Annis, as you know, is betrothed to the son of his French friends, Malcolm is to study at the Paris University, and Davie to be in the Scottish Guards to learn chivalry like his father. And the Leddy of Glenuskie—our Cousin Lilian—is going with them.'

'And she will see Margaret,' said Eleanor. 'Meg the dearie! Dost remember Meg, Jeanie?'

'Well, well do I remember her, and how she used to let us nestle in her lap and sing to us. She sang like thee, Elleen, and was as mother-like as Mary is to the weans, but she was much blithesomer—at least before our father was slain.'

'Sweetest Meg! My whole heart leaps after her,' cried Eleanor, with a fervent gesture.

'I loved her better than Isabel, though she was not so bonnie,' said Jean.

'Jeanie, Jeanie,' cried Eleanor, turning round with a vehemence strangely contrasting with her previous language, 'wherefore should we not go with Glenuskie to be with Meg at Bourges?'

Jeanie opened her blue eyes wide.

'Go to the French King's Court?' she said.

'To the land of chivalry and song,' exclaimed Eleanor, 'where they have courts of love and poetry, and tilts and tourneys and minstrelsy, and the sun shines as it never does in this cold bleak north; and above all there is Margaret, dear tender Margaret, almost a queen, as a queen she will be one day. Oh! I almost feel her embrace.'

'It might be well,' said Jean, in the matter-of-fact tone of a practical young lady; 'mewed up in these dismal castles, we shall never get princely husbands like our sisters. I might be Queen of Beauty, I doubt me whether you are fair enough, Eleanor.'

'Oh, that is not what I think of,' said Eleanor. 'It is to see our own Margaret, and to see and hear the minstrel knights, instead of the rude savages here, scarce one of whom knows what knighthood means!'

'Ay, and they will lay hands on us and wed us one of these days,' returned Jean, 'unless we vow ourselves as nuns, and I have no mind for that.'

'Nor would a convent always guard us,' said Eleanor; 'these reivers do not stick at sanctuary. Now in that happy land ladies meet with courtesy, and there is a minstrel king like our father, Rene is his name, uncle to Margaret's husband. Oh! it would be a very paradise.'

'Let us go, let us go!' exclaimed Jean.

'Go!' said Mary, who had drawn nearer to them while they spoke. 'Whither did ye say?'

'To France—to sister Margaret and peace and sunshine,' said Eleanor.

'Eh!' said the girl, a pale fair child of twelve; 'and what would poor Jamie and the weans do, wanting their titties?'

'Ye are but a bairn, Mary,' was Jean's answer. 'We shall do better for Jamie by wedding some great lords in the far country than by waiting here at home.'

'And James will soon have a queen of his own to guide him,' added Eleanor.

'I'll no quit Jamie or the weans,' said little Mary resolutely, turning back as the three-year-old boy elicited a squall from the eighteen-months one.

'Johnnie! Johnnie! what gars ye tak' away wee Andie's claw? Here, my mannie.'

And she was kneeling on the leads, making peace over the precious crab's claw, which, with a few cockles and mussels, was the choicest toy of these forlorn young Stewarts; for Stewarts they all were, though the three youngest, the weans, as they were called, were only half-brothers to the rest.

Nothing, in point of fact, could have been much more forlorn than the condition of all. The father of the elder ones, James I., the flower of the whole Stewart race, had nine years before fallen a victim to the savage revenge and ferocity of the lawless men whom he had vainly endeavoured to restrain, leaving an only son of six years old and six young daughters. His wife, Joanna, once the Nightingale of Windsor, had wreaked vengeance in so barbarous a manner as to increase the dislike to her as an Englishwoman. Forlorn and in danger, she tried to secure a protector by a marriage with Sir James Stewart, called the Black Knight of Lorn; but he was unable to do much for her, and only added the feuds of his own family to increase the general danger. The two eldest daughters, Margaret and Isabel, were already contracted to the Dauphin and the Duke of Brittany, and were soon sent to their new homes. The little King, the one darling of his mother, was snatched from her, and violently transferred from one fierce guardian to another; each regarding the possession of his person as a sanction to tyranny. He had been introduced to the two winsome young Douglases only as a prelude to their murder, and every day brought tidings of some fresh violence; nay, for the second time, a murder was perpetrated in the Queen's own chamber.

The poor woman had never been very tender or affectionate, and had the haughty demeanour with which the house of Somerset had thought fit to assert their claims to royalty. The cruel slaughter of her first husband, perhaps the only person for whom she had ever felt a softening love, had hardened and soured her. She despised and domineered over her second husband, and made no secret that the number of her daughters was oppressive, and that it was hard that while the royal branch had produced, with one exception, only useless pining maidens, her second marriage in too quick succession should bring her sons, who could only be a burthen. No one greatly marvelled when, a few weeks after the birth of little Andrew, his father disappeared, though whether he had perished in some brawl, been lost at sea, or sought foreign service as far as possible from his queenly wife and inconvenient family, no one knew.

Not long after, the Queen, with her four daughters and the infants, had been seized upon by a noted freebooter, Patrick Hepburn of Hailes, and carried to Dunbar Castle, probably to serve as hostages, for they were fairly well treated, though never allowed to go beyond the walls. The Queen's health had, however, been greatly shaken, the cold blasts of the north wind withered her up, and she died in the beginning of the year 1445.

The desolateness of the poor girls had perhaps been greater than their grief. Poor Joanna had been exacting and tyrannical, and with no female attendants but the old, worn-out English nurse, had made them do her all sorts of services, which were requited with scoldings and grumblings instead of the loving thanks which ought to have made them offices of affection as well as duty; while the poor little boys would indeed have fared ill if their half-sister Mary, though only twelve years old, had not been one of those girls who are endowed from the first with tender, motherly instincts.

Beyond providing that there was a supply of some sort of food, and that they were confined within the walls of the Castle, Hepburn did not trouble his head about his prisoners, and for many weeks they had no intercourse with any one save Archie Scott, an old groom of their mother's; Ankaret, nurse to baby Andrew; and the seneschal and his wife, both Hepburns.

Eleanor and Jean, who had been eight and seven years old at the time of the terrible catastrophe which had changed all their lives, had been well taught under their father's influence; and the former, who had inherited much of his talent and poetical nature, had availed herself of every scanty opportunity of feeding her imagination by book or ballad, story-teller or minstrel; and the store of tales, songs, and fancies that she had accumulated were not only her own chief resource but that of her sisters, in the many long and dreary hours that they had to pass, unbrightened save by the inextinguishable buoyancy of young creatures together. When their mother was dying, Hepburn could not help for very shame admitting a priest to her bedside, and allowing the clergy to perform her obsequies in full form. This had led to a more complete perception of the condition of the poor Princesses, just at the time when the two worst tyrants over the young King, Crichton and Livingstone, had fallen out, and he had been able to put himself under the guidance of his first cousin, James Kennedy, Bishop of St. Andrews and now Chancellor of Scotland, one of the wisest, best, and truest-hearted men in Scotland, and imbued with the spirit of the late King.

By his management Hepburn was induced to make submission and deliver up Dunbar Castle to the King with all its captives, and the meeting between the brother and sisters was full of extreme delight on both sides. They had been together very little since their father's death, only meeting enough to make them long for more opportunities; and the boy at fifteen years old was beginning to weary after the home feeling of rest among kindred, and was so happy amidst his sisters that no attempt at breaking up the party at Dunbar had yet been made, as its situation made it a convenient abode for the Court. Though he had never had such advantages of education as, strangely enough, captivity had afforded to his father, he had not been untaught, and his rapid, eager, intelligent mind had caught at all opportunities afforded by those palace monasteries of Scotland in which he had stayed for various periods of his vexed and stormy minority. Good Bishop Kennedy, with whom he had now spent many months, had studied at Paris and had passed four years at Rome, so as to be well able both to enlarge and stimulate his notions. In Eleanor he had found a companion delighted to share his studies, and full likewise of original fancy and of that vein of poetry almost peculiar to

Scottish women; and Jean was equally charming for all the sports in which she could take part, while the little ones, whom, to his credit be it spoken, he always treated as brothers, were pleasant playthings.

His presence, with all that it involved, had made a most happy change in the maidens' lives; and yet there was still great dreariness, much restraint in the presence of constant precaution against violence, much rudeness and barbarism in the surroundings, absolute poverty in the plenishing, a lack of all beauty save in the wild and rugged face of northern nature, and it was hardly to be wondered at that young people, inheritors of the cultivated instincts of James I. and of the Plantagenets, should yearn for something beyond, especially for that sunny southern land which report and youthful imagination made them believe an ideal world of peace, of poetry, and of chivalry, and the loving elder sister who seemed to them a part of that golden age when their noble and tender-hearted father was among them.

The boy's foot was on the turret-stairs, and he was out on the battlements—a tall lad for his age, of the same colouring as Eleanor, and very handsome, except for the blemish of a dark-red mark upon one cheek.

'How now, wee Andie?' he exclaimed, tossing the baby boy up in his arms, and then on the cry of 'Johnnie too!' 'Me too!' performing the same feat with the other two, the last so boisterously that Mary screamed that 'the bairnie would be coupit over the crag.'

'What, looking out over the sea?' he cried to his elder sisters. 'That's the wrang side! Ye should look out on the other, to see Glenuskie coming with Davie and Malcolm, so we'll have no lack of minstrelsy and tales to-night, that is if the doited old council will let me alone. Here, come to the southern tower to watch for them.'

The sisters had worked themselves to the point of eagerness where propitious moments are disregarded, and both broke out—

'Glenuskie is going to Margaret. We want to go with him!'

'Go! Go to Margaret and leave me!' cried James, the red spot on his face spreading.

'Oh, Jamie, it is so dull and dreary, and folks are so fierce and rude.'

'That might be when that loon Hepburn had you, but now you have me, who can take order with them.'

'You cannot do all, Jamie,' persisted Eleanor; 'and we long after that fair smooth land of peace. Lady Glenuskie would take good care of us till we came to Margaret.'

'Ay! And 'tis little you heed how it is with me,' exclaimed James, 'when you are gone to your daffing and singing and dancing—with me that have saved you from that reiver Hepburn.'

'Jamie, dear, I'll never quit ye,' said little Mary's gentle voice.

He laughed.

'You are a leal faithful little lady, Mary; but you are no good as yet, when Angus is speiring for my sister for his heir.'

'And do you trow,' said Jean hotly, 'that when one sister is to be a queen, and the other is next thing to it, we are going to put up with a raw-boned, red-haired, unmannerly Scots earl?'

'And do you forget who is King of Scotland, ye proud peat?' her brother cried in return.

'A braw sort of king,' returned Jean, 'who could not hinder his mother and sisters from being stolen by an outlaw.'

The pride and hot temper of the Beauforts had descended to both brother and sister, and James lifted his hand with 'Dare to say that again'; and Jean was beginning 'I dare,' when little Annaple opportunely called, 'There's a plump of spears coming over the hill.'

There was an instant rush to watch them, James saying—

'The Drummond banner! Ye shall see how Glenuskie mocks at this same fine fancy of yours'; and he ran downstairs at no kingly pace, letting the heavy nail-studded door bang after him.

'He will never let us go,' sighed Jean.

'You worked him into one of his tempers,' returned Eleanor. 'You should have broached it to him more by degrees.'

'And lost the chance of going with Sir Patie and his wife, and got plighted to the red-haired Master of Angus—never see sweet Meg and her braw court, and the tilts and tourneys, but live among murderous caitiffs and reivers all my days,' sobbed Jean.

'I would not be such a fule body as to give in for a hasty word or two, specially of Jamie's,' said Eleanor composedly.

'And gin ye bide here,' added gentle Mary, 'we shall be all together, and you will have Jamie and the bairnies.'

'Fine consolation,' muttered Jean.

'Eh well,' said Eleanor, we must go down and meet them.'

'This fashion!' exclaimed Jean. 'Look at your hair, Ellie—blown wild about your ears like a daft woman's, and your kirtle all over mortar and smut. My certie, you would be a bonnie lady to be Queen of Love and Beauty at a jousting-match.'

'You are no better, Jeanie,' responded Eleanor.

'That I ken full well, but I'd be shamed to show myself to knights and lairds that gate. And see Mary and all the lave have their hands as black as a caird's.'

'Come and let Andie's Mary wash them,' said that little personage, picking up fat Andrew in her arms, while he retained his beloved crab's claw. 'Jeanie, would you carry Johnnie, he's not sure-footed, over the stair? Annaple, take Lorn's hand over the kittle turning.'

One chamber was allotted to the entire party and their single nurse. Being far up in the tower, it ventured to have two windows in the massive walls, so thick that five-and-twenty steps from the floor were needed to reach the narrow slips of glass in a frame that could be removed at will, either to admit the air or to be exchanged for solid wooden shutters to exclude storms by sea or arrows and bolts by land. The lower part of the walls was hung with very grim old tapestry, on which Holofernes' head, going into its bag, could just be detected; there were two great solid box-beds, two more pallets rolled up for the day, a chest or two, a rude table, a cross-legged chair, a few stools, and some deer and seal skins spread on the floor completed the furniture of this ladies' bower. There was, unusual luxury, a chimney with a hearth and peat fire, and a cauldron on it, with a silver and a copper basin beside it for washing purposes, never discarded by poor Queen Joanna and her old English nurse Ankaret, who had remained beside her through all the troubles of the stormy and barbarous country, and, though crippled by a fall and racked with rheumatism, was the chief comfort of the young children. She crouched at the hearth with her spinning and her beads, and exclaimed at the tossed hair and soiled hands and faces of her charges.

Mary brought the little ones to her to be set to rights, and the elder girls did their best with their toilette. Princesses as they were, the ruddy golden tresses of Eleanor and the flaxen locks of Jean and Mary were the only ornaments that they could boast of as their own; and though there were silken and embroidered garments of their mother's in one of the chests, their mourning forbade the use of them. The girls only wore the plain black kirtles that had been brought from Haddington at the time of the funeral, and the little boys had such homespun garments as the shepherd lads wore.

Partly scolding, partly caressing, partly bemoaning the condition of her young ladies, so different from the splendours of the house of Somerset, Ankaret saw that Eleanor was as fit to be seen as circumstances would permit; as to Jean and Mary, there was no trouble on that score.

The whole was not accomplished till a horn was sounded as an intimation that supper was ready, at five o'clock, for the entire household, and all made their way down—Jean first, in all the glory of her fair face and beautiful hair; then Eleanor with little Lorn, as he was called, his Christian name being James; then Annaple and Johnnie hand-in-hand, Mary carrying Andrew, and lastly old Ankaret, hobbling along with her stick, and, when out of sight, a hand on Annaple's shoulder. In public, nothing would have made her presume so far. The hall was a huge, vaulted, stone-walled room, with a great fire on the wide hearth, and three long tables—one was cross-wise, on the dais near the fire, the other two ran the length of the hall. The upper one was furnished with tolerably clean napery and a few silver vessels; as to the lower ones, they were in two degrees of comparison, and the less said of the third the better. It was for the men-at-arms and the lowest servants, whereas the second belonged to those of the suite of the King and Chancellor, who were not of rank to be at his table. The Lord Lion King-at-Arms was high-table company, but he was absent, and the inferior royal pursuivant was entertaining two of his fellows, one with the Douglas Bloody Heart, the other with the Lindsay Lion on a black field, besides two messengers of the different clans, who looked askance at one another.

Leaning against the wall near the window stood the young King with two or three youths beside him, laughing and talking over three great deer-hounds, and by the hearth were two elder men—one, a tall dignified figure in the square cap and purple robe of a Bishop, with a face of great wisdom and sweetness; the other, still taller, with slightly grizzled hair and the weather-beaten countenance of a valiant and sagacious warrior, dressed in the leathern garments usually worn under armour.

As Jean emerged from the turret she was met and courteously greeted by Sir Patrick Drummond and his sons, as were also her sisters, with a grace and deference to their rank such as they hardly ever received from the nobles, and whose very rarity made Eleanor shy and uncomfortable, even while she was gratified and accepted it as her due.

The Bishop inclined his head and gave them a kind smile; but they had already seen him in the morning, as he was residing in the castle. He was the most fatherly friend and kinsman the young things knew, and though really their first cousin, they looked to him like an uncle. He insisted on due ceremony with them, though he had much difficulty in enforcing it, except with those Scottish knights and nobles who, like Sir Patrick Drummond, had served in France, and retained their French breeding.

So Jean, hawk and all, had to be handed to her seat by Sir Patrick as the guest, Eleanor by her brother, not without a little fraternal pinch, and Mary by the Bishop, who answered with a paternal caress to her murmured entreaty that she might keep wee Andie on her lap and give him his brose.

It was not a sumptuous repast, the staple being a haggis, also broth with chunks of meat and barleycorns floating in it, the meat in strings by force of boiling. At the high table each person had a bowl, either silver or wood, and each had a private spoon, and a dagger to serve as knife, also a drinking-cup of various materials, from the King's gold goblet downwards to horns, and a bannock to eat with the brose. At the middle table trenchers and bannocks served the purpose of plates; and at the third there was nothing interposed between the boards of the table and the lumps of meat from which the soup had been made.

Jean's quick eyes soon detected more men-at-arms and with different badges from the thyme spray of Drummond, and her brother was evidently bursting with some communication, held back almost forcibly by the Bishop, who had established a considerable influence over the impetuous boy, while Sir Patrick maintained a wise and tedious political conversation about the peace between France and England, which was to be cemented by the marriage of the young King of England to the daughter of King Rene and the cession of Anjou and Maine to her father.

'Solid dukedoms for a lassie!' cried young James. 'What a craven to make such a bargain!'

'Scarce like his father's son,' returned Sir Patrick, 'who gat the bride with a kingdom for her tocher that these folks have well-nigh lost among them.'

'The saints be praised if they have.'

'I cannot forget, my liege, how your own sainted father loved and fought for King Harry of Monmouth. Foe as he was, I own that I shall never look on his like again.'

'I hold with you in that, Patie,' said Bishop Kennedy; 'and frown as you may, my young liege, a few years with such as he would do more for you—as it did with your blessed father—than ever we can.'

'I can hold mine own, I hope, without lessons from the enemy,' said James, holding his head high, while his ruddy locks flew back, his eyes glanced, and the red scar on his cheek widened. 'And is it true that you are for going through false England, Patie?'

'I made friends there when I spent two years there with your Grace's blessed father,' returned Sir Patrick, 'and so did my good wife. She longs to see the lady who is now Sister Clare at St. Katharine's in London, and it is well not to let her and Annis brook the long sea voyage.'

'There, Jean! I'd brook ten sea voyages rather than hold myself beholden to an Englishman!' quoth James.

'Nevertheless, there are letters and messages that it is well to confide to so trusty and wise-headed a knight as Glenuskie,' returned the Bishop.

The meal over, the silver bowls were carried round with water to wash the hands by the two young Drummonds, sons of Glenuskie, and by the King's pages, youths of about the same age, after which the Bishop and Sir Patrick asked licence of the King to retire for consultation to the Bishop's apartment, a permission which, as may well be believed, he granted readily, only rejoicing that he was not wanted.

The little ones were carried off by Mary and Nurse Ankaret; and the King, his elder sisters, and the other youths of condition betook themselves, followed by half-a-dozen great dogs, to the court, where the Drummonds wanted to exhibit the horses procured for the journey, and James and Jean to show the hawks that were the pride of their heart.

By and by came an Italian priest, who acted as secretary to the Bishop—a poor little man who grew yellower and yellower, was always shivering, and seemed to be shrivelled into growing smaller and smaller by the Scottish winds, but who had a most keen and intelligent face.

'How now, Father Romuald,' called out James. 'Are ye come to fetch me?'

'Di grazia, Signor Re', began the Italian in some fear, as the dogs smelted his lambskin cape. 'The Lord Bishop entreats your Majesty's presence.'

His Majesty, who, by the way, never was so called by any one else, uttered some bitter growls and grumbles, but felt forced to obey the call, taking with him, however, his beautiful falcon on his wrist, and the two huge deer-hounds, who he declared should be of the council if he was.

Jean and Eleanor then closed upon David and Malcolm, eagerly demanding of them what they expected in that wonderful land to which they were going, much against the will of young David, who was sure there would be no hunting of deer, nor hawking for grouse, nor riding after an English borderer or Hieland cateran—nothing, in fact, worth living for! It would be all a-wearying with their manners and their courtesies and such like daft woman's gear! Why could not his father be content to let him grow up like his fellows, rough and free and ready?

'And knowing nothing better—nothing beyond,' said Eleanor.

'What would you have better than the hill and the brae? To tame a horse and fly a hawk, and couch a lance and bend a bow! That's what a man is made for, without fashing himself with letters and Latin and manners, no better than a monk; but my father would always have it so!'

'Ye'll be thankful to him yet, Davie,' put in his graver brother.

'Thankful! I shall forget all about it as soon as I am knighted, and make you write all my letters—and few enough there will be.'

'And you, Malcolm!' said Eleanor, 'would you be content to hide within four walls, and know nothing by your own eyes?'

'No indeed, cousin,' replied the lad; 'I long for the fair churches and cloisters and the learned men and books that my father tells of. My mother says that her brother, that I am named for, yearned to make this a land of peace and godliness, and to turn these high spirits to God's glory instead of man's strife and feud, and how it might have been done save for the slaying of your noble father—Saints rest him!—which broke mine uncle's heart, so that he died on his way home from pilgrimage. She hopes to pray at his tomb that I may tread in his steps, and be a blessing and not a curse to the land we love.'

Eleanor was silent, seeing for the first time that there might be higher aims than escaping from dulness, strife, and peril; whilst Jean cried—

"Tis the titles and jousts, the knights and ladies that I care for—men that know what fair chivalry means, and make knightly vows to dare all sorts of foes for a lady's sake.'

'As if any lass was worth it,' said David contemptuously.

'Ay, that's what you are! That's what it is to live in this savage realm,' returned Jean.

At this moment, however, Brother Romuald was again seen advancing, and this time with a request for the presence of the ladies Jean and Eleanor.

'Could James be relenting on better advice?' they asked one another as they went.

'More likely,' said Jean, with a sigh, amounting to a groan, 'it is only to hear that we are made over, like a couple of kine, to some ruffianly reivers, who will beat a princess as soon as a scullion.'

They reached the chamber in time. Though the Bishop slept there it also served for a council chamber; and as he carried his chapel and household furniture about with him, it was a good deal more civilised-looking than even the princesses' room. Large folding screens, worked with tapestry, representing the lives of the saints, shut off the part used as an oratory and that which served as a bedchamber, where indeed the good man slept on a rush mat on the floor. There were a table and several chairs and stools, all capable of being folded up for transport. The young King occupied a large chair of state, in which he twisted himself in a very undignified manner; the Bishop-Chancellor sat beside him, with the Great Seal of Scotland and some writing materials, parchments, and letters before him, and Sir Patrick came forward to receive and seat the young ladies, and then remained standing—as few of his rank in Scotland would have done on their account.

'Well, lassies,' began the King, 'here's lads enow for you. There's the Master of Angus, as ye ken—'(Jean tossed her head)—'moreover, auld Crawford wants one of you for his son.'

'The Tyger Earl,' gasped Eleanor.

'And with Stirling for your portion, the modest fellow,' added James. 'Ay, and that's not all. There's the MacAlpin threats me with all his clan if I dinna give you to him; and Mackay is not behindhand, but will come down with pibroch and braidsword and five hundred caterans to pay his court to you, and make short work of all others. My certie, sisters seem but a cause for threats from reivers, though maybe they would not be so uncivil if once they had you.'

'Oh, Jamie! oh! dear holy Father,' cried Eleanor, turning from the King to the Bishop, 'do not, for mercy's sake, give me over to one of those ruffians.'

'They are coming, Eleanor,' said James, with a boy's love of terrifying; 'the MacAlpin and Mackay are both coming down after you, and we shall have a fight like the Clan Chattan and Clan Kay. There's for the demoiselle who craved for knights to break lances for her!'

'Knights indeed! Highland thieves,' said Jean; 'and 'tis for what tocher they may force from you, James, not for her face.'

'You are right there, my puir bairn,' said the Bishop. 'These men—save perhaps the young Master of Angus—only seek your hands as a pretext for demands from your brother, and for spuilzie and robbery among themselves. And I for my part would never counsel his Grace to yield the lambs to the wolves, even to save himself.'

'No, indeed,' broke in the King; we may not have them fighting down here, though it would be rare sport to look on, if you were not to be the prize. So my Lord Bishop here trows, and I am of the same mind, that the only safety is that the birds should be flown, and that you should have your wish and be away the morn, with Patie of Glenuskie here, since he will take the charge of two such silly lasses.'

The sudden granting of their wish took the maidens' breath away. They looked from one to the other without a word; and the Bishop, in more courtly language, explained that amid all these contending parties he could not but judge it wiser to put the King's two marriageable sisters out of reach, either of a violent abduction, or of being the cause of a savage contest, in either case ending in demands that would be either impossible or mischievous for the Crown to grant, and moreover in misery for themselves.

Sir Patrick added something courteous about the honour of the charge.

'So soon!' gasped Jean; 'are we really to go the morn?'

'With morning light, if it be possible, fair ladies,' said Sir Patrick.

'Ay,' said James, 'then will we take Mary and the weans to the nunnery in St. Mary's Wynd, where none will dare to molest them, and I shall go on to St. Andrews or Stirling, as may seem fittest; while we leave old Seneschal Peter to keep the castle gates shut. If the Hielanders come, they'll find the nut too hard for them to crack, and the kernel gone, so you'd best burn no more daylight, maidens, but busk ye, as women will.'

'Oh, Jamie, to speak so lightly of parting!' sighed Eleanor.

'Come—no fule greeting, now you have your will,' hastily said James, who could hardly bear it himself.

'Our gear!' faltered Jeanie, with consternation at their ill-furnished wardrobes.

'For that,' said the Bishop, 'you must leave the supply till you are over the Border, when the Lady Glenuskie will see to your appearing as nigh as may be as befits the daughters of Scotland among your English kin.'

'But we have not a mark between us,' said Jean, 'and all my mother's jewels are pledged to the Lombards.'

'There are moneys falling due to the Crown,' said the Bishop, 'and I can advance enow to Sir Patrick to provide the gear and horses.'

'And my gude wife's royal kin are my guests till they win to their sister,' added Sir Patrick.

And so it was settled. It was an evening of bustle and a night of wakefulness. There were floods of tears poured out by and over sweet little Mary and good old Ankaret, not to speak of those which James scorned to shed. Had a sudden stop been put to the journey, perhaps, Eleanor would have been relieved but Jean sorely disappointed.

It was further decided that Father Romuald should accompany the party, both to assist in negotiations with Henry VI. and Cardinal Beaufort, and to avail himself of the opportunity of returning to his native land, fa north, and to show cause to the Pope for erecting St. Andrews into an archiepiscopal see, instead of leaving Scotland under the primacy of York.

Hawk and harp were all the properties the princesses-errant took with them; but Jean, as her old nurse sometimes declared, loved Skywing better than all the weans, and Elleen's small travelling-harp was all that she owned of her father's—except the spirit that loved it.

CHAPTER 2. DEPARTURE

  'I bowed my pride,
  A horse-boy in his train to ride.'—SCOTT.

The Lady of Glenuskie, as she was commonly called, was a near kinswoman of the Royal House, Lilias Stewart, a grand-daughter of King Robert II., and thus first cousin to the late King. Her brother, Malcolm Stewart, had resigned to her the little barony of Glenuskie upon his embracing the life of a priest, and her becoming the wife of Sir Patrick Drummond, the son of his former guardian.

Sir Patrick had served in France in the Scotch troop who came to the assistance of the Dauphin, until he was taken prisoner by his native monarch, James I., then present with the army of Henry V. He had then spent two years at Windsor, in attendance upon that prince, until both were set at liberty by the treaty made by Cardinal Beaufort. In the meantime, his betrothed, Lilias, being in danger at home, had been bestowed in the household of the Countess of Warwick, where she had been much with an admirable and saintly foreign lady, Esclairmonde de Luxembourg, who had taken refuge from the dissensions of her own vexed country among the charitable sisterhood of St. Katharine in the Docks in London.

Sir Patrick and his lady had thus enjoyed far more training in the general

European civilisation than usually fell to the lot of their countrymen; and they had moreover imbibed much of the spirit of that admirable King, whose aims at improvement, religious, moral, and political, were so piteously cut short by his assassination. During the nine miserable years that had ensued it had not been possible, even in conjunction with Bishop Kennedy, to afford any efficient support or protection to the young King and his mother, and it had been as much as Sir Patrick could do to protect his own lands and vassals, and do his best to bring up his children to godly, honourable, and chivalrous ways; but amid all the evil around he had decided that it was well-nigh impossible to train them to courage without ruffianism, or to prevent them from being tainted by the prevailing standard. Even among the clergy and monastic orders the type was very low, in spite of the endeavours of Bishop Kennedy, who had not yet been able to found his university at St. Andrews; and it had been agreed between him and Sir Patrick that young Malcolm Drummond, a devout and scholarly lad of earnest aspiration, should be trained at the Paris University, and perhaps visit Padua and Bologna in preparation for that foundation, which, save for that cruel Eastern's E'en, would have been commenced by the uncle whose name he bore.

The daughter had likewise been promised in her babyhood to the Sire de Terreforte, a knight of Auvergne, who had come on a mission to the Scotch Court in the golden days of the reign of James I., and being an old companion-in-arms of Sir Patrick, had desired to unite the families in the person of his infant son Olivier and of Annis Drummond.

Lady Drummond had ever since been preparing her little daughter and her wardrobe. The whole was in a good state of forwardness; but it must be confessed that she was somewhat taken aback when she beheld two young ladies riding up the glen with her husband, sons, and their escort; and found, on descending to welcome them, that they were neither more nor less than the two eldest unmarried princesses of Scotland.

'And Dame Lilias,' proceeded her knight, 'you must busk and boune you to be in the saddle betimes the morn, and put Tweed between these puir lasses and their foes—or shall I say their ower well wishers?'

The ladies of Scotland lived to receive startling intelligence, and Lady Drummond's kind heart was moved by the two forlorn, weary-looking figures, with traces of tears on their cheeks. She kissed them respectfully, conducted them to the guest-chamber, which was many advances beyond their room at Dunbar in comfort, and presently left her own two daughters, Annis and Lilias, and their nurse, to take care of them, since they seemed to have neither mails nor attendants of their own, while she sought out her husband, as he was being disarmed by his sons, to understand what was to be done.

He told her briefly of the danger and perplexity in which the presence of the two poor young princesses might involve themselves, their brother, and the kingdom itself, by exciting the greed, jealousy, and emulation of the untamed nobles and Highland chiefs, who would try to gain them, both as an excuse for exactions from the King and out of jealousy of one another. To take them out of reach was the only ready means of preventing mischief, and the Bishop of St.

Andrews had besought Sir Patrick to undertake the charge.

'We are bound to do all we can for their father's daughters,' Dame Lilias owned, 'alike as our King and the best friend that ever we had, or my dear brother Malcolm, Heaven rest them both! But have they no servants, no plenishing?'

'That must we provide,' said Sir Patrick. 'We must be their servants, Dame. Our lasses must lend them what is fitting, till we come where I can make use of this, which my good Lord of St. Andrews gave me.'

'What is it, Patie? Not the red gold?'

'Oh no! I have heard of the like. Ye ken Morini, as they call him, the Lombard goldsmith in the Canongate? Weel, for sums that the Bishop will pay to Morini, sums owing, he says, by himself to the Crown—though I shrewdly suspect 'tis the other way, gude man!—then the Lombard's fellows in York, London, or Paris, or Bourges will, on seeing this bit bond, supply us up to the tune of a hundred crowns. Thou look'st mazed, Lily, but I have known the like before. 'Tis no great sum, but mayhap the maidens' English kin will do somewhat for them before they win to their sister.'

'I would not have them beholden to the English,' said Dame Lilias, not forgetting that she was a Stewart.

Her husband perhaps scarcely understood the change made in the whole aspect of the journey to her. Not only had she to hurry her preparations for the early start, but instead of travelling as the mistress of the party, she and her daughter would, in appearance at least, be the mere appendages of the two princesses, wait upon them, give them the foremost place, supply their present needs from what was provided for themselves, and it was quite possible have likewise to control girlish petulance and inexperience in the strange lands where her charges must appear at their very best, to do honour to their birth and their country.

But the loyal woman made up her mind without a word of complaint after the first shock, and though a busy night was not the best preparation for a day's journey, she never lay down; nor indeed did her namesake daughter, who was to be left at a Priory on their way, there to decide whether she had a vocation to be a nun.

So effectually did she bestir herself that by six o'clock the next morning the various packages were rolled up for bestowal on the sumpter horses, and the goods to be left at home locked up in chests, and committed to the charge of the trusty seneschal and his wife; a meal, to be taken in haste, was spread on the table in the hall, to be swallowed while the little rough ponies were being laden.

Mass was to be heard at the first halting-place, the Benedictine nunnery of Trefontana on Lammermuir, where Lilias Drummond was to be left, to be passed on, when occasion served, to the Sisterhood at Edinburgh.

The fresh morning breezes over the world of heather brightened the cheeks and the spirits of the two sisters; the first wrench of parting was over with them, and they found themselves treated with much more observance than usual, though they did not know that the horses they were riding had been trained for the special use of the Lady of Glenuskie and her daughter Annis upon the journey.

They rode on gaily, Jean with her inseparable falcon Skywing, Eleanor with her father's harp bestowed behind her—she would trust it to no one else. They were squired by their two cousins, David and Malcolm, who, in spite of David's murmurs, felt the exhilaration of the future as much as they did, as they coursed over the heather, David with two great greyhounds with majestic heads at his side, Finn and Finvola, as they were called.

The graver and sadder ones of the party, father, mother, and the two young sisters, rode farther back, the father issuing directions to the seneschal, who accompanied them thus far, and the mother watching over the two fair young girls, whose hearts were heavy in the probability that they would never meet again, for how should a Scottish Benedictine nun and the wife of a French seigneur ever come together? nor would there be any possibility of correspondence to bridge over the gulf.

The nunnery was strong, but not with the strength of secular buildings, for, except when a tempting heiress had taken refuge there, convents were respected even by the rudest men.

Numerous unkempt and barely-clothed figures were coming away from the gates, a pilgrim or two with brown gown, broad hat, and scallop shell, the morning's dole being just over; but a few, some on crutches, some with heads or limbs bound up, were waiting for their turn of the sister-infirmarer's care. The pennon of the Drummond had already been recognised, and the gate-ward readily admitted the party, since the house of Glenuskie were well known as pious benefactors to the Church.

They were just in time for a mass which a pilgrim priest was about to say, and they were all admitted to the small nave of the little chapel, beyond which a screen shut off the choir of nuns. After this the ladies were received into the refectory to break their fast, the men folk being served in an outside building for the purpose. It was not sumptuous fare, chiefly consisting of barley bannocks and very salt and dry fish, with some thin and sour ale; and David's attention was a good deal taken up by a man-at-arms who seemed to have attached himself to the party, but whom he did not know, and who held a little aloof from the rest—keeping his visor down while eating and drinking, in a somewhat suspicious manner, as though to avoid observation.

Just as David had resolved to point this person out to his father, Sir Patrick was summoned to speak to the Lady Prioress. Therefore the youth thought it incumbent upon him to deal with the matter, and advancing towards the stranger, said, 'Good fellow, thou art none of our following. How, now!' for a pair of gray eyes looked up with recognition in them, and a low voice whispered, 'Davie Drummond, keep my secret till we be across the Border.'

'Geordie, what means this?'

'I canna let her gang! I ken that she scorns me.'

'That proud peat Jean?'

'Whist! whist! She scorns me, and the King scarce lent a lug to my father's gude offer, so that he can scarce keep the peace with their pride and upsettingness. But I love her, Davie, the mere sight of her is sunshine, and wha kens but in the stour of this journey I may have the chance of standing by her and defending her, and showing what a leal Scot's heart can do? Or if not, if I may not win her, I shall still be in sight of her blessed blue een!'

David whistled his perplexity. 'The Yerl,' said he, 'doth he ken?'

'I trow not! He thinks me at Tantallon, watching for the raid the Mackays are threatening—little guessing the bird would be flown.'

'How cam' ye to guess that same, which was, so far as I know, only decided two days syne?'

'Our pursuivant was to bear a letter to the King, and I garred him let me bear him company as one of his grooms, so that I might delight mine eyes with the sight of her.'

David laughed. His time was not come, and this love and admiration for his young cousin was absurd in his eyes. 'For a young bit lassie,' he said; 'gin it had been a knight! But what will your father say to mine?'

'I will write to him when I am well over the Border,' said Geordie, 'and gin he kens that your father had no hand in it he will deem no ill-will. Nor could he harm you if he did.'

David did not feel entirely satisfied, on one side of his mind as to his own loyalty to his father, or Geordie's to 'the Yerl,' and yet there was something diverting to the enterprising mind in the stolen expedition; and the fellow-feeling which results in honour to contemporaries made him promise not to betray the young man and to shield him from notice as best he might. With Geordie's motive he had no sympathy, having had too many childish squabbles with his cousin for her to be in his eyes a sublime Princess Joanna, but only a masterful Jeanie.

Sir Patrick, absorbed in orders to his seneschal, did not observe the addition to his party; and as David acted as his squire, and had been seen talking to the young man, no further demur was made until the time when the home party turned to ride back to Glenuskie, and Sir Patrick made a roll-call of his followers, picked men who could fairly be trusted not to embroil the company by excesses or imprudences in England or France.

Besides himself, his wife, sons and daughters, and the two princesses, the party consisted of Christian, female attendant for the ladies, the wife of Andrew of the Cleugh, an elderly, well-seasoned man-at-arms, to whom the banner was entrusted; Dandie their son, a stalwart youth of two or three-and-twenty, who, under his father, was in charge of the horses; and six lances besides. Sir Patrick following the French fashion, which gave to each lance two grooms, armed likewise, and a horse-boy. For each of the family there was likewise a spare palfrey, with a servant in charge, and one beast of burthen, but these last were to be freshly hired with their attendants at each stage.

Geordie, used to more tumultuous and irregular gatherings, where any man with a good horse and serviceable weapons was welcome to join the raid, had not reckoned on such a review of the party as was made by the old warrior accustomed to more regular warfare, and who made each of his eight lances—namely, the two Andrew Drummonds, Jock of the Glen, Jockie of Braeside, Willie and Norman Armstrong, Wattie Wudspurs, and Tam Telfer—answer to

18

their names, and show up their three followers.

'And who is yon lad in bright steel?' Sir Patrick asked.

'Master Davie kens, sir,' responded old Andrew. David, being called, explained that he was a leal lad called Geordie, whom he had seen in Edinburgh, and who wished to join them, go to France, and see the world under Sir Patrick's guidance, and that he would be at his own charges. 'And I'll be answerable for him, sir,' concluded the lad.

'Answer! Ha! ha! What for, eh? That he is a long-legged lad like your ain self. What more? Come, call him up!'

The stranger had no choice save to obey, and came up on a strong white mare, which old Andrew scanned, and muttered to his son, 'The Mearns breed—did he come honestly by it?'

'Up with your beaver, young man,' said Sir Patrick peremptorily; 'no man rides with me whose face I have not seen.'

A face not handsome and thoroughly Scottish was disclosed, with keen intelligence in the gray eyes, and a certain air of offended dignity, yet self-control, in the close-shut mouth. The cheeks were sunburnt and freckled, a tawny down of young manhood was on the long upper lip, and the short-cut hair was red; but there was an intelligent and trustworthy expression in the countenance, and the tall figure sat on horseback with the upright ease of one well trained.

'Soh!' said Sir Patrick, looking him over, 'how ca' they you, lad?'

'Geordie o' the Red Peel,' he answered.

'That's a by-name,' said the knight sternly; 'I must have the full name of any man who rides with me.'

'George Douglas, then, if nothing short of that will content you!'

'Are ye sib to the Earl?'

'Ay, sir, and have rid in his company.'

'Whose word am I to take for that?'

'Mine, sir, a word that none has ever doubted,' said the youth boldly. 'By that your son kens me.'

David here vouched for having seen the young man in the Angus following, when he had accompanied his father in the last riding of the Scots Parliament at Edinburgh; and this so far satisfied Sir Patrick that he consented to receive the stranger into his company, but only on condition of an oath of absolute obedience so long as he remained in the troop.

David could see that this had not been reckoned on by the high-spirited Master of Angus; and indeed obedience, save to the head of the name, was so little a Scottish virtue that Sir Patrick was by no means unprepared for reluctance.

'I give thee thy choice, laddie,' he said, not unkindly; 'best make up your mind while thou art still in thine own country, and can win back home. In England and France I can have no stragglers nor loons like to help themselves, nor give cause for a fray to bring shame on the haill troop in lands that are none too friendly. A raw carle like thyself, or even these lads of mine, might give offence unwittingly, and then I'd have to give thee up to the laws, or to stand by thee to the peril of all, and of the ladies themselves. So there's nothing for it but strict keeping to orders of myself and Andrew Drummond of the Cleugh, who kens as well as I do what sorts to be done in these strange lands. Wilt thou so bind thyself, or shall we part while yet there is time?'

'Sir, I will,' said the young man, 'I will plight my word to obey you, and faithfully, so long as I ride under your banner in foreign parts—provided such oath be not binding within this realm of Scotland, nor against my lealty to the head of my name.'

'Nor do I ask it of thee,' returned Sir Patrick heartily, but regarding him more attentively; 'these are the scruples of a true man. Hast thou any following?'

'Only a boy to lead my horse to grass,' replied George, giving a peculiar whistle, which brought to his side a shock-headed, barefooted lad, in a shepherd's tartan and little else, but with limbs as active as a wild deer, and an eye twinkling and alert.

'He shall be put in better trim ere the English pock-puddings see him,' said Douglas, looking at him, perhaps for the first time, as something unsuited to that orderly company.

'That is thine own affair,' said Sir Patrick. 'Mine is that he should comport himself as becomes one of my troop. What's his name?'

'Ringan Raefoot,' replied Geordie Sir Patrick began to put the oath of obedience to him, but the boy cried out—

'I'll ne'er swear to any save my lawful lord, the Yerl of Angus, and my lord the Master.'

'Hist, Ringan,' interposed Geordie. 'Sir, I will answer for his faith to me, and so long as he is leal to me he will be the same to thee; but I doubt whether it be expedient to compel him.'

So did Sir Patrick, and he said—

'Then be it so, I trust to his faith to thee. Only remembering that if he plunder or brawl, I may have to leave him hanging on the next bush.'

'And if he doth, the Red Douglas will ken the reason why,' quoth Ringan, with head aloft.

It was thought well to turn a deaf ear to this observation. Indeed, Geordie's effort was to elude observation, and to keep his uncouth follower from attracting it. Ringan was not singular in running along with bare feet. Other 'bonnie boys,' as the ballad has it, trotted along by the side of the horses to which they were attached in the like fashion, though they had hose and shoon slung over their shoulders, to be donned on entering the good town of Berwick-upon-Tweed.

Not without sounding of bugle and sending out a pursuivant to examine into the intentions and authorisation of the party, were they admitted, Jean and Eleanor riding first, with the pursuivant proclaiming—'Place, place for the high and mighty princesses of Scotland.'

It was an inconvenient ceremony for poor Sir Patrick, who had to hand over to the pursuivant, in the name of the princesses, a ring from his own finger. Largesse he could not attempt, but the proud spirit of himself and his train could not but be chafed at the expectant faces of the crowd, and the intuitive certainty that 'Beggarly Scotch' was in every disappointed mind.

And this was but a foretaste of what the two royal maidens' presence would probably entail throughout the journey. His wife added to this care uneasiness as to the deportment of her three maidens. Of Annis she had not much fear, but she suspected Jean and Eleanor of being as wild and untamed as hares, and she much doubted whether any counsels might not offend their dignity, and drive them into some strange behaviour that the good people of Berwick would never forget.

They rode in, however, very upright and stately, with an air of taking possession of the place on their brother's behalf; and Jean bowed with a certain haughty grace to the deputy-warden who came out to receive them, Eleanor keeping her eye upon Jean and imitating her in everything. For Eleanor, though sometimes the most eager, and most apt to commit herself by hasty words and speeches, seemed now to be daunted by the strangeness of all around, and to commit herself to the leading of her sister, though so little her junior.

She was very silent all through the supper spread for them in the hall of the castle, while Jean exchanged conversation with their host upon Iceland hawks and wolf and deer hounds, as if she had been a young lady keeping a splendid court all her life, instead of a poverty-stricken prisoner in castle after castle.

'Jeanie,' whispered Eleanor, as they lay down on their bed together, 'didst mark the tall laddie that was about to seat himself at the high table and frowned when the steward motioned him down?'

'What's that to me? An ill-nurtured carle,' said Jean; 'I marvel Sir Patie brooks him in his meinie!'

Eleanor was a little in awe of Jeanie in this mood, and said no more, but Annis, who slept on a pallet at their feet, heard all, and guessed more as to the strange young squire.

Fain would she and Eleanor have discussed the situation, but Jean's blue eyes glanced heedfully and defiantly at them, and, moreover, the young gentleman in question, after that one error, effaced himself, and was forgotten for the time in the novelty of the scenes around.

The sub-warden of Berwick, mindful of his charge to obviate all occasions of strife, insisted on sending a knight and half-a-dozen men to escort the Scottish travellers as far as Durham. David Drummond and the young ladies murmured to one another their disgust that the English pock-pudding should not suppose Scots able to keep their heads with their own hands; but, as Jean sagely observed, 'No doubt he would not wish them to have occasion to hurt any of the English, nor Jamie to have to call them to account.'

This same old knight consorted with Sir Patrick, Dame Lilias, and Father Romuald, and kept a sharp eye on the little party, allowing no straggling on any pretence, and as Sir Patrick enforced the command, all were obliged to obey, in spite of chafing; and the scowls of the English Borderers, with the scant courtesy vouchsafed by these sturdy spirits, proved the wisdom of the precaution.

At Durham they were hospitably entertained in the absence of the Bishop. The splendour of the cathedral and its adjuncts much impressed Lady Drummond, as it had done a score of years previously; but, though Malcolm ventured to share her admiration, Jean was far above allowing that she could be astonished at anything in England. In fact, she regarded the stately towers of St. Cuthbert as so much stolen family property which 'Jamie' would one day regain; and all the other young people followed suit. David even made all the observations his own sense of honour and the eyes of his hosts would permit, with a view to a future surprise. The escort of Sir Patrick was asked to York by a Canon who had to journey thither, and was anxious for protection from the outlaws—who had begun to renew the doings of Robin Hood under the laxer rule of the young Henry VI, though things were expected to be better since the young Duke of York had returned from France.

Perhaps this arrangement was again a precaution for the preservation of peace, and at York there was a splendid entertainment by Cardinal Kemp; but all the 'subtleties' and wonders—stags' heads in their horns, peacocks in their pride, jellies with whole romances depicted in them, could not reconcile the young Scots to the presumption of the Archbishop reckoning Scotland into his province. Durham was at once too monastic and too military to have afforded much opportunity for recruiting the princesses' wardrobe; but York was the resort of the merchants of Flanders, and Christie was sent in quest of them and their wares, for truly the black serge kirtles and shepherd's tartan screens that had made the journey from Dunbar were in no condition to do honour to royal damsels.

Jean was in raptures with the graceful veils depending from the horned headgear, worn, she was told, by the Duchess of Burgundy; but Eleanor wept at the idea of obscuring the snood of a Scottish maiden, and would not hear of resigning it.

'I feel as Elleen no more,' she said, 'but a mere Flanders popinjay. It has changed my ain self upon me, as well as the country.'

'Thou shouldst have been born in a hovel!' returned Jean, raising her proud little head. 'I feel more than ever what I am—a true princess!'

And she looked it, with beauty enhanced by the rich attire which only made Eleanor embarrassed and uncomfortable.

Malcolm, the more scrupulous of the Drummond brothers, begged of George Douglas, when at Durham, to write to his father and declare himself to Sir Patrick, but the youth would do neither. He did not think himself sufficiently out of reach, and, besides, the very sight of a pen was abhorrent to him. There was something pleasing to him in the liberty of a kind of volunteer attached to the expedition, and he would not give it up. Nor was he without some wild idea of winning Jean's notice by some gallant exploit on her behalf before she knew him for the object of her prejudice, the Master of Angus. As to Sir Patrick, he was far too busy trying to compose Border quarrels, and gleaning information about the Gloucester and Beaufort parties at Court, to have any attention to spare for the young man riding in his suite with the barefooted lad ever at his stirrup.

Geordie never attempted to secure better accommodation than the other lances; he groomed his steed himself, with a little assistance from Ringan, and slept in the straw of its bed, with the lad curled up at his feet; the only difference observable between him and the rest being that he always groomed himself every night and morning as carefully as the horse, a ceremony they thought entirely needless.

CHAPTER 3. FALCON AND FETTERLOCK

'Ours is the sky
Where at what fowl we please our hawk shall fly.'
—T. Randolph.

Beyond York that species of convoy, which ranged between protection and supervision, entirely ceased; the Scottish party moved on their own wa oftener through heath, rock, and moor, for England was not yet thickly inhabited, though there was no lack of hostels or of convents to receive them on this the great road to the North, and to its many shrines for pilgrimage.

Perhaps Sir Patrick relaxed a little of his vigilance, since the good behaviour of his troop had won his confidence, and they were less likely to be regarded as invaders than by the inhabitants of the district nearer their own frontier.

Hawking and coursing within bounds had been permitted by both the Knight of Berwick and the Canon of Durham on the wide northern moors; but Sir Patrick, on starting in the morning of the day when they were entering Northamptonshire, had given a caution that sport was not free in the more frequented parts of England, and that hound must not be loosed nor hawk flown without special permission from the lord of the manor.

He was, however, riding in the rear of the rest, up a narrow lane leading uphill, anxiously discussing with Father Romuald the expediency of seeking hospitality from any of the great lords whose castles might be within reach before he had full information of the present state of factions at the Court, when suddenly his son Malcolm came riding back, pushing up hastily.

'Sir! father!' he cried, 'there's wud wark ahead, there's a flight of unco big birds on before, and Lady Jean's hawk is awa' after them, and Jeanie's awa' after the hawk, and Geordie Red Peel is awa' after Jean, and Davie's awa' after Geordie; and there's the blast of an English bugle, and my mither sent me for you to redd the fray!'

'Time, indeed!' said Sir Patrick with a sigh, and, setting spurs to his horse, he soon was beyond the end of the lane, on an open heath, where some of his troop were drawn up round his banner, almost forcibly kept back by Dame Lilias and the elder Andrew. He could not stop for explanation from them, indeed his wife only waved him forward towards a confused group some hundred yards farther off, where he could see a number of his own men, and, too plainly, long bows and coats of Lincoln green, and he only hoped, as he galloped onward, that they belonged to outlaws and not to rangers. Too soon he saw that his hope was vain; there were ten or twelve stout archers with the white rosette of York in their bonnets, the falcon and fetterlock on their sleeves, and the Plantagenet quarterings on their breasts. In the midst was a dead bustard, also an Englishman sitting up, with his head bleeding; Jean was on foot, with her dagger-knife in one hand, and holding fast to her breast her beloved hawk, whose jesses were, however, grasped by one of the foresters. Geordie of the Red Peel stood with his sword at his feet, glaring angrily round, while Sir Patrick, pausing, could hear his son David's voice in loud tones—

'I tell you this lady is a royal princess! Yes, she is'—as there was a kind of scoff—'and we are bound on a mission to your King from the King of Scots, and woe to him that touches a feather of ours.'

'That may be,' said the one who seemed chief among the English, 'but that gives no licence to fly at the Duke's game, nor slay his foresters for doing their duty. If we let the lady go, hawk and man must have their necks wrung, after forest laws.'

'And I tell thee,' cried Davie, 'that this is a noble gentleman of Scotland, and that we will fight for him to the death.'

'Let it alone, Davie,' said George. 'No scathe shall come to the lady through me.'

'Save him, Davie! save Skywing!' screamed Jean.

'To the rescue—a Drummond,' shouted David; but his father pushed his horse forward, just as the men in green, were in the act of stringing, all at the same moment, their bows, as tall as themselves. They were not so many but that his escort might have overpowered them, but only with heavy loss, and the fact of such a fight would have been most disastrous.

'What means this, sirs?' he exclaimed, in a tone of authority, waving back his own men; and his dignified air, as well as the banner with which Andrew followed him, evidently took effect on the foresters, who perhaps had not believed the young men.

'Sir Patie, my hawk!' entreated Jean. 'She did but pounce on yon unco ugsome bird, and these bloodthirsty grasping loons would have wrung her neck.'

'She took her knife to me,' growled the wounded man, who had risen to his feet, and showed bleeding fingers.

'Ay, for meddling with a royal falcon,' broke in Jean. "Tis thou, false loon, whose craig should be raxed.'

Happily this was an unknown tongue to the foresters, and Sir Patrick gravely silenced her.

'Whist, lady, brawls consort not with your rank. Gang back doucely to my leddy.'

'But Skywing! he has her jesses,' said the girl, but in a lower tone, as though rebuked.

'Sir ranger,' said Sir Patrick courteously, 'I trust you will let the young demoiselle have her hawk. It was loosed in ignorance and heedlessness, no doubt, but I trow it is the rule in England, as elsewhere, that ladies of the blood royal are not bound by forest laws.'

'Sir, if we had known,' said the ranger, who was evidently of gentle blood, as he took his foot off the jesses, and Jean now allowed David to remount her.

'But my Lord Duke is very heedful of his bustards, and when Roger there went to seize the bird, my young lady was over-ready with her knife.'

'Who would not be for thee, my bird?' murmured Jean.

'And yonder big fellow came plunging down and up with his sword—so as he was nigh on being the death of poor Roger again for doing his duty. If such be the ways of you Scots, sir, they be not English ways under my Lord Duke, that is to say, and if I let the lady and her hawk go, forest law must have its due on the young man there—I must have him up to Fotheringay to abide the Duke's pleasure.'

'Heed me not, Sir Patrick!' exclaimed Geordie. 'I would not have those of your meinie brought into jeopardy for my cause.'

David was plucking his father's mantle to suggest who George was, which in fact Sir Patrick might suspect enough to be conscious of the full awkwardness of the position, and to abandon the youth was impossible. Though it was not likely that the Duke of York would hang him if aware of his rank, he might be detained as a hostage or put to heavy ransom, or he might never be brought to the Duke's presence at all, but be put to death by some truculent underling, incredulous of a Scotsman's tale, if indeed he were not too proud to tell it. Anyway, Sir Patrick felt bound to stand by him.

'Good sir,' said he to the forester, 'will it content thee if we all go with thee to thy Duke? The two Scottish princesses are of his kin, and near of blood to King Henry, whom they are about to visit at Windsor. I am on a mission thither on affairs of state, but I shall be willing to make my excuses to him for any misdemeanour committed on his lands by my followers.'

The forester was consenting, when George cried—

'I'll have no hindrance to your journey on my account, Sir Patrick. Let me answer for myself.'

'Foolish laddie,' said the knight. 'Father Romuald and I were only now conferring as to paying the Duke a visit on our way. Sir forester, we shall be beholden to you for guiding us.'

He further inquired into the ranger's hurts, and salved them with a piece of gold, while David thought proper to observe to George—

'So much for thy devoir to thy princess! It was for Skywing's craig she cared, never thine.'

George turned a deaf ear to the insinuation. He was allowed free hands and his own horse, which was perhaps well for the Englishmen, for Ringan Raefoot, running by his stirrup, showed him a long knife, and said with a grin—

'Ready for the first who daurs to lay hands on the Master! Gin I could have come up in time, the loon had never risen from the ground.'

George endeavoured in vain to represent how much worse this would have made their condition.

Sir Patrick, joining the ladies, informed them of the necessity of turning aside to Fotheringay, which he had done not very willingly, being ignorant of the character of the Duke of York, except as one of the war party against France and Scotland, whereas the Beauforts were for peace. As a vigorous governor of Normandy, he had not commended himself to one whose sympathies were French. Lady Drummond, however, remembered that his wife, Cicely Nevil, the Rose of Raby, was younger sister to that Ralf Nevil who had married the friend of her youth, Alice Montagu, now Countess of Salisbury in her own right.

Sir Patrick did not let Jean escape a rebuke.

'So, lady, you see what perils to brave men you maids can cause by a little heedlessness.'

'I never asked Geordie to put his finger in,' returned Jean saucily. 'I could have brought off Skywing for myself without such a clamjamfrie after me.'

But Eleanor and Annis agreed that it was as good as a ballad, and ought to be sung in one, only Jean would have to figure as the 'dour lassie.' For she continued to aver, by turns, that Geordie need never have meddled, and that of course it was his bounden duty to stand by his King's sister, and that she owed him no thanks. If he were hanged for it he had run his craig into the noose.

So she tossed her proud head, and toyed with her falcon, as all rode on their way to Fotheringay, with Geordie in the midst of the rangers.

It was so many years since there had been serious war in England, that the castles of the interior were far less of fortresses than of magnificent abodes for the baronage, who had just then attained their fullest splendour. It may be observed that the Wars of the Roses were for the most part fought out in battles, not by sieges. Thus Fotheringay had spread out into a huge pile, which crowned the hill above, with a strong inner court and lofty donjon tower indeed, and with mighty walls, but with buildings for retainers all round, reaching down to the beautiful newly-built octagon-towered church; and with a great park stretching for miles, for all kinds of sport.

'All this enclosed! Yet they make sic a wark about their bustards, as they ca' them,' muttered Jean.

The forester had sent a messenger forward to inform the Duke of York of his capture. The consequence was that the cavalcade had no sooner crossed the first drawbridge under the great gateway of the castle, where the banner of Plantagenet was displayed, than before it were seen a goodly company, in the glittering and gorgeous robes of the fifteenth century.

There was no doubt of welcome. Foremost was a graceful, slenderly-made gentleman about thirty years old, in rich azure and gold, who doffed his cap of maintenance, turned up with fur, and with long ends, and, bowing low, declared himself delighted that the princesses of Scotland, his good cousins, should honour his poor dwelling.

He gave his hand to assist Jean to alight, and an equally gorgeous but much younger gentleman in the same manner waited on Eleanor. A tall, grizzled, sunburnt figure received Lady Drummond with recognition on both sides, and the words, 'My wife is fain to see you, my honoured lady: is this your daughter?' with a sign to a tall youth, who took Annis from her horse. Dame Lilias heard with joy that the Countess of Salisbury was actually in the castle, and in a few moments more she was in the great hall, in the arms of the sweet Countess Alice of her youth, who, middle-aged as she was, with all her youthful impulsiveness had not waited for the grand and formal greeting bestowed on the princesses by her stately young sister-in-law, the Duchess of York.

There seemed to be a perfect crowd of richly-dressed nobles, ladies, children; and though the Lady Joanna held her head up in full state, and kept her eye on her sister to make her do the same, their bewilderment was great; and when they had been conducted to a splendid chamber, within that allotted to the Drummond ladies, tapestry-hung, and with silver toilette apparatus, to prepare for supper, Jean dropped upon a high-backed chair, and insisted that Dame Lilias should explain to her exactly who each one was.

'That slight, dark-eyed carle who took me off my horse was the Duke of York, of course,' said she. 'My certie, a bonnie Scot would make short work of him, bones and all! And it would scarce be worth while to give a clout to the sickly lad that took Elleen down.'

'Hush, Jean,' said Eleanor; 'some one called him King! Was he King Harry himself?'

'Oh no,' said Dame Lilias, smiling; 'only King Harry of the Isle of Wight—a bit place about the bigness of Arran; but it pleased the English King to crown him and give him a ring, and bestow on him the realm in a kind of sport. He is, in sooth, Harry Beauchamp, Earl of Warwick, and was bred up as the King's chief comrade and playfellow.'

'And what brings him here?'

'So far as I can yet understand, the family and kin have gathered for the marriage of his sister, the Lady Anne—the red-cheeked maiden in the rose-coloured kirtle—to the young Sir Richard Nevil, the same who gave his hand to thee, Annis—the son of my Lord of Salisbury.'

'That was the old knight who led thee in, mother,' said Annis. 'Did you say he was brother to the Duchess?'

'Even so. There were fifteen or twenty Nevils of Raby—he was one of the eldest, she one of the youngest. Their mother was a Beaufort, aunt to yours.'

'Oh, I shall never unravel them!' exclaimed Eleanor, spreading out her hands in bewilderment.

Lady Drummond laughed, having come to the time of life when ladies enjoy genealogies.

'It will be enough,' she said, 'to remember that almost all are, like yourselves, grandchildren or great-grandchildren to King Edward of Windsor.'

Jean, however, wanted to know which were nearest to herself, and which were noblest. The first question Lady Drummond said she could hardly answer; perhaps the Earl of Salisbury and the Duchess, but the Duke was certainly noblest by birth, having a double descent from King Edward, and in the male line.

'Was not his father put to death by this King's father?' asked Eleanor.

'Ay, the Earl of Cambridge, for a foul plot. I have heard my Lord of Salisbury speak of it; but this young man was of tender years, and King Harry of Monmouth did not bear malice, but let him succeed to the dukedom when his uncle was killed in the Battle of Agincourt.'

'They have not spirit here to keep up a feud,' said Jean.

'My good brother—ay, and your father, Jeanie—were wont to say they were too Christian to hand on a feud,' observed Dame Lilias, at which Jean tossed her head, and said—

'That may suit such a carpet-knight as yonder Duke. He is not so tall as Elleen there, nor as his own Duchess.'

'I do not like the Duchess,' said Annis; 'she looks as if she scorned the very ground she walks on.'

'She is wondrous bonnie, though,' said Eleanor; 'and so was the bairnie by her side.'

In some degree Jean changed her opinion of the Duke, in consequence, perhaps, of the very marked attention that he showed her when the supper was spread. She had never been so made to feel what it was to be at once a king's daughter and a beauty; and at the most magnificent banquet she had ever known.

Durham had afforded a great advance on Scottish festivities; but in the absence of its Prince Bishop, another Nevil, it had lacked much of what was to be found at Fotheringay in the full blossoming of the splendours of the princely nobility of England, just ere the decimation that they were to perpetrate on one another.

The hall itself was vast, and newly finished in the rich culmination of Gothic work, with a fan tracery-vaulted roof, a triumph of architecture, each stalactite glowing with a shield or a badge of England, France, Mortimer, and Nevil—lion or lily, falcon and fetterlock, white rose and dun cow, all and many others—likewise shining in the stained glass of the great windows.

The high table was loaded with gold and silver plate, and Venice glasses even more precious; there were carpets under the feet of the nobler guests, and even the second and third tables were spread with more richness and refinement than ever the sisters of James II had known in their native land. In a gallery above, the Duke's musicians and the choristers of his chapel were ready to enliven the meal; and as the chief guest, the Lady Joanna of Scotland was handed to her place by the Duke of York, who, as she now perceived, though small in stature, was eminently handsome and graceful, and conversed with her, not as a mere child, but as a fair lady of full years.

Eleanor, who sat on his other hand beside the Earl of Salisbury, was rather provoked with her sister for never asking after the fate of her champion; but was reassured by seeing his red head towering among the numerous squires and other retainers of the second rank. It certainly was not his proper place, but it was plain that he was not in disgrace; and in fact the whole affair had been treated as a mere pardonable blunder of the rangers. The superior one was sitting next to the young Scot, making good cheer with him. Grand as the whole seemed to the travellers, it was not an exceptional banquet; indeed, the Duchess apologised for its simplicity, since she had been taken at unawares, evidently considering it as the ordinary family meal. There was ample provision, served up in by no means an unrefined manner, even to the multitudinous servants and retainers of the various trains; and beyond, on the steps and in the court, were a swarm of pilgrims, friars, poor, and beggars of all kinds, waiting for the fragments.

It was a wet evening, and when the tables were drawn the guests devoted themselves to various amusements. Lord Salisbury challenged Sir Patrick to a game at chess, Lady Salisbury and Dame Lilias wished for nothing better than to converse over old times at Middleham Castle; but the younger people began with dancing, the Duke, who was only thirty years old, leading out the elder Scottish princess, and the young King of the Isle of Wight the stately and beautiful Duchess Cicely. Eleanor, who knew she did not excel in anything that required grace, and was, besides, a good deal fatigued, would fain have excused herself when paired with the young Richard Nevil; but there was a masterful look about him that somewhat daunted her, and she obeyed his summons, though without acquitting herself with anything approaching to the dexterity of her sister, who, with quite as little practice as herself, danced well—by quickness of eye and foot, and that natural elegance of movement which belongs to symmetry.

The dance was a wreathing in and out of the couples, including all of rank to dance together, and growing more and more animated, till excitement took the place of weariness; and Eleanor's pale cheeks were flushed, her eyes glowing, when the Duchess's signal closed the dance.

Music was then called for, and several of the princely company sang to the lute; Jean, pleased to show there was something in which her sister excelled, and gratified at some recollections that floated up of her father's skill in minstrelsy, insisted on sending for Eleanor's harp.

'Oh, Jean, not now; I canna,' murmured Eleanor, who had been sitting with fixed eyes, as though in a dream.

But the Duke and other nobles came and pressed her, and Jean whispered to her not to show herself a fule body, and disgrace herself before the English, setting the harp before her and attending to the strings. Eleanor's fingers then played over them in a dreamy, fitful way, that made the old Earl raise his head and say—

'That twang carries me back to King Harry's tent, and the good old time when an Englishman's sword was respected.'

''Tis the very harp,' said Sir Patrick; 'ay, and the very tune—'

'Come, Elleen, begin. What gars thee loiter in that doited way?' insisted Jean. 'Come, "Up atween."'

And, led by her sister in spite of herself, almost, as it were, without volition, Eleanor's sweet pathetic voice sang—

'Up atween yon twa hill-sides, lass,
 Where I and my true love wont to be,
A' the warld shall never ken, lass,
 What my true love said to me.

'Owre muckle blinking blindeth the ee, lass,
 Owre muckle thinking changeth the mind,
Sair is the life I've led for thee, lass,
 Farewell warld, for it's a' at an end.'

Her voice had been giving way through the last verse, and in the final line, with a helpless wail of the harp, she hid her face, and sank back with a strange choked agony.

'Why, Elleen! Elleen, how now?' cried Jean. 'Cousin Lilias, come!'

Lady Drummond was already at her side, and the Duchess and Lady Salisbury proffering essences and cordials, the gentlemen offering support; but in a moment or two Eleanor recovered enough to cling to Lady Drummond, muttering—

'Oh, take me awa', take me awa'!'

And hushing the scolding which Jean was commencing by way of bracing, and rejecting all the kind offers of service, Dame Lilias led the girl away, leaving Jean to make excuses and explanations about her sister being but 'silly' since they had lost their mother, and the tune minding her of home and of her father.

When, with only Annis following, the chambers had been reached, Eleanor let herself sink on a cushion, hiding her face against her friend, and sobbing hysterically—

'Oh, take me awa', take me awa'! It's all blood and horror!'

'My bairnie, my dearie! You are over-weary—'tis but a dreamy fancy. Look up! All is safe; none can harm you here.'

With soothings, and with some of the wine on the table, Lady Drummond succeeded in calming the girl, and, with Annis's assistance, she undressed her and placed her in the bed.

'Oh, do not gang! Leave me not,' she entreated. And as the lady sat by her, holding her hand, she spoke, 'It was all dim before me as the music played, and—'

'Thou wast sair forefaughten, dearie.'

Eleanor went on—

'And then as I touched mine harp, all, all seemed to swim in a mist of blood and horror. There was the old Earl and the young bridegroom, and many and many more of them, with gaping wounds and deathly faces—all but the young King of the Isle of Wight and his shroud, his shroud, Cousin Lily, it was up to his breast; and the ladies' faces that were so blithe, they were all weeping, ghastly, and writhen; and they were whirling round a great sea of blood right in the middle of the hall, and I could—I could bear it no longer.'

Lady Drummond controlled herself, and for the sake both of the sobbing princess and of her own shuddering daughter said that this terrible vision came of the fatigue of the day, and the exhaustion and excitement that had followed. She also knew that on poor Eleanor that fearful Eastern's Eve had left an indelible impression, recurring in any state of weakness or fever. She scarcely marvelled at the strange and frightful fancies, except that she believed enough in second-sight to be concerned at the mention of the shroud enfolding the young Beauchamp, who bore the fanciful title of the King of the Isle of Wight.

For the present, however, she applied herself to the comforting of Eleanor with tender words and murmured prayers, and never left her till she had slept and wakened again, her full self, upon Jean coming up to bed at nine o'clock—a very late hour—escorted by sundry of the ladies to inquire for the patient.

Jean was still excited, but she was, with all her faults, very fond of her sister, and obeyed Lady Drummond in being as quiet as possible. She seemed to take it as a matter of course that Elleen should have her strange whims.

'Mother used to beat her for them,' she said, 'but Nurse Ankaret said that made her worse, and we kept them secret as much as we could. To think of her having them before all that English folk! But she will be all right the morn.'

This proved true; after the night's rest Eleanor rose in the morning as if nothing had disturbed her, and met her hosts as if no visions had hung around them. It was well, for Sir Patrick had accepted the invitation courteously given by the Duke of York to join the great cavalcade with which he, with his brothers-in-law, the

Earl of Salisbury and Bishop of Durham, and the Earl of Warwick, alias the King of the Isle of Wight, were on their way to the Parliament that was summoned anent the King's marriage. The unwilling knights of the shire and burgesses of Northampton who would have to assist in the money grant had asked his protection; and all were to start early on the Monday—for Sunday was carefully observed as a holiday, and the whole party in all their splendours attended high mass in the beautiful church.

After time had been given for the ensuing meal, all the yeomen and young men of the neighbourhood came up to the great outer court of the castle, where there was ample space for sports and military exercises, shooting with the long and cross bow, riding at the quintain and the like, in competitions with the grooms and men-at-arms attached to the retinue of the various great men; and the wives, daughters, and sweethearts came up to watch them. For the most successful there were prizes of leathern coats, bows, knives, and the like, and refreshments of barley-bread, beef, and very small beer, served round with a liberal hand by the troops of servants bearing the falcon and fetterlock badge, and all was done not merely in sport but very much in earnest, in the hope on the part of the Duke, and all who were esteemed patriotic, that these youths might serve in retaining at least, if not in recovering, the English conquests.

Those of gentle blood abstained from their warlike exercises on this day of the week, but they looked on from the broad walk in the thickness of the massive walls; the Duke with his two beautiful little boys by his side, the young Earls of March and Rutland, handsome fair children, in whom the hereditary blue eyes and fair complexion of the Plantagenets recurred, and who bade fair to surpass their father in stature. Their mother was by right and custom to distribute the prizes, but she always disliked doing so, and either excused herself, or reached them out with the ungracious demeanour that had won for her the muttered name of 'Proud Cis'. On this day she had avoided the task on the plea of the occupations caused by her approaching journey, and the Duke put in her place his elder boy and his little cousin, Lady Anne Beauchamp, the child of the young King of the Isle of Wight—a short-lived little delicate being, but very fair and pretty, so that the two children together upon a stone chair, cushioned with red velvet, were like a fairy king and queen, and there was many a murmur of admiration, and 'Bless their little hearts' or 'their sweet faces,' as Anne's dainty fingers handled the prizes, big bows or knives, arrows or belts, and Edward had a smile and appropriate speech for each, such as 'Shoot at a Frenchman's breast next time, Bob'; 'There's a knife to cut up the deer with, Will,' and the like amenities, at which his father nodded, well pleased to see the arts of popularity coming to him by nature. Sir Patrick watched with grave eyes, as he thought of his beloved sovereign's desire to see his people thus practised in arms without peril of feud and violence to one another.

Jean looked on, eager to see some of the Scots of their own escort excel the English pock-puddings, but though Dandie and two or three more contended, the habits were too unfamiliar for them to win any great distinction, and George Douglas did not come forward; the competition was not for men of gentle blood, and success would have brought him forward in a manner it was desirable to avoid. There was a good deal of merry talk between Jean and the hosts, enemies though she regarded them. The Duke of York was evidently much struck with her beauty and liveliness, and he asked Sir Patrick in private whether there were any betrothal or contract in consequence of which he was taking her to France.

'None,' said Sir Patrick, 'it is merely to be with her sister, the Dauphiness.'

'Then,' said young Richard Nevil, who was standing by him, and seemed to have instigated the question, 'there would be no hindrance supposing she struck the King's fancy.'

'The King is contracted,' said Sir Patrick.

'Half contracted! but to the beggarly daughter of a Frenchman who calls himself king of half-a-dozen realms without an acre in any of them. It is not gone so far but that it might be thrown over if he had sense and spirit not to be led by the nose by the Cardinal and Suffolk.'

'Hush-hush, Dick! this is dangerous matter,' said the Duke, and Sir Patrick added—

'These ladies are nieces to the Cardinal.'

'That is well, and it would win the more readily consent—even though Suffolk and his shameful peace were thrown over,' eagerly said the future king-maker.

'Gloucester would be willing,' added the Duke. 'He loved the damsel's father, and hateth the French alliance.'

'I spoke with her,' added Nevil, 'and, red-hot little Scot as she is, she only lacks an English wedlock to make her as truly English, which this wench of Anjou can never be.'

'She would give our meek King just the spring and force he needs,' said the Duke; 'but thou wilt hold thy peace, Sir Knight, and let no whisper reach the women-folk.'

This Sir Patrick readily promised. He was considerably tickled by the idea of negotiating such an important affair for his young King and his protegee, feeling that the benefit to Scotland might outweigh any qualms as to the disappointment to the French allies. Besides, if King Henry of Windsor should think proper to fall in love with her, he could not help it; he had not brought her away from home or to England with any such purpose; he had only to stand by and let things take their course, so long as the safety and honour of her, her brother, and the kingdom were secure. So reasoned the canny Scot, but he held his tongue to his Lilias.

CHAPTER 4. ST. HELEN S

'I thought King Henry had resembled thee,
In courage, courtship, and proportion:
But all his mind is bent to holiness,
To number Ave-Maries on his beads:
His champions are the prophets and apostles;

His weapons, holy saws of sacred writ.'
King Henry VI.

George Douglas's chivalrous venture in defence of the falcon of his lady-love had certainly not done much for him hitherto, as Davie observed. The Lady Joanna, as every one now called her, took it as only the bounden duty and natural service of one of her suite, and would have cared little for his suffering for it personally, except so far as it concerned her own dignity, which she understood much better than she had done in Scotland, where she was only one of 'the lassies,' an encumbrance to every one.

The York retainers had dropped all idea of visiting his offence upon Douglas when they found that he had acted in the service of an honoured guest of their lord, but they did not look with much favour on him or on any other of the Scottish troop, whom their master enjoined them to treat as guests and comrades.

The uniting of so many suites of the mighty nobles of the fifteenth century formed quite a little army, amounting to some two or three hundred horsemen, mostly armed, and well appointed, with their masters' badges on their sleeves,—falcon and fetterlock, dun cow, bear and ragged staff and the cross of Durham, while all likewise wore in their caps the white rose. Waggons with household furniture and kitchen needments had been sent in advance with the numerous 'black guard,' and a provision of cattle for slaughter accompanied these, since it was one of the considerate acts that already had won affection to Richard of York that, unlike many of the great nobles, he always avoided as much as possible letting his train be oppressive to the country-people.

David Drummond had been seeing that all his father's troop were duly provided with the Drummond badge, the thyme, which was requisite as showing them accepted of the Duke of York's company, but as George and his follower had never submitted to wear it, he was somewhat surprised to find the gray blossom prominent in George's steel-guarded cap, and to hear him saying—

'Don it, Ringan, as thou wouldst obey me.'

'His father's son is not his own father,' said Ringan sulkily.

'Then tak' thy choice of wearing it, or winning hame as thou canst—most like hanging on the nearest oak.'

'And I'd gey liefer than demean myself in the Drummond thyme!' replied Ringan, half turning away. 'But then what would come of Gray Meg wi' only the Master to see till her,' muttered he, caressing the mare's neck. 'Weel, aweel, sir'—and he held out his hand for the despised spray.

'Is yon thy wild callant, Geordie?' said David in some surprise, for Ringan was not only provided with a pony, but his thatch of tow-like hair had been trimmed and covered with a barret cap, and his leathern coat and leggings were like those of the other horse-boys.

'Ay,' said George, 'this is no place to be ower kenspeckle.'

'I was coming to ask,' said David, 'if thou wouldst not own thyself to my father, and take thy proper place ere ganging farther south. It irks me to see some of the best blood in Scotland among the grooms.'

'It must irk thee still, Davie,' returned George. 'These English folk might not thole to see my father's son in their hands without winning something out of him, and I saw by what passed the other day that thou and thy father would stand by me, hap what hap, and I'll never embroil him and peril the lady by my freak.'

'My father kens pretty well wha is riding in his companie,' said David.

'Ay, but he is not bound to ken.'

'And thou winna write to the Yerl, as ye said ye would when ye were ower the Border? There's a clerk o' the Bishop of Durham ganging back, and my father is writing letters that he will send forward to the King, and thou couldst get a scart o' the pen to thy father.'

'And what wad be thought of a puir man-at-arms sending letters to the Yerl?' said George. 'Na, na; I may write when we win to France, a friendly land, but while we are in England, the loons shall make naething out of my father's son.'

'Weel, gang thine ain gait, and an unco strange one it is,' said David. 'I marvel what thou count'st on gaining by it!'

'The sicht of her at least,' said George. 'Nay, she needed a stout hand once, she may need it again.'

Whereat David waved his hands in a sort of contemptuous wonder.

'If it were the Duchess of York now!' he said. 'She is far bonnier and even prouder, gin that be what tak's your fancy! And as to our Jeanie, they are all cockering her up till she'll no be content with a king. I doot me if the Paip himself wad be good enough for her!'

It was true that the brilliant and lively Lady Joanna was in high favour with the princely gallants of the cavalcade. The only member of the party at all equal to her in beauty was the Duchess of York, who travelled in a whirlicote with her younger children and her ladies, and at the halting-places never relaxed the stiff dignity with which she treated every one. Eleanor did indeed accompany her sister, but she had not Jean's quick power of repartee, and she often answered at haphazard, and was not understood when she did reply; nor had she Jean's beauty, so that in the opinion of most of the young nobles she was but a raw, almost dumb, Scotswoman, and was left to herself as much as courtesy permitted, except by the young King of the Isle of Wight, a gentle, poetical personage, in somewhat delicate health, with tastes that made him the chosen companion of the scholarly King Henry. He could repeat a great deal of Chaucer's poetry by heart, the chief way in which people could as yet enjoy books, and there was an interchange between them of "Blind Harry" and of the "Canterbury Tales", as they rode side by side, sometimes making their companions laugh, and wonder that the youthful queen was not jealous. Dame Lilias found her congenial companion in the Countess Alice of Salisbury, who could talk with her of that golden age of the two kings, Henry and James, of her brother Malcolm, and of Esclairmonde de Luxembourg, now Sister Clare, whom they hoped soon to see in the sisterhood of St. Katharine's.

'Hers hath been the happy course, the blessed dedication,' said Countess Alice.

'We have both been blessed too, thanks to the saints,' returned Lilias.

'That is indeed sooth,' replied the other lady. 'My lord hath ever been most good to me, and I have had joy of my sons. Yet there is much that my mind forbodes and shrinks back from in dread, as I watch my son Richard's overmastering spirit.'

'The Cardinal and the Duke of Gloucester have long been at strife, as we heard,' said Lady Drummond, 'but sure that will be appeased now that the Cardinal is an old man and your King come to years of discretion.'

'The King is a sweet youth, a very saint already,' replied the Countess, 'but I misdoubt whether he have the stout heart and strong hand of his father, and he is set on peace.'

'Peace is to be followed,' said Lilias, amazed at the tone in which her friend mentioned it.

'Peace at home! Ay, but peace at home is only to be had by war abroad. Peace abroad without honour only leaves these fiery spirits to fume, and fly at one another's throats, or at those who wrought it. My mind misgives me, mine old friend, lest wrangling lead to blows. I had rather see my Richard spurring against the French than against his cousins of Somerset, and while they advance themselves and claim to be nearer in blood to the King than our good host of York, so long will there be cause of bitterness.'

'Our kindly host seems to wish evil to no man.'

'Nay, he is content enough, but my sister his wife, and alas! my son, cannot let him forget that after the Duke of Gloucester he is highest in the direct male line to King Edward of Windsor, and in the female line stands nearer than this present King.'

'In Scotland he would not forget that his father suffered for that very cause.'

'Ah, Lilias, thou hast seen enow of what such blood-feuds work in Scotland to know how much I dread and how I pray they may never awaken here. The blessed King Harry of Monmouth kept them down by the strong hand, while he won all hearts to himself. It is my prayer that his young son may do the like, and that my Lord of York be not fretted out of his peaceful loyalty by the Somerset "outrecuidance", and above all that my own son be not the make-bate; but Richard is proud and fiery, and I fear—I greatly fear, what may be in store for us.'

Lilias thought of Eleanor's vision, but kept silence respecting it.

Forerunners had been sent on by the Duke of York to announce his coming, and who were in his company; and on the last stage these returned, bringing with them a couple of knights and of clerks on the part of the Cardinal of Winchester to welcome his great-nieces, whom he claimed as his guests.

'I had hoped that the ladies of Scotland would honour my poor house,' said the Duke.

'The Lord Cardinal deems it thus more fitting,' said the portly priest who acted as Beaufort's secretary, and who spoke with an authority that chafed the Duke.

Richard Nevil rode up to him and muttered—'He hath divined our purpose, and means to cross it.'

The clerk, however, spoke with Sir Patrick, and in a manner took possession of the young ladies. They were riding between walled courts, substantially built, with intervals of fields and woods, or sometimes indeed of morass; for London was still an island in the middle of swamps, with the great causeways of the old Roman times leading to it. The spire of St. Paul's and the square keep of the

Tower had been pointed out to them, and Jean exclaimed—

'My certie, it is a braw toon!'

But Eleanor, on her side, exclaimed—

"Tis but a flat! Mine eye wearies for the sea; ay, and for Arthur's Seat and the Castle! Oh, I wadna gie Embro' for forty of sic toons!'

Perhaps Jean had guessed enough to make her look on London with an eye of possession, for her answer was—

'Hear till her; and she was the first to cry out upon Embro' for a place of reivers and land-loupers, and to want to leave it.'

There was so much that was new and wonderful that the sisters pursued the question no further. They saw the masts of the shipping in the Thames, and what seemed to them a throng of church towers and spires; while, nearer, the road began to be full of market-folk, the women in hoods and mantles and short petticoats, the men in long frocks, such as their Saxon forefathers had worn, driving the rough ponies or donkeys that had brought in their produce. There were begging friars in cowl and frock, and beggars, not friars, with crutch and bowl; there were gleemen and tumbling women, solid tradesfolk going out to the country farms they loved, troops of 'prentices on their way to practice with the bow or cudgel, and parties of gaily-coloured nobles, knights, squires, and burgesses, coming, like their own party, to the meeting of Parliament.

There were continual greetings, the Duke of York showing himself most markedly courteous to all, his dark head being almost continuously uncovered, and bending to his saddle-bow in response to the salutations that met him; and friendly inquiries and answers being often exchanged. The Earl of Salisbury and his son were almost equally courteous; but in the midst of all the interest of these greetings, soon after entering the city at Bishopsgate, the clerk caused the two Scottish sisters to draw up at an arched gateway in a solid-looking wall, saying that it was here that my Lord Cardinal wished his royal kinswomen to be received, at the Priory of St. Helen's. A hooded lay-sister looked out at a wicket, and on his speaking to her, proceeded to unbar the great gates, while the Duke of York took leave in a more than kindly manner, declaring that they would meet again, and that he knew 'My Lady of St. Helen's would make them good cheer.'

Indeed, he himself and the King of Wight rode into the outer court, and lifted the two ladies down from horseback, at the inner gate, beyond which they might not go. Jean, crossed now for the first time since she had left home, was in tears of vexation, and could hardly control her voice to respond to his words, muttering—

'As if I looked for this. Beshrew the old priest!'

None but female attendants could be admitted. Sir Patrick, with his sons and the rest of the train, was to be lodged at the great palace of the Bishop of Winchester at Southwark, and as he came up to take leave of Jean, she said, with a stamp of her foot and a clench of her hand—

'Let my uncle know that I am no cloister-bird to be mewed up here. I demand to be with the friends I have made, and who have bidden me.'

Shrewd Sir Patrick smiled a little as he said—

'I will tell the Lord Cardinal what you say, lady; but methinks you will find that submission to him with a good grace carries you farther here than does ill-humour.'

He said something of the same kind to his wife as he took leave of her, well knowing who were predominant with the King, and who were in opposition, the only link being the King of Wight, or rather Earl of Warwick, who, as the son of Henry's guardian, had been bred up in the closest intimacy with the monarch, and, indeed, had been invested with his fantastic sovereignty that he might be treated as a brother and on an equality.

Jean, however, remained very angry and discontented. After her neglected and oppressed younger days, the courtesy and admiration she had received for the last ten days had the effect of making her like a spoilt child; and when they entered the inner cloistered court within, and were met by the Lady Prioress, at the head of all her sisters in black dresses, she hardly vouchsafed an inclination of the head in reply to the graceful and courtly welcome with which the princesses, nieces to the great Cardinal, were received. Eleanor, usually in the background, was left in surprise and confusion to stammer out thanks in broad Scotch, seconded by Lady Drummond, who could make herself far more intelligible to these south-country ears.

There was a beautiful cloister, a double walk with clustered columns running down the centre and a vaulted roof, and with a fountain in the midst of the quadrangle. There was a chapel on one side, the buildings of the Priory on the others. It was only a Priory, for the parent Abbey was in the country; but the Prioress was a noble lady of the house of Stafford, a small personage as to stature, but thoroughly alert and business-like, and, in fact, the moving spring, not only of the actual house, but of the parent Abbey, manager of the property it possessed in the city, and of all its monastic politics.

Without apparent offence, she observed that no doubt the ladies were weary, and that Sister Mabel should conduct them to the guest-chamber. Accordingly one of the black figures led the way, and as soon as they were beyond ear-shot there were observations that would not have gratified Jean.

'The ill-nurtured Scots!' cried one young nun. ''Tis ever the way with them,' returned a much older one. 'I mind when one was captive in my father's castle who was a mere clown, and drank up the water that was meant to wash his fingers after meat. The guest-chamber will need a cleaning after they are gone!'

'Methinks it was less lack of manners than lack of temper,' said the Prioress. 'She hath the Beaufort face and the Beaufort spirit.'

The chapel bell began to ring, and the black veils and white filed in long procession to the pointed doorway, while the two Scottish damsels, with Lady Drummond, her daughter, and Christie, were conducted to three chambers looking out on the one side on the cloistered court, on the other over a choicely-kept garden, walled in, but planted with trees shading the turf walks. The rooms were, as Sister Mabel explained with some complacency, reserved for the lodging of the noble ladies who came to London as guests of my Lord Cardinal, or with petitions to the King; and certainly there was nothing of asceticism about them;

but they were an advance even on those at Fotheringay. St. Helena discovering the Cross was carved over the ample chimney, and the hangings were of Spanish leather, with all the wondrous history of Santiago's relics, including the miracle of the cock and hen, embossed and gilt upon them. There was a Venetian mirror, in which the ladies saw more of themselves than they had ever done before, and with exquisite work around; there were carved chests inlaid with ivory, and cushions, perfect marvels of needlework, as were the curtains and coverlets of the mighty bed, and the screens to be arranged for privacy. There were toilette vessels of beautifully shaped and brightly polished brass, and on a silver salver was a refection of manchet bread, comfits, dried cherries, and wine.

Sister Mabel explained that a lay-sister would be at hand, in case anything was needed by the noble ladies, and then hurried away to vespers.

Jean threw herself upon the cross-legged chair that stood nearest.

'A nunnery forsooth! Does our uncle trow that is what I came here for? We have had enow of nunneries at home.'

'Oh, fie for shame, Jeanie!' cried Eleanor.

"Twas thou that saidst it,' returned Jean. 'Thou saidst thou hadst no call to the veil, and gin my Lord trows that we shall thole to be shut up here, he will find himself in the wrong.'

'Lassie, lassie,' exclaimed Lady Drummond, 'what ails ye? This is but a lodging, and sic a braw chamber as ye hae scarce seen before. Would you have your uncle lodge ye among all his priests and clerks? Scarce the place for douce maidens, I trow.'

'Leddy of Glenuskie, ye're not sae sib to the bluid royal of Scotland as to speak thus! Lassie indeed!'

Again Eleanor remonstrated. 'Jeanie, to speak thus to our gude kinswoman!'

'I would have all about me ken their place, and what fits them,' said the haughty young lady, partly out of ill-temper and disappointment, partly in imitation of the demeanour of Duchess Cicely. 'As to the Cardinal, I would have him bear in mind that we are a king's own daughters, and he is at best but the grandson of a king! And if he deems that he has a right to shut us up here out of sight of the King and his court, lest we should cross his rule over his King and disturb his French policy and craft, there are those that will gar him ken better!'

'Some one else will ken better,' quietly observed Dame Lilias. 'Gin ye be no clean daft, Leddy Joanna, since naething else will serve ye, canna ye see that to strive with the Cardinal is the worst gait to win his favour with the King, gin that be what ye be set upon?'

'There be others that can deal with the King, forbye the Cardinal,' said Jean, tossing her head.

Just then arrived a sister, sent by the Mother Prioress, to invite the ladies to supper in her own apartments.

Her respectful manner so far pacified Jean's ill-humour that a civil reply was returned; the young ladies bestirred themselves to make preparations, though Jean grumbled at the trouble for 'a pack of womenfolk'—and supposed they were to make a meal of dried peas and red herrings, like their last on Lammermuir.

It was a surprise to be conducted, not to the refectory, where all the nuns took their meal together, but to a small room opening into the cloister on one side, and with a window embowered in vines on the other, looking into the garden. It was by no means bare, like the typical cells of strict convents. The Mother, Margaret Stafford, was a great lady, and the Benedictines of the old foundation of St. Helen's in the midst of the capital were indeed respectable and respected, but very far from strict observers of their rule—and St. Helen's was so much influenced by the wealth and display of the city that the nuns, many of whom were these great merchants' daughters, would have been surprised to be told that they had departed from Benedictine simplicity. So the Prioress's chamber was tapestried above with St. Helena's life, and below was enclosed with drapery panels. It was strewed with sweet fresh rushes, and had three cross-legged chairs, besides several stools; the table, as usual upon trestles, was provided with delicate napery, and there was a dainty perfume about the whole; a beautiful crucifix of ivory and ebony, with images of Our Lady and St. John on either side, and another figure of St. Helena, cross in hand, presiding over the holy water stoup, were the most ecclesiastical things in the garniture, except the exquisitely illuminated breviary that lay open upon a desk.

Mother Margaret rose to receive her guests with as much dignity as Jean herself could have shown, and made them welcome to her poor house, hoping that they would there find things to their mind.

Something restrained Jean from bursting out with her petulant complaint, and it was Eleanor who replied with warm thanks. 'My Lord Cardinal would come to visit them on the morn,' the Prioress said; 'and in the meantime, she hoped,' looking at Jean, 'they would condescend to the hospitality of the poor daughters of St. Helen.'

The hospitality, as brought in by two plump, well-fed lay-sisters, consisted of 'chickens in cretyne,' stewed in milk, seasoned with sugar, coloured with saffron, of potage of oysters, butter of almond-milk, and other delicate meats, such as had certainly never been tasted at Stirling or Dunbar. Lady Drummond's birth entitled her and Annis to sit at table with the Princesses and the Prioress, and she ventured to inquire after Esclairmonde de Luxembourg, or, as she was now called, Sister Clare of St. Katharine's.

'I see her at times. She is the head of the sisters,' said the Prioress; 'but we have few dealings with uncloistered sisters.'

'They do a holy work,' observed Lady Lilias.

'None ever blamed the Benedictines for lack of alms-deeds,' returned the Prioress haughtily, scarcely attending to the guest's disclaimer. 'Nor do I deem it befitting that instead of the poor coming to us our sisters should run about to all the foulest hovels of the Docks, encountering men continually, and those of the rudest sort.'

'Yet there are calls and vocations for all,' ventured Lady Drummond. 'And the sick are brethren in need.'

'Let them send to us for succour then,' answered Mother Margaret. 'I grant that it is well that some one should tend them in their huts, but such tasks are for sisters of low birth and breeding. Mine are ladies of noble rank, though I do admit daughters of Lord Mayors and Aldermen.'

'Our Saint Margaret was a queen, Reverend Mother,' put in Eleanor.

'She was no nun, saving your Grace,' said the Prioress. 'What I speak of is that which beseems a daughter of St. Bennet, of an ancient and royal foundation! The saving of the soul is so much harder to the worldly life, specially to a queen, that it is no marvel if she has to abase herself more—even to the washing of lepers—than is needful to a vowed and cloistered sister.'

It was an odd theory, that this Benedictine seclusion saved trouble, as being actually the strait course; but the young maidens were not scholars enough to question it, and Dame Lilias, though she had learnt more from her brother and her friend, would have deemed it presumptuous to dispute with a Reverend Mother. So only Eleanor murmured, 'The holy Margaret no saint'—and Jean, 'Weel, I had liefer take my chance.'

'All have not a vocation,' piously said the Mother. 'Taste this Rose Dalmoyne, Madame; our lay-sister Mold is famed for making it. An alderman of the Fishmongers' Company sent to beg that his cook might know the secret, but that was not to be lightly parted with, so we only send them a dish for their banquets.'

Rose Dalmoyne was chiefly of peas, flavoured with almonds and milk, but the guests grew weary of the varieties of delicacies, and were very glad when the tables were removed, and Eleanor asked permission to look at the illuminations in the breviary on the desk.

And exquisite they were. The book had been brought from Italy and presented to the Prioress by a merchant who wished to place his daughter in St. Helen's, and the beauty was unspeakable. There were natural flowers painted so perfectly that the scattered violets seemed to invite the hand to lift them up from their gold-besprinkled bed, and flies and beetles that Eleanor actually attempted to drive away; and at all the greater holy days, the type and the antitype covering the two whole opposite pages were represented in the admirable art and pure colouring of the early Cinquecento.

Eleanor and Annis were entranced, and the Prioress, seeing that books had an attraction for her younger guest, promised her on the morrow a sight of some of the metrical lives of the saints, especially of St. Katharine and of St. Cecilia. It must be owned that Jean was not fretted as she expected by chapel bells in the middle of the night, nor was even Lady Drummond summoned by them as she intended, but there was a conglomeration of the night services in the morning, with beautiful singing, that delighted Eleanor, and the festival mass ensuing was also more ornate than anything to be seen in Scotland. And that the extensive almsgiving had not been a vain boast was evident from the swarms of poor of all kinds who congregated in the outer court for the attention of the Sisters Almoner and Infirmarer, attended by two or three novices and some lay-sisters.

There were genuine poor, ragged forlorn women, and barefooted, almost naked children, and also sturdy beggars, pilgrims and palmers on their way to various shrines, north or south, and many more for whom a dole of broth or bread sufficed; but there were also others with heads or limbs tied up, sometimes injured in the many street fights, but oftener with the terrible sores only too common from the squalid habits and want of vegetable diet of the poor. These were all attended to with a tenderness and patience that spoke well for the charity of Sister Anne and her assistants, and indeed before long Dame Lilias perceived that, however slack and easy-going the general habits might be, there were truly meek and saintly women among the sisterhood.

The morning was not far advanced before a lay-sister came hurrying in from the portress's wicket to announce that my Lord Cardinal was on his way to visit the ladies of Scotland. There was great commotion. Mother Margaret summoned all her nuns and drew them up in state, and Sister Mabel, who carried the tidings to the guests, asked whether they would not join in receiving him.

'We are king's daughters,' said Jean haughtily.

'But he is a Prince of the Church and an aged man,' said Lady Drummond, who had already risen, and was adjusting that headgear of Eleanor's that never would stay in its place. And her matronly voice acted upon Jean, so as to conquer the petulant pride, enough to make her remember that the Lady of Glenuskie was herself a Stewart and king's grandchild, and moreover knew more of courts and their habits than herself.

So down they went together, in time to join the Prioress on the steps, as the attendants of the great stately, princely Cardinal Bishop began to appear. He did not come in state, so that he had only half a dozen clerks and as many gentlemen in attendance, together with Sir Patrick and his two sons.

Few of the Plantagenet family had been long-lived, and Cardinal Beaufort was almost a marvel in the family at seventy. Much evil has been said and written of him, and there is no doubt that he was one of those mediaeval prelates who ought to have been warriors or statesmen, and that he had been no model for the Episcopacy in his youth. But though far from having been a saint, it would seem that his unpopularity in his old age was chiefly incurred by his desire to put an end to the long and miserable war with France, and by his opposition to a much worse man, the Duke of Gloucester, whose plausible murmurs and amiable manners made him a general favourite. At this period of his life the old man had lived past his political ambitions, and his chief desire was to leave the gentle young king freed from the wasting war by a permanent peace, to be secured by a marriage with a near connection of the French monarch, and daughter to the most honourable and accomplished Prince in Europe. That his measures turned out wretchedly has been charged upon his memory, and he has been supposed guilty of a murder, of which he was certainly innocent, and which probably was no murder at all.

He had become a very grand and venerable old man, when old men were scarce, and his white hair and beard (a survival of the customs of the days of Edward III) contrasted well with his scarlet hat and cape, as he came slowly into the cloistered court on his large sober-paced Spanish mule; a knight and the chaplain of the convent assisted him from it, and the whole troop of the convent knelt as he lifted his fingers to bestow his blessing, Jean casting a quick glance around to satisfy her proud spirit. The Prioress then kissed his hand, but he raised and kissed the cheeks of his two grand-nieces, after which he moved on to the Prioress's chamber, and there, after being installed in her large chair, and waving to the four favoured inmates to be also seated, he looked critically at the two sisters, and observed, 'So, maidens! one favours the mother, the other the father! Poor Joan, it is two-and-twenty years since we bade her good-speed, she and her young king—who behoved to be a minstrel—on her way to her kingdom, as if it were the land of Cockayne, for picking up gold and silver. Little of that she found, I trow, poor wench. Alack! it was a sore life we sent her to. And you are mourning her freshly, my maidens! I trust she died at peace with God and man.'

'That reiver, Patrick Hepburn, let the priest from Haddington come to assoilzie and housel her,' responded Jean.

'Ah! Masses shall be said for her by my bedesmen at St. Cross, and at all my churches,' said the Cardinal, crossing himself. 'And you are on your way to your sister, the Dolfine, as your knight tells me. It is well. You may be worthily wedded in France, and I will take order for your safe going. Meantime, this is a house where you may well serve your poor mother's soul by prayers and masses, and likewise perfect yourselves in French.'

This was not at all what Jean had intended, and she pouted a little, while the Cardinal asked, changing his language, 'Ces donzelles, ont elles appris le Francais?'

Jean, who had tried to let Father Romuald teach her a little in conversation during the first part of the journey, but who had dropped the notion since other ideas had been inspired at Fotheringay, could not understand, and pouted the more; but Eleanor, who had been interested, and tried more in earnest, for Margaret's sake, answered diffidently and blushing deeply, 'Un petit peu, beau Sire Oncle.'

He smiled, and said, 'You can be well instructed here. The Reverend Mother hath sisters here who can both speak and write French of Paris.'

'That have I truly, my good Lord,' replied the Prioress. 'Sisters Isabel and Beata spent their younger days, the one at Rouen, the other at Bordeaux, and have learned many young ladies in the true speaking of the French tongue.'

'It is well!' said the Cardinal, 'my fair nieces will have good leisure. While sharing the orisons that I will institute for the repose of your mother, you can also be taught the French.'

Jean could not help speaking now, so far was this from all her hopes. 'Sir, sir, the Duke and Duchess of York, and the Countess of Salisbury, and the Queen of the Isle of Wight all bade us to be their guests.'

'They could haply not have been aware of your dool,' said the Cardinal gravely.

'But, my Lord, our mother hath been dead since before Martinmas,' exclaimed Jean.

'I know not what customs of dool be thought befitting in a land like Scotland,' said the Cardinal, in such a repressive manner that Jean was only withheld by awe from bursting into tears of disappointment and anger at the slight to her country.

Lady Drummond ventured to speak. 'Alack, my Lord,' she said, 'my poor Queen died in the hands of a freebooter, leaving her daughters in such stress and peril that they had woe enough for themselves, till their brother the King came to their rescue.'

'The more need that they should fulfil all that may be done for the grace of her soul,' replied the uncle; but just at this crisis of Jean's mortification there was a knocking at the door, and a sister breathlessly entreated—

'Pardon! Merci! My Lord, my Lady Mother! Here's the King, the King himself—and the King and Queen of the Isle of Wight asking licence to enter to visit the ladies of Scotland.'

Kings were always held to be free to enter anywhere, even far more dangerous monarchs than the pious Henry VI. Jean's heart bounded up again, with a sense of exultation over the old uncle, as the Prioress went out to receive her new guest, and the Cardinal emitted a sort of grunting sigh, without troubling himself to go out to meet the youth, whom he had governed from babyhood, and in whose own name he had, as one of the council, given permission for wholesome chastisements of the royal person.

King Henry entered. He was then twenty-four years old, tall, graceful, and with beautiful features and complexion, almost feminine in their delicacy, and with a wonderful purity and sweetness in the expression of the mouth and blue eyes, so that he struck Eleanor as resembling the angels in the illuminations that she had been studying, as he removed his dark green velvet jewelled cap on entering, and gave a cousinly, respectful kiss lightly to each of the young ladies on her cheek, somewhat as if he were afraid of them. Then after greeting the Cardinal, who had risen on his entrance, he said that, hearing that his fair cousins were arrived, he had come to welcome them, and to entreat them to let him do them such honour as was possible in a court without a queen.

'The which lack will soon be remedied,' put in his grand-uncle.

'Truly you are in holy keeping here,' said the pious young King, crossing himself, 'but I trust, my sweet cousins, that you will favour my poor house at Westminster with your presence at a supper, and share such entertainment as is in our power to provide.'

'My nieces are keeping their mourning for their mother, from which they have hitherto been hindered by the tumults of their kingdom,' said the Cardinal.

'Ah!' said the King, crossing himself, and instantly moved, 'far be it from me to break into their holy retirement for such a purpose.' (Jean could have bitten the Cardinal.) 'But I will take order with my Lord Abbot of Westminster for a grand requiem mass for the good Queen Joanna, at which they will, I trust, be present, and they will honour my poor table afterwards.'

To refuse this was quite impossible, and the day was to be fixed after reference to the Abbess. Meantime the King's eye was caught by the illuminated breviary. He was a connoisseur in such arts, and eagerly stood up to look at it as it lay on the desk. Eleanor could not but come and direct him to the pages with which she had been most delighted. She found him looking at Jacob's dream on the one side, the Ascension on the other.

'How marvellous it is!' she said. 'It is like the very light from the sky!'

'Light from heaven,' said the King; 'Jacob has found it among the stones. Wandering and homelessness are his first step in the ladder to heaven!'

'Ah, sir, did you say that to comfort and hearten us?' said Eleanor.

There was a strange look in the startled blue eyes that met hers. 'Nay, truly, lady, I presumed not so far! I was but wondering whether those who are born to have all the world are in the way of the stair to heaven.'

Meantime the King of Wight had made his request for the presence of the ladies at a supper at Warwick House, and Jean, clasping her hands, implored her uncle to consent.

'I am sure our mother cannot be the better for our being thus mewed up,' she cried, 'and I'll rise at prime, and tell my beads for her.'

She looked so pretty and imploring that the old man's heart was melted, all the more that the King was paying more attention to the book and the far less beautiful Eleanor, than to her and the invitation was accepted.

The convent bell rang for nones, and the King joined the devotions of the nuns, though he was not admitted within the choir; and just as these were over, the Countess of Salisbury arrived to take the Lady of Glenuskie to see their old friend, the Mother Clare at St. Katharine's, bringing a sober palfrey for her conveyance.

'A holy woman, full of alms-deeds,' said the King. 'The lady is happy in her friendship.'

Which words were worth much to Lady Drummond, for the Prioress sent a lay-sister to invite Mother Clare to a refection at the convent.

CHAPTER 5. THE MEEK USURPER

'Henry, thou of holy birth,
Thou to whom thy Windsor gave
Nativity and name and grave!
Heavily upon his head
Ancestral crimes were visited.'—SOUTHEY.

It suits not with the main thread of our story to tell of the happy and peaceful meetings between the Lady of Glenuskie and her old friend, who had given up almost princely rank and honour to become the servant of the poor and suffering strangers at the wharves of London. To Dame Lilias, Mother Clare's quiet cell at St. Katharine's was a blessed haven of rest, peace, and charity, such as was neither the guest-chamber nor the Prioress's parlour at St. Helen's, with all the distractions of the princesses' visitors and invitations, and with the Lady Joanna continually pulling against the authority that the Cardinal, her uncle, was exerting over his nieces.

His object evidently was to keep them back, firstly, from the York party, and secondly, from the King, under pretext of their mourning for their mother; and in this he might have succeeded but for the interest in them that had been aroused in Henry by his companion, namesake, and almost brother, the King of Wight. The King came or sent each day to St. Helen's to arrange about the requiem at Westminster, and when their late travelling companions invited the young ladies to dinner or to supper expressly to meet the King and the Cardinal—not in state, but at what would be now called a family party—Beaufort had no excuse for a refusal, such as he could not give without dire offence. And, indeed, he was even then obliged to yield to the general voice, and, recalling his own nephew from Normandy, send the Duke of York to defend the remnant of the English conquests.

He could only insist that the requiem should be the first occasion of the young ladies going out of the convent; but they had so many visitors there that they had not much cause for murmuring, and the French instructions of Sister Beata did not amount to much, even with Eleanor, while Jean loudly protested that she was not going to school.

The great day of the requiem came at last. The Cardinal had, through Sir Patrick Drummond and the Lady, provided handsome robes of black and purple for his nieces, and likewise palfreys for their conveyance to Westminster; and made it understood that unless Lady Joanna submitted to be completely veiled he should send a closed litter.

'The doited auld carle!' she cried, as she unwillingly hooded and veiled herself. 'One would think we were basilisks to slay the good folk of London with our eyes.'

The Drummond following, with fresh thyme sprays, beginning to turn brown, were drawn up in the outer court, all with black scarves across the breast— George Douglas among them, of course—and they presently united with the long train of clerks who belonged to the household of the Cardinal of Winchester. Jean managed her veil so as to get more than one peep at the throng in the streets through which they passed, so as to see and to be seen; and she was disappointed that no acclamations greeted the fair face thus displayed by fits. She did not understand English politics enough to know that a Beaufort face and Beaufort train were the last things the London crowd was likely to applaud. They had not forgotten the penance of the popular Duke Humfrey's wife, which, justly or unjustly, was imputed to the Cardinal and his nephews of Somerset.

But the King, in robes of purple and black, came to assist her from her palfrey before the beautiful entry of the Abbey Church, and led her up the nave to the desks prepared around what was then termed 'a herce,' but which would now be called a catafalque, an erection supposed to contain the body, and adorned with the lozenges of the arms of Scotland and Beaufort, and of the Stewart, in honour of the Black Knight of Lorn.

The Cardinal was present, but the Abbot of Westminster celebrated. All was exceedingly solemn and beautiful, in a far different style from the maimed rites that had been bestowed upon poor Queen Joanna in Scotland. The young King's face was more angelic than ever, and as psalm and supplication, dirge and hymn arose, chanted by the full choir, speaking of eternal peace, Eleanor bowed her head under her veil, as her bosom swelled with a strange yearning longing, not exactly grief, and large tears dropped from her eyes as she thought less of her mother than of her noble-hearted father; and the words came back to her in which Father Malcolm Stewart, in his own bitter grief, had told the desolate children to remember that their father was waiting for them in Paradise. Even Jean was so touched by the music and carried out of herself that she forgot the spectators, forgot the effect she was to produce, forgot her struggle with her uncle, and sobbed and wept with all her heart, perhaps with the more abandon because she, like all the rest, was fasting.

With much reverence for her emotion, the King, when the service was over, led her out of the church to the adjoining palace, where the Queen of Wight and the Countess of Suffolk, a kinswoman through the mother of the Beauforts, conducted the ladies to unveil themselves before they were to join the noontide refection with the King.

There was no great state about it, spread, as it was, not in the great hall, but in the richly-tapestried room called Paradise. The King's manner was most gently and sweetly courteous to both sisters. His three little orphan half-brothers, the Tudors, were at table; and his kind care to send them dainties, and the look with which he repressed an unseasonable attempt of Jasper's to play with the dogs, and Edmund's roughness with little Owen, reminded the sisters of Mary with 'her weans,' and they began to speak of them when the meal was over, while he showed them his chief treasures, his books. There was St. Augustine's City of God, exquisitely copied; there was the History of St. Louis, by the bon Sire de Joinville; there were Sir John Froissart's Chronicles, the same that the good Canon had presented to King Richard of Bordeaux.

Jean cast a careless glance at the illuminations, and exclaimed at Queen Isabel's high headgear and her becloaked greyhound. Eleanor looked and longed, and sighed that she could not read the French, and only a very little of the Latin.

'This you can read,' said Henry, producing the Canterbury Tales; 'the fair minstrelsy of my Lady of Suffolk's grandsire.'

Eleanor was enchanted. Here were the lines the King of Wight had repeated to her, and she was soon eagerly listening as Henry read to her the story of 'Patient Grisell.'

'Ah! but is it well thus tamely to submit?' she asked.

'Patience is the armour and conquest of the godly,' said Henry, quoting a saying that was to serve 'the meek usurper' well in after-times.

'May not patience go too far?' said Eleanor.

'In this world, mayhap,' said he; 'scarcely so in that which is to come.'

'I would not be the King's bride to hear him say so,' laughed the Lady of Suffolk. 'Shall I tell her, my lord, that this is your Grace's ladder to carry her to heaven?'

Henry blushed like a girl, and said that he trusted never to be so lacking in courtesy as the knight; and the King of Wight, wishing to change the subject, mentioned that the Lady Eleanor had sung or said certain choice ballads, and Henry eagerly entreated for one. It was the pathetic 'Wife of Usher's Well' that Eleanor chose, with the three sons whose hats were wreathen with the birk that

> 'Neither grew in dyke nor ditch,
> Nor yet in any shaugh,
> But at the gates of Paradise

That birk grew fair eneugh.'

Henry was greatly delighted with the verse, and entreated her, if it were not tedious, to repeat it over again.

In return he promised to lend her some of the translations from the Latin of Lydgate, the Monk of Bury, and sent them, wrapped in a silken neckerchief, by the hands of one of his servants to the convent.

'Was that a token?' anxiously asked young Douglas, riding up to David Drummond, as they got into order to ride back to Winchester House, after escorting the ladies to St. Helen's.

'Token, no; 'tis a book for Lady Elleen. Never fash yourself, man; the King, so far as I might judge, is far more taken with Elleen than ever he is with Jean. He seems but a bookish sort of bodie of Malcolm's sort.'

'My certie, an' that be sae, we may look to winning back Roxburgh and Berwick!' returned the Douglas, his eye flashing. 'He's welcome to Lady Elleen! But that ane should look at her in presence of her sister! He maun be mair of a monk than a man!'

Such was, in truth, Jean's own opinion when she flounced into her chamber at the Priory and turned upon her sister.

'Weel, Elleen, and I hope ye've had your will, and are a bit shamed, taking up his Grace so that none by yersell could get in a word wi' him.'

'Deed, Jeanie, I could not help it; if he would ask me about our ballants and buiks, that ye would never lay your mind to—'

'Ballants and buiks! Bonnie gear for a king that should be thinking of spears and jacks, lances and honours. Ye're welcome to him, Elleen, sin ye choose to busk your cockernnonny at ane that's as good as wedded! I'll never have the man who's wanting the strick of carle hemp in the making of him!'

Eleanor burst into tears and pleaded that she was incapable of any such intentions towards a man who was truly as good as married. She declared that she had only replied as courtesy required, and that she would not have her harp taken to Warwick House the next day, as she had been requested to do.

Dame Lilias here interposed. With a certain conviction that Jean's dislike to the King was chiefly because the grapes were sour, she declared that Lady Elleen had by no means gone beyond the demeanour of a douce maiden, and that the King had only shown due attention to guests of his own rank, and who were nearly of his own age. In fact, she said, it might be his caution and loyalty to his espoused lady that made him avoid distinguishing the fairest.

It was not complimentary to Eleanor, but Jean's superior beauty was as much an established fact as her age, and she was pacified in some degree, agreeing with the Lady of Glenuskie that Eleanor was bound to take her harp the next day.

Warwick House was a really magnificent place, its courts, gardens, and offices covering much of the ground that still bears the name in the City, and though the establishment was not quite as extensive as it became a few years later, when Richard Nevil had succeeded his brother-in-law, it was already on a magnificent scale.

All the party who had travelled together from Fotheringay were present, besides the King, young Edmund and Jasper Tudor, and the Earl and Countess of Suffolk; and the banquet, though not a state one, nor encumbered with pageants and subtilties, was even more refined and elegant than that at Westminster, showing, as all agreed, the hand of a mistress of the household. The King's taste had been consulted, for in the gallery were the children of St. Paul's choir and of the chapel of the household, who sang hymns with sweet trained voices. Afterwards, on the beautiful October afternoon, there was walking in the garden, where Edmund and Jasper played with little Lady Anne Beauchamp, and again King Henry sought out Eleanor, and they had an enjoyable discussion of the Tale of Troie, which he had lent her, as they walked along the garden paths. Then she showed him her cousin Malcolm, and told of Bishop Kennedy and the schemes for St. Andrews, and he in return described Winchester College, and spoke of his wish to have such another foundation as Wykeham's under his own eye near Windsor, to train up the godly clergy, whom he saw to be the great need and lack of the Church at that day.

By and by, on going in from the garden, the King and Eleanor found that a tall, gray-haired gentleman, richly but darkly clad, had entered the hall. He had been welcomed by the young King and Queen of Wight, who had introduced Jean to him. 'My uncle of Gloucester,' said the King, aside. 'It is the first time he has come among us since the unhappy affair of his wife. Let me present you to him.'

Going forward, as the Duke rose to meet him, Henry bent his knee and asked his fatherly blessing, then introduced the Lady Eleanor of Scotland—'who knows all lays and songs, and loves letters, as you told me her blessed father did, my fair uncle,' he said, with sparkling eyes.

Duke Humfrey looked well pleased as he greeted her. 'Ever the scholar, Nevoy Hal,' he said, as if marvelling at the preference above the beauty, 'but each man knows his own mind. So best.' Eleanor's heart began to beat high! What did this bode? Was this King fully pledged? She had to fulfil her promise of singing and playing to the King, which she did very sweetly, some of the pathetic airs of her country, which reach back much farther than the songs with which they have in later times been associated. The King thoroughly enjoyed the music, and the Duke of York came and paid her several compliments, begging for the song she had once begun at Fotheringay. Eleanor began—not perhaps so willingly as before. Strangely, as she sang—

'Owre muckle blinking blindeth the ee, lass,
Owre muckle thinking changeth the mind,'—

her face and voice altered. Something of the same mist of tears and blood seemed to rise before her eyes as before—enfolding all around. Such a winding-sheet which had before enwrapt the King of Wight, she saw it again—nay, on the Duke of Gloucester there was such another, mounting—mounting to his neck. The face of Henry himself grew dim and ghastly white, like that of a marble saint. She kept herself from screaming, but her voice broke down, and she gave a choking sob.

King Henry's arm was the first to support her, though she shuddered as he touched her, calling for essences, and lamenting that they had asked too much of her in begging her to sing what so reminded her of her home and parents.

'She hath been thus before. It was that song,' said Jean, and the Lady of Glenuskie coming up at the same time confirmed the idea, and declined all help except to take her back to the Priory. The litter that had brought the Countess of Salisbury was at the door, and Henry would not be denied the leading her to it. She was recovering herself, and could see the extreme sweetness and solicitude of his face, and feel that she had never before leant on so kind and tender a supporting arm, since she had sat on her father's knee. 'Ah! sir, you mind me of my blessed father,' she said.

'Your father was a holy man, and died well-nigh a martyr's death,' said Henry. ''Tis an honour I thank you for to even me to him—such as I am.'

'Oh, sir! the saints guard you from such a fate,' she said, trembling.

'Was it so sad a fate—to die for the good he could not work in his life?' said Henry.

They had reached the arch into the court. A crowd was round them, and no more could be said. Henry kissed Eleanor's hand, as he assisted her into the litter, and she was shut in between the curtains, alone, for it only held one person. There was a strange tumult of feeling. She seemed lifted into a higher region, as if she had been in contact with an angel of purity, and yet there was that strange sense of awful fate all round, as if Henry were nearer being the martyr than the angel. And was she to share that fate? The generous young soul seemed to spring forward with the thought that, come what might, it would be hallowed and sweetened with such as he! Yet withal there was a sense of longing to protect and shield him.

As usual, she had soon quite recovered, but Jean pronounced it 'one of Elleen's megrims—as if she were a Hielander to have second sight.'

'But,' said the young lady, 'it takes no second sight to spae ill to yonder King. He is not one whose hand will keep his head, and there are those who say that he had best look to his crown, for he hath no more right thereto than I have to be Queen of France!'

'Fie, Jean, that's treason.'

'I'm none of his, nor ever will be! I have too much spirit for a gudeman who cares for nothing but singing his psalter like a friar.'

Jean was even more of that opinion when, the next day, at York House, only Edmund and Jasper Tudor appeared with their brother's excuses. He had been obliged to give audience to a messenger from the Emperor. 'Moreover,' added Edmund disconsolately, 'to-morrow he is going to St. Albans for a week's penitence. Harry is always doing penance, I cannot think what for. He never eats marchpane in church—nor rolls balls there.'

'I know,' said Jasper sagely. 'I heard the Lord Cardinal rating him for being false to his betrothed—that's the Lady Margaret, you know.'

'Ha!' said the Duke of York, before whom the two little boys were standing. 'How was that, my little man?'

'Hush, Jasper,' said Edmund; 'you do not know.'

'But I do, Edmund; I was in the window all the time. Harry said he did not know it, he only meant all courtesy; and then the Lord Cardinal asked him if he called it loyalty to his betrothed to be playing the fool with the Scottish wench. And then Harry stared—like thee, Ned, when thy bolt had hit the Lady of Suffolk: and my Lord went on to say that it was perilous to play the fool with a king's sister, and his own niece. Then, for all that Harry is a king and a man grown, he wept like Owen, only not loud, and he went down on his knees, and he cried, "Mea peccata, mea peccata, mea infirmitas," just as he taught me to do at confession. And then he said he would do whatever the Lord Cardinal thought fit, and go and do penance at St. Albans, if he pleased, and not see the lady that sings any more.'

'And I say,' exclaimed Edmund, 'what's the good of being a king and a man, if one is to be rated like a babe?'

'So say I, my little man,' returned the Duke, patting him on the head, then adding to his own two boys, 'Take your cousins and play ball with them, or spin tops, or whatever may please them.'

'There is the king we have,' quoth Richard Nevil 'to be at the beck of any misproud priest, and bewail with tears a moment's following of his own will, like other men.'

Most of the company felt such misplaced penitence and submission, as they deemed it, beneath contempt; but while Eleanor had pride enough to hold up her head so that no one might suppose her to be disappointed, she felt a strange awe of the conscientiousness that repented when others would only have felt resentment—relief, perhaps, at not again coming into contact with one so unlike other men as almost to alarm her.

Jean tossed up her head, and declared that her brother knew better than to let any bishop put him into leading-strings. By and by there was a great outcry among the children, and Edmund Tudor and Edward of York were fighting like a pair of mastiff-puppies because Edward had laughed at King Harry for minding what an old shaveling said. Edward, though the younger, was much the stronger, and was decidedly getting the best of it, when he was dragged off and sent into seclusion with his tutor for misbehaviour to his guest.

No one was amazed when the next day the Cardinal arrived, and told his grand-nieces and the Lady of Glenuskie that he had arranged that they should go forward under the escort of the Earl and Countess of Suffolk, who were to start immediately for Nanci, there to espouse and bring home the King's bride, the Lady Margaret. There was reason to think that the French Royal Family would be present on the occasion, as the Queen of France was sister to King Rene of Sicily and Jerusalem, and thus the opportunity of joining their sister was not to be missed by the two Scottish maidens. The Cardinal added that he had undertaken, and made Sir Patrick Drummond understand, that he would be at all charges for his nieces, and further said that merchants with women's gear would presently be sent in, when they were to fit themselves out as befitted their rank for appearance at the wedding. At a sign from him a large bag, jingling heavily, was laid on the table by a clerk in attendance. There was nothing to be done but to make a low reverence and return thanks.

Jean had it in her to break out with ironical hopes that they would see something beyond the walls of a priory abroad, and not be ordered off the moment any one cast eyes on them; but my Lord of Winchester was not the man to be impertinent to, especially when bringing gifts as a kindly uncle, and when, moreover, King Henry had the bad taste to be more occupied with her sister than with herself.

It was Eleanor who chiefly felt a sort of repugnance to being thus, as it were, bought off or compensated for being sent out of reach. She could have found it in her heart to be offended at being thought likely to wish to steal the King's heart, and yet flattered by being, for the first time, considered as dangerous, even while her awe, alike of Henry's holiness and of those strange visions that had haunted her, made her feel it a relief that her lot was not to be cast with him.

The Cardinal did not seem to wish to prolong the interview with his grand-nieces, having perhaps a certain consciousness of injury towards them; and, after assuring brilliant marriages for them, and graciously blessing them, he bade them farewell, saying that the Lady of Suffolk would come and arrange with them for the journey. No doubt, though he might have been glad to place a niece on the throne, it would have been fatal to the peace he so much desired for Henry to break his pledges to so near a kinswoman of the King of France. And when the bag was opened, and the rouleaux of gold and silver crowns displayed, his liberality contradicted the current stories of his avarice.

And by and by arrived a succession of merchants bringing horned hoods, transparent veils, like wings, supported on wire projections, long trained dresses of silk and sendal, costly stomachers, bands of velvet, buckles set with precious stones, chains of gold and silver—all the fashions, in fact, enough to turn the head of any young lady, and in which the staid Lady Prioress seemed to take quite as much interest as if she had been to wear them herself—indeed, she asked leave to send Sister Mabel to fetch a selection of the older nuns given to needlework and embroidery to enjoy the exhibition, though it was to be carefully kept out of sight of the younger ones, and especially of the novices.

The excitement was enough to put the Cardinal's offences out of mind, while the delightful fitting and trying on occupied the maidens, who looked at themselves in the little hand-mirrors held up to them by the admiring nuns, and demanded every one's opinion. Jean insisted that Annis should have her share, and Eleanor joined in urging it, when Dame Lilias shook her head, and said that was not the use the Lord Cardinal intended for his gold.

'He gave it to us to do as we would with it,' argued Eleanor.

'And she is our maiden, and it befits us not that she should look like ane scrub,' added Jean, in the words used by her brother's descendant, a century later.

'I thank you, noble cousins,' replied Annis, with a little haughtiness, 'but Davie would never thole to see me pranking it out of English gold.'

'She is right, Jeanie,' cried Eleanor. 'We will make her braw with what we bought at York with gude Scottish gold.'

'All the more just,' added Jean, 'that she helped us in our need with her ain.'

'And we are sib—near cousins after a',' added Eleanor; 'so we may well give and take.'

So it was settled, and all was amicable, except that there was a slight contest between the sisters whether they should dress alike, as Eleanor wished, while Jean had eyes and instinct enough to see that the colours and forms that set her fair complexion and flaxen tresses off to perfection were damaging to Elleen's freckles and general auburn colouring. Hitherto the sisters had worn only what they could get, happy if they could call it ornamental, and the power of choice was a novelty to them. At last the decision fell to the one who cared most about it, namely Jean. Elleen left her to settle for both, being, after the first dazzling display, only eager to get back again to Saint Marie Maudelin before the King should reclaim it.

There was something in the legend, wild and apocryphal as it is, together with what she had seen of the King, that left a deep impression upon her.

>'And by these things ye understand maun
> The three best things which this Mary chose,
> As outward penance and inward contemplation,
> And upward bliss that never shall cease,
> Of which God said withouten bees
> That the best part to her chose Mary,
> Which ever shall endure and never decrease,
> But with her abideth eternally.'

Stiff, quaint, and awkward sounds old Bokenham's translation of the 'Golden Legend,' but to Eleanor it had much power. The whole history was new to her, after her life in Scotland, where information had been slow to reach her, and books had been few. The gewgaws spread out before Jean were to her like the gloves, jewels, and braiding of hair with which Martha reproached her sister in the days of her vanity, and the cloister with its calm services might well seem to her like the better part. These nuns indeed did not strike her as models of devotion, and there was something in the Prioress's easy way of declaring that being safe there might prevent any need of special heed, which rung false on her ear; and then she thought of King Henry, whose rapt countenance had so much struck her, turning aside from enjoyment to seclude himself at the first hint that his pleasure might be a temptation. She recollected too what Lady Drummond had told her of Father Malcolm and Mother Clare, and how each had renounced the world, which had so much to offer them, and chosen the better part! She remembered Father Malcolm's sweet smile and kind words, and Mother Clare's face had impressed her deeply with its lofty peace and sweetness. How much better than all these agitations about princely bridegrooms! and broken lances and queens of beauty seemed to fade into insignificance, or to be only incidents in the tumult of secular life and worldly struggle, and her spirit quailed at the anticipation of the journey she had once desired, the gay court with its follies, empty show, temptations, coarsenesses and cruelties, and the strange land with its new language. The alternative seemed to her from Maudelin in her worldly days to Maudelin at the Saviour's feet, and had Mother Margaret Stafford been one whit more the ideal nun, perhaps every one would have been perplexed by a vehement request to seclude herself at once in the cloister of St. Helen's.

Looking up, she saw a figure slowly pacing the turf walk. It was the Mother Clare, who had come to see the Lady of Glenuskie, but finding all so deeply engaged, had gone out to await her in the garden.

Much indeed had Dame Lilias longed to join her friend, and make the most of these precious hours, but as purse-bearer and adviser to her Lady Joanna, it was impossible to leave her till the arrangements with the merchants were over. And the nuns of St. Helen's did not, as has already been seen, think much of an uncloistered sister. In her twenty years' toils among the poor it had been pretty well forgotten that Mother Clare was Esclairmonde de Luxembourg, almost of princely rank, so that no one took the trouble to entertain her, and she had slipped out almost unperceived to the quiet garden with its grass walks. And there Eleanor came up to her, and with glistening tears, on a sudden impulse exclaimed, 'Oh, holy Mother, keep me with you, tell me to choose the better part.'

'You, lady? What is this?'

'Not lady, daughter—help me! I kenned it not before—but all is vanity, turmoil, false show, except the sitting at the Lord's feet.'

'Most true, my child. Ah! have I not felt the same? But we must wait His time.'

'It was I—it was I,' continued Eleanor, 'who set Jean upon this journey, leaving my brother and Mary and the bairns. And the farther we go, the more there is of vain show and plotting and scheming, and I am weary and heartsick and homesick of it all, and shall grow worse and worse. Oh! shelter me here, in your good and holy house, dear Reverend Mother, and maybe I could learn to do the holy work you do in my own country.'

How well Esclairmonde knew it all, and what aspirations had been hers! She took Elleen's hand kindly and said, 'Dear maid, I can only aid you by words! I could not keep you here. Your uncle the Cardinal would not suffer you to abide here, nor can I take sisters save by consent of the Queen—and now we have no Queen, of the King, and—'

'Oh no, I could not ask that,' said Eleanor, a deep blush mounting, as she remembered what construction might be put on her desire to remain in the King's neighbourhood. 'Ah! then must I go on—on—on farther from home to that Court which they say is full of sin and evil and vanity? What will become of me?'

'If the religious life be good for you, trust me, the way will open, however unlikely it may seem. If not, Heaven and the saints will show what your course should be.'

'But can there be such safety and holiness, save in that higher path?' demanded Eleanor.

'Nay, look at your own kinswoman, Dame Lilias—look at the Lady of Salisbury. Are not these godly, faithful women serving God through their duty to man— husband, children, all around? And are the longings and temptations to worldly thoughts and pleasures of the flesh so wholly put away in the cloister?'

'Not here,' began Eleanor, but Mother Clare hushed her.

'Verily, my child,' she added, 'you must go on with your sister on this journey, trusting to the care and guidance of so good a woman as my beloved old friend,

Dame Lilias; and if you say your prayers with all your heart to be guarded from sin and temptation, and led into the path that is fittest for you, trust that our blessed Master and our Lady will lead you. Have you the Pater Noster in the vulgar tongue?' she added.

'We—we had it once ere my father's death. And Father Malcolm taught us; but we have since been so cast about that—that—I have forgotten.'

'Ah! Father Malcolm taught you,' and Esclairmonde took the girl's hand. 'You know how much I owe to Father Malcolm,' she softly added, as she led the maiden to a carved rood at the end of the cloister, and, before it, repeated the vernacular version of the Lord's Prayer till Eleanor knew it perfectly, and promised to follow up her 'Pater Nosters' with it.

And from that time there certainly was a different tone and spirit in Eleanor.

David, urged by his father, who still publicly ignored the young Douglas, persuaded him to write to his father now that there could be no longer any danger of pursuit, and the messenger Sir Patrick was sending to the King would afford the last opportunity. George growled and groaned a good deal, but perhaps Father Romuald pressed the duty on him in confession, for in his great relief at his lady's going off unplighted from London, he consented to indite, in the chamber Father Romuald shared with two of the Cardinal's chaplains, in a crooked and crabbed calligraphy and language much more resembling Anglo-Saxon than modern English, a letter to the most high and mighty, the Yerl of Angus, 'these presents.'

But when he was entreated to assume his right position in the troop, he refused. 'Na, na, Davie,' he said, 'gin my father chooses to send me gear and following, 'tis all very weel, but 'tisna for the credit of Scotland nor of Angus that the Master should be ganging about like a land-louper, with a single laddie after him—still less that he should be beholden to the Drummonds.'

'Ye would win to the speech of the lassie,' suggested David, 'gin that be what ye want!'

'Na kenning me, she willna look at me. Wait till I do that which may gar her look at me,' said the chivalrous youth.

He was not entirely without means, for the links of a gold chain which he had brought from home went a good way in exchange, and though he had spoken of being at his own charges, he had found himself compelled to live as one of the train of the princesses, who were treated as the guests first of the Duke of York, then of the Cardinal, who had given Sir Patrick a sum sufficient to defray all possible expenses as far as Bourges, besides having arranged for those of the journey with Suffolk whose rank had been raised to that of a Marquis, in honour of his activity as proxy for the King.

CHAPTER 6. THE PRICE OF A GOOSE

> 'We would have all such offenders cut off, and we give
> express charge that, in the marches through the country,
> there be nothing compelled from the villages.'
> —King Henry V.

The Marquis of Suffolk's was a slow progress both in England and abroad, with many halts both on account of weather and of feasts and festivals. Cardinal Beaufort had hurried the party away from London partly in order to make the match with Margaret of Anjou irrevocable, partly for the sake of removing Eleanor of Scotland, the only maiden who had ever produced the slightest impression on the monastic-minded Henry of Windsor.

When once out of London there were, however, numerous halts on the road,— two or three days of entertainment at every castle, and then a long delay at Canterbury to give time for Suffolk's retainers, and all the heralds, pursuivants, and other adjuncts of pomp and splendour, to join them. They were the guests of Archbishop Stafford, one of the peace party, and a friend of Beaufort and Suffolk, so that their entertainment was costly and magnificent, as befitted the mediaeval notions of a high-born gentleman, Primate of all England. A great establishment for the chase was kept by almost all prelates as a necessity; and whenever the weather was favourable, hunting and hawking could be enjoyed by the princesses and their suite. Indeed Jean, if not in the saddle, was pretty certain to be visiting the hawks all the morning, or else playing at ball or some other sport with her cousins or some of the young gentlemen of Suffolk's train, who were all devoted to her.

Lady Drummond found that to try to win her to quieter occupations was in vain. The girl would not even try to learn French from Father Romuald by reading, though she would pick up words and phrases by laughing and chattering with the young knights who chanced to know the language. But as by this time Dame Lilias had learnt that there were bounds that princely pride and instinct prevented from overpassing, she contented herself with seeing that there was fit attendance, either by her daughter Annis, Sir Patrick himself, or one or other of Lady Suffolk's ladies.

To some degree Eleanor shared in her sister's outdoor amusements, but she was far more disposed to exercise her mind than her body. After having pined in weariness for want of intellectual food, her opportunities were delightful to her. Not only did she read with Father Romuald with intense interest the copy of the bon Sire Jean Froissart in the original, which he borrowed from the Archbishop's library, but she listened with great zest to the readings which the Lady of Suffolk extracted from her chaplains and unwilling pages while the ladies sat at work, for the Marchioness, a grandchild of Geoffrey Chaucer, had a strong taste for literature. Moreover, from one of the choir Eleanor obtained lessons on the lute, as well as her beloved harp, and was taught to train her voice, and sing from 'pricke-song,' so that she much enjoyed this period of her journey.

Nothing could be more courteous and punctilious than the Marquis of Suffolk to the two princesses, and indeed to every one of his own degree; but there was something of the parvenu about him, and, unlike the Duke of York or Archbishop Stafford, who were free, bright, and good-natured to the meanest persons, he was haughty and harsh to every one below the line of gentle blood, and in his own train he kept up a discipline, not too strict in itself, but galling in the manner in which it was enforced by those who imitated his example. By the time the suite was collected, Christmas and the festival of St. Thomas a Becket were so near that it would have been neglect of a popular saint to have left his shrine without keeping his day. And after the Epiphany, though the party did reach Dover in a day's ride, a stormy period set in, putting crossing out of the question, and detaining the suite within the massive walls of the castle.

At last, on a brisk, windless day of frost, the crossing to Calais was effected, and there was another week of festivals spread by the hospitality of the Captain of Calais, where everything was as English as at Dover. When they again started on their journey, Suffolk severely insisted on the closest order, riding as travellers in a hostile country, where a misadventure might easily break the existing truce, although the territories of the Duke of Burgundy, through which their route chiefly lay, were far less unfavourable to the English than actual French countries; indeed, the Flemings were never willingly at war with the English, and some of the Burgundian nobles and knights had been on intimate terms with Suffolk. Still, he caused the heralds always to keep in advance, and allowed no stragglers behind the rearguard that came behind the long train of waggons loaded with much kitchen apparatus, and with splendid gifts for the bride and her family, as well as equipments for the wedding-party, and tents for such of the troop as could not find shelter in the hostels or monasteries where the slowly-moving party halted for the night. It was unsafe to go on after the brief hours of daylight, especially in the neighbourhood of the Forest of Ardennes, for wolves might be near on the winter nights. It was thus that the first trouble arose with Sir Patrick Drummond's two volunteer followers. Ringan Raefoot had become in his progress a very different looking being from the wild creature who had come with 'Geordie of the Red Peel,' but there was the same heart in him. He had endured obedience to the Knight of Glenuskie as a Scot, and with the Duke of York and through England the discipline of the troop had not been severe; but Suffolk, though a courtly, chivalrous gentleman to his equals, had not the qualities of popularity, and chafed his inferiors.

There were signs of confusion in the cavalcade as they passed between some of the fertile fields of Namur, and while Suffolk was halting and about to send a squire to the rear to interfere, a couple of his retainers hurried up, saying, 'My Lord, those Scottish thieves will bring the whole country down on us if order be not taken with them.'

Sir Patrick did not need the end of the speech to gallop off at full speed to the rear of all the waggons, where a crowd might be seen, and there was a perfect Babel of tongues, rising in only too intelligible shouts of rage. Swords and lances were flashing on one side among the horsemen, on the other stones were flying from an ever-increasing number of leather-jerkined men and boys, some of them with long knives, axes, and scythes.

George Douglas's high head seemed to be the main object of attack, and he had Ringan Raefoot before him across his horse, apparently retreating, while David, Malcolm, and a few more made charges on the crowd to guard him. When he was seen, there was a cry of which he could distinguish nothing but 'Ringan! Geordie! goose—Flemish hounds.'

Riding between, regardless of the stones, he shouted in the Burgundian French he had learnt in his campaigns, to demand the cause of the attack. The stones ceased, and the head man of the village, a stout peasant, came forward and complained that the varlet, as he called Ringan, had been stealing the village geese on their pond, and when they were about to do justice on him, yonder man-at-arms had burst in, knocked down and hurt several, and carried him off.

Before there had been time for further explanation, to Sir Patrick's great vexation, the Marshal of the troop and his guard came up, and the complaint was repeated. George, at the same time, having handed Ringan over to some others of the Scots, rode up with his head very high.

'Sir Patrick Drummond,' said the Marshal stiffly, 'you know my Lord's rules for his followers, as to committing outrages on the villeins of the country.'

'We are none of my Lord of Suffolk's following,' began Douglas; but Sir Patrick, determined to avoid a breach if possible, said—

'Sir Marshal, we have as yet heard but one side of the matter. If wrong have been done to these folk, we are ready to offer compensation, but we should hear how it has been—'

'Am I to see my poor laddie torn to bits, stoned, and hanged by these savage loons,' cried George, 'for a goose's egg and an old gander?'

Of course his defence was incomprehensible to the Flemings, but on their side a man with a bound-up head and another limping were produced, and the head man spoke of more serious damage to others who could not appear, demanding both the aggressors to be dealt with, i.e. to be hanged on the next tree.

'These men are of mine, Master Marshal,' said Sir Patrick.

'My Lord can permit no violence by those under his banner,' said the Marshal stiffly. 'I must answer it to him.'

'Do so then,' said Sir Patrick. 'This is a matter for him.'

The Marshal, who had much rather have disposed of the Scottish thieves on his own responsibility, was forced to give way so far as to let the appeal be carried to the Marquis of Suffolk, telling the Flemings, in something as near their language as he could accomplish, that his Lord was sure to see justice done, and that they should follow and make their complaint.

Suffolk sat on his horse, tall, upright, and angry. 'What is this I hear, Sir Patrick Drummond,' said he, 'that your miscreants of wild Scots have been thieving from the peaceful peasant-folk, and then beating them and murdering them? I deemed you were a better man than to stand by such deeds and not give up the fellows to justice.'

'It were shame to hang a man for one goose,' said Sir Patrick.

'All plunder is worthy of death,' returned the Englishman. 'Your Border law may be otherwise, but 'tis not our English rule of honest men. And here's this other great lurdane knave been striking the poor rogues down right and left! A halter fits both.'

'My Lord, they are no subjects of England. I deny your rights over them.'

'Whoever rides in my train is under me, I would have you to know, sir.'

'Hark ye, my Lord of Suffolk,' said Sir Patrick, coming near enough to speak in an undertone, 'that lurdane, as you call him, is heir of a noble house in Scotland, come here on a young man's freak of chivalry. You will do no service to the peace of the realms if you give him up to these churls, for making in to save his servant.'

Before Sir Patrick had done speaking, while Suffolk was frowning grimly in perplexity, a wild figure, with blood on the face, rushed forth with a limping run, crying 'Let the loons hang me and welcome, if they set such store by their lean old gander, but they shanna lay a finger on the Master.'

And he had nearly precipitated himself into the hands of the sturdy rustics, who shouted with exultation, but with two strides Geordie caught him up. 'Peace, Ringan! They shall no more hang thee than me,' and he stood with one hand on Ringan's shoulder and his sword in the other, looking defiant.

'If he be a young gentleman masking, I am not bound to know it,' said Suffolk impatiently to Drummond; 'but if he will give up that rascal, and make compensation, I will overlook it.'

'Who touches my fellow does so at his peril,' shouted George, menacing with his sword.

'Peace, young man!' said Sir Patrick. 'Look here, my Lord of Suffolk, we Scots are none of your men. We need no favour of you English with our allies. There be enough of us to make our way through these peasants to the French border, so unless you let us settle the matter with a few crowns to these rascallions, we part company.'

'The ladies were entrusted to my charge,' began Lord Suffolk.

At that instant, however, both Jean and Eleanor came on the scene, riding fast, having in truth been summoned by Malcolm, who shrewdly suspected that thus an outbreak might be best averted.

It was Eleanor who spoke first. In spite of all her shyness, when her blood was up, she was all the princess.

'What is this, my Lord of Suffolk?' she said. 'If one of our following have transgressed, it is the part of ourselves and of Sir Patrick Drummond to see to it, as representing the King my brother.'

'Lady,' replied Suffolk, bowing low and doffing his cap, 'yonder ill-nurtured knave hath been robbing the country-folk, and the—the man-at-arms there not only refuses to give him up to justice, but has hurt, well-nigh slain, some of them in violently taking him from them. They ride in my train and I am responsible.'

Jean broke in: 'He only served the cowardly loons right. A whole crowd of the rogues to hang one poor laddie for one goose! Shame on a gentleman for hearkening to the foul-mouthed villains one moment. Come here, Ringan. King

Jamie's sister will never see them harm thee.'

Perhaps Suffolk was not sorry to see a way out of the perplexity. 'Far be it from a knight to refuse a boon to a fair lady in her selle, farther still to *two* royal damsels. The lives are granted, so satisfaction in coin be made to yon clamorous hinds.'

'I do not call it a boon but a right, said Eleanor gravely; 'nevertheless I thank you, my Lord Marquis.'

George would have thrown himself at their feet, but Jean coldly said, 'Spare thanks, sir. It was for my brother's right,' and she turned her horse away, and rode off at speed, while Eleanor could not help pausing to say, 'She is more blithe than she lists to own! Sir Patrick, what the fellows claim must come from my uncle's travelling purse.'

George's face was red. This was very bitter to him, but he could only say, 'It shall be repaid so soon as I have the power.'

The peasants meanwhile were trying to make the best bargain they could by representing that they were tenants of an abbey, so that the death of the gander was sacrilegious on that account as well as because it was in Lent. To this, however, Sir Patrick turned a deaf ear: he threw them a couple of gold pieces, with which, as he told them, they were much better off than with either the live goose or the dead Ringan.

Suffolk had halted for the mid-day rest and was waiting for him till this matter was disposed of. 'Sir Patrick Drummond,' he said with some ceremony, 'this company of yours may be Scottish subjects, but while they are riding with me I am answerable for them. It may be the wont in Scotland, but it is not with us English, to let unnamed adventurers ride under our banner.'

'The young man is not unnamed,' said Sir Patrick, on his mettle.

'You know him?'

'I'll no say, but I have an inkling. My son David kenn'd him and answered for him when he joined himself to my following; nor has he hitherto done aught to discredit himself.'

'What is his name, or the name he goes by?'

'George Douglas.'

'H'm! Your Scottish names may belong to any one, from your earls down to your herdboys; and they, forsooth, are as like as not to call themselves gentlemen.'

'And wherefore not, if theirs is gentle blood?' said Sir Patrick.

'Nay, now, Sir Patrick, stand not on your Scotch pride. Gentlemen all, if you will, but you gave me to understand that this was none of your barefoot gentlemen, and I ask if you can tell who he truly is?'

'I have never been told, my Lord, and I had rather you put the question to himself than to me.'

'Call him then, an' so please you.'

Sir Patrick saw no alternative save compliance; and he found Ringan undergoing a severe rating, not unaccompanied by blows from the wood of his master's lance. The perfect willingness to die for one another was a mere natural incident, but the having transgressed, and caused such a serious scrape, made George very indignant and inflict condign punishment. 'Better fed than he had ever been in his life, the rogue' (and he looked it, though he muttered, 'A bannock and a sup of barley brose were worth the haill of their greasy beeves!'). 'Better fed than ever before. Couldn't the daft loon keep the hands of him off poor folks' bit goose? In Lent, too!' (by far the gravest part of the offence).

George did, however, transfer Ringan's explanation to Sir Patrick, and make some apology. A nest of goose eggs apparently unowned had been too much for him, incited further by a couple of English horseboys, who were willing to share goose eggs for supper, and let the Scotsman bear the wyte of it. The goose had been nearer than expected, and summoned her kin; the gander had shown fight; the geese had gabbled, the gooseherd and his kind came to the rescue, the horseboys had made off; Ringan, impeded by his struggle with the ferocious gander, was caught; and Geordie had come up just in time to see him pricked with goads and axes to a tree, where a halter was making ready for him. Of course, without asking questions, George hurried to save him, pushing his horse among the angry crew, and striking right and left, and equally of course the other Scots came to his assistance.

Sir Patrick agreed that he could not have done otherwise, though better things might have been hoped of Ringan by this time.

'But,' said he, 'there's not an end yet of the coil. Here has my Lord of Suffolk been speiring after your name and quality, till I told him he must ask at you and not at me.'

'Tell'd you the dour meddling Englishman my name?' asked George.

'I told him only what ye told me yerself. In that there was no lie. But bethink you, royal maidens dinna come to speak for lads without a cause.'

George's colour mounted high in his sunburnt, freckled cheek.

'Kens—ken they, trow ye, Sir Pate?'

'Cannie folk, even lassies, can ken mair than they always tell,' said the knight of Glenuskie. 'Yonder is my Lord Marquis, as they ca' him; so bethink you weel how you comport yourself with him, and my counsel is to tell him the full truth. He is a dour man towards underlings, whom he views as made not of the same flesh and blood with himself, but he is the very pink of courtesy to men of his own degree.'

'Set him up,' quoth the heir of the Douglas, with a snort. 'His own degree, indeed! scarce even a knight's son!'

'What he deems his own degree, then,' corrected Sir Patrick; 'but he holds himself full of chivalry to them, and loves a spice of the errant knight; ye may trust his honour. And mind ye,' he added, laughing, 'I've never been told your name and quality.'

Which the Master of Angus returned with an equally canny laugh. The young man, as he approached the Marquis, drew his head up, straightened his tall form, brushed off the dust that obscured the bloody heart on his breast, and altogether advanced with a step and bearing far more like the great Earl's son than the man-at-arms of the Glenuskie following; his eyes bespoke equality or more as they met those of William de la Pole, and yet there was that in the glance which forbade the idea of insolence, so that Suffolk, instead of remaining seated rose to meet him and took him aside, standing as they talked.

'Sir Squire,' he said, 'for such I understand your degree in chivalry to be.'

'I have not won my spurs,' said George.

'It is not our rule to take to foreign courts gentlemen from another realm unknown to us,' proceeded Suffolk, with much civility; 'therefore, unless any vow of chivalry binds you, I should be glad to know who it is who does my banner the honour of riding in its company for a time. If a secret, it is safe with me.'

George gave his name.

'That is the name of one of the chief nobles in Scotland,' said Suffolk. 'Do I see before me his son?' George bowed.

'Then, my Lord Douglas, am I permitted to ask wherefore this mean disguise? Is it for some vow of chivalry, or for that which is the guerdon of chivalry?' the Marquis added in a lower, softer tone, which, however, extremely chafed the proud young Scot, all the more that he felt himself blushing.

'My Lord,' he said, 'I am not bound to render a reason to any save my father, from whom I hope for letters shortly.'

To his further provocation Suffolk smiled meaningly, and answered—

'I understand. But if my Lord Douglas would honour my suite by assuming the place that befits him, I should be happy that aught of mine should serve—'

'I am beholden to you, my Lord, for the offer,' replied George, somewhat roughly. 'Whatever I make use of must be my father's or my own. All I crave of you is to keep my secret, and not make me the common talk. Have I your licence to depart?'

Wherewith, tall, irate, and shamefaced, the Master of Angus stalked away to meet David Drummond, to whom he confided his disgusts.

'The parlous fulebody! As though I were like to make myself a mere sport for ballad-mongers, such as Lady Elleen is always mooning after; or as if I would stoop to borrow a following of the English blackguard, to bolster up my state like King Herod in a mystery play. If my father lists, he may send me out a band, but the Douglas shall have Douglas's men, or none at all.'

David approved the sentiment, but added—

'Ye could win to Jeanie if ye took your right place.'

'What good would that do me while she is full of her fine daffing, singing, clacking, English knights, that would only gibe at the red-haired Scot? Let her wait to see what the Red Douglas's hand can do in time of need! But, Davie, you that can speak to her, let her know how deeply I thank her for what she did even now on my behalf, or rather on puir Ringan's, and that I am trebly bound to her service though I make no minstrel fule's work.'

David delivered his message, but did not obtain much by it for his friend's satisfaction, for Jeanie only tossed her head and answered—

'Does the gallant cock up his bonnet because he thinks it was for his sake. It was Elleen's doing there, firstly; and next, wadna we have done the like for the meanest of Jamie's subjects?'

'Dinna credit her, Davie,' said Eleanor. 'Ye should have seen her start in her saddle, and wheel round her palfrey at Malcolm's first word.'

'It wasna for him,' replied Jean hotly. 'They dinna hang the like of him for twisting a goose's neck; it was for the puir leal laddie; and ye may tak' that to him.'

'Shall I, Elleen?' asked David, with a twinkle in his eye of cousinly teasing.

'An' ye do not, I shall proclaim ye in the lists at Nanci as a corbie messenger and mansworn squire, unworthy of your spurs,' threatened Jeanie, in all good humour however.

Suffolk, baffled in his desire to patronise the young Master of Angus, examined both Sir Patrick and Lady Drummond as far as their caution would allow, telling that the youth had confessed his rank and admitted the cause—making inquiry whether the match would be held suitable in Scotland, and why it had not taken place there—a matter difficult to explain, since it did not merely turn upon the young lady's ambition—which would have gone for nothing—but on the danger to the Crown of offending rival houses. Suffolk had a good deal about him of the flashy side of chivalry, and loved its brilliance and romance; he was an honourable man, and the weak point about him was that he never understood that knighthood should respect men of meaner birth. He was greatly flattered by the idea of having the eldest son of the great Earl of Angus riding as an unknown man-at-arms in his troop, and on the way likewise to the most chivalrous of kings. His scheme would have been to equip the youth fully with horse and arms, and at some brilliant tourney see him carry all before him, like Du Gueselin in his boyhood, and that the eclat of the affair should reflect itself upon his sponsor. But there were two difficulties in the way—the first that the proud young Scot showed no intention of being beholden to any Englishman, and secondly, that the tall, ungainly youth did not look as if he had attained to the full strength or management of his own limbs; and though in five or ten years' time he might be a giant in actual warfare, he did not appear at all likely to be a match for the highly-trained champions of the tilt-yard. Moreover, he was not a knight as yet, and on sounding Sir Patrick it was elicited that he was likely to deem it high treason to be dubbed by any hand save that of his King or his father.

So the Marquis could only feel sagacious, and utter a hint or two before the ladies which fell the more short, since he was persuaded, by Eleanor's having been the foremost in the defence, that she was the object of the quest; and he now and then treated her to hints which she was slow to understand, but which exasperated while they amused her sister.

The journey was so slow that it was not until the fourth week in Lent that they were fairly in Lorraine. It had of course been announced by couriers, and at Thionville a very splendid herald reached them, covered all over with the blazonry of Jerusalem and the Two Sicilies, to say nothing of Provence and Anjou. He brought letters from King Rene, explaining that he and his daughters were en route from Provence, and he therefore designated a nunnery where he requested that the Scottish princesses and their ladies would deign to be entertained, and a monastery where my Lord Marquis of Suffolk and his suite would be welcomed, and where they were requested to remain till Easter week, by which time the King of France, the Dauphin, and Dauphiness would be near at hand, and there could be a grand entrance into Nanci. Of course there was nothing to be done but to obey though the Englishmen muttered that the delay was in order to cast the expense upon the rich abbeys, and to muster all the resources of Lorraine and Provence to cover the poverty of the many-titled King.

The Abbey where the gentlemen were lodged was so near Nanci that it was easy to ride into the city and make inquiries whether any tidings had arrived from Scotland; but nothing had come from thence for either the princesses, Sir Patrick, or Geordie of the Red Peel, so that the strange situation of the latter must needs continue as long as he insisted on being beholden for nothing to the English upstart, as he scrupled not to call Lord Suffolk, whose new-fashioned French title was an offence in Scottish ears.

The ladies on their side had not the relaxation of these expeditions. The Abbey was a large and wealthy one, but decidedly provincial. Only the Lady Abbess and one sister could speak 'French of Paris,' the others used a dialect so nearly German that Lady Suffolk could barely understand them, and the other ladies, whose French was not strong, could hold no conversation with them.

To insular minds, whether Scottish or English, every deviation of the Gallican ritual from their own was a sore vexation. If Lady Drummond had devotion enough not to be distracted by the variations, the young ladies certainly had not, and Jean very decidedly giggled during some of the most solemn ceremonies, such as the creeping to the cross—the large carved cross in the middle of the graveyard, to which all in turn went upon their knees on Good Friday and kissed it.

Last year, at this season, they had been shut up in their prison-castle, and had not shared in any of these ceremonies; and Eleanor tried to think of King Henry and Sister Esclairmonde, and how they were throwing their hearts into the great thoughts of the day, and she felt distressed at being infected by Jean's suppressed laughter at the movements of the fat Abbess, and at the extraordinary noises made by the younger nuns with clappers, as demonstrations against Judas on the way to the Easter Sepulchre.

She was so much shocked at herself that she wanted to confess; but Father Romuald had gone with the male members of the party, and the chaplain did not half understand her French, though he gave her absolution.

Meantime all the nuns were preparing Easter eggs, whereof there was a great exchange the next day, when the mass was as splendid as the resources of the Abbey could furnish, and all were full of joy and congratulation, the sense of oneness for once inspiring all.

Moreover, after mass, Sir Patrick and an Englishman rode over with tidings that King Rene had sent a messenger, who was on the Tuesday to guide them all to a glade where the King hoped to welcome the ladies as befitted their rank and beauty, and likewise to meet the royal travellers from Bourges, so that all might make their entry into Nanci together.

The King himself, it was reported, did nothing but ride backwards and forwards between Nanci and the convent where he had halted, arranging the details of the procession, and of the open-air feast at the rendezvous upon the way.

'I hope,' said Lady Suffolk, 'that King Rene's confections will not be as full of rancid oil as those of the good sisters. I know not which was more distasteful—their Lenten Fast or their Easter Feast. We have, certes, done our penance this Lent!'

To which the rest of the ladies could not but agree, though Lady Drummond felt it somewhat treasonable to the good nuns, their entertainers; and both she and Eleanor recollected how differently Esclairmonde would have felt the matter, and how little these matters of daily fare would have concerned her.

'To-day we shall see her!' exclaimed Eleanor, springing to the floor, as, early on a fine spring morning, the ladies in the guest-chamber of the nunnery began to bestir themselves at the sound of one of the many convent bells. 'They are at Toul, and we shall meet this afternoon. I have not slept all night for thinking of it.'

'No, and hardly let me sleep,' said Jean, slowly sitting up in bed. 'Thou hast waked me so often that I shall be pale and heavy-eyed for the pageant.'

'Little fear of that, my bonnie bell,' said old Christie, laughing.

'Besides,' said Eleanor, 'nobody will fash themselves to look at us in the midst of the pageant. There will be the King to see, and the bride. Oh, I wish we were not to ride in it, and could see it instead at our ease.'

'Thou wast never meant for a princess,' said Jean; 'Christie, Annis, for pity's sake, see till her. She is busking up her hair just as was gude enough for the old nuns, but no for kings and queens.'

'I hate the horned cap, in which I feel like a cow, and methought Meg wad feel the snood a sight for sair een,' said Eleanor.

'Meg indeed! Thou must frame thy tongue to Madame la Dauphine.'

'Before the lave of them, but not with sweet Meg herself.'

'Our sister behoves to have learnt what suits her station, and winna bide sic ways from an ower forward sister. Dinna put us all to shame, and make the folk trow we came from some selvage land,' said Jean, tossing her head.

'Hast ever seen me carry myself unworthy of King James's daughter?' proudly demanded Eleanor.

'Nay, now, bairnies, fash not yoursells that gate,' interfered old Christie; 'nae fear but Lady Elleen will be douce and canny enow when folks are there to see. She kens what fits a king's daughter.'

Jean made a little hesitation over kirtles and hoods, but fortunately ladies, however royal, had no objection to wearing the same robes twice, and both she and her sister were objects to delight the eyes of the crowding and admiring nuns when they mounted their palfreys in the quadrangle, and, attended by the Lady of Glenuskie and her daughter, rode forth with the Marchioness of Suffolk at the great gateway to join the cavalcade, headed by Suffolk and Sir Patrick.

After about two miles' riding on a woodland road they became aware of fitful strains of music and a continuous hum of voices, heard through the trees and presently a really beautiful scene opened before them, as the trees seemed to retreat, so as to unfold a wide level space, further enclosed by brilliant tapestry hangings, their scarlet, blue, gold and silver hues glittering in an April sun, and the fastenings concealed by garlands of spring flowers. An awning of rich gold embroidery on a green ground was spread so as to shelter a cloth glittering with plate and bestrewn with flowers; horses, in all varieties of ornamental housings, were being led about; there was a semicircle of musicians in the rear; and, as soon as the guests came in sight, there came forward, doffing his embroidered and jewelled cap, a gentleman of middle stature and of exceeding grace and courtesy, whose demeanour, no less than the attendance around him, left no doubt that this was no other than Rene, Duke of Anjou and of Lorraine, Count of Provence, and King of the Two Sicilies and of Jerusalem.

'Welcome,' he exclaimed in French, 'welcome, fair and royal maidens; welcome, noble lord, the representative of our dear brother and son of England. Deign on your journey to partake of the humble and rural fare of the poor minstrel shepherd.'

Wherewith the music broke out in strains of welcome from the grove, with voices betweenwhiles Rene himself assisted each princess to dismount, and respectfully kissed her on the cheek as she stood on the ground. Then, taking a hand of each, he led them to a great chestnut tree, the shade of whose branches was assisted by hangings of blue embroidered with white, beneath which cushions, mantles, and seats were spread, and a bevy of ladies in bright garments stood. From these came forward two beautiful young girls, with fair complexions and flowing golden hair, scarcely confined by the bands whence transparent veils descended. King Rene presented them as his two daughters, Yolande and Margaret, to the two Scottish maidens, and there were kindly as well as courtly embraces on either side. The Lady of Glenuskie, as a king's grand-daughter, with Annis and Lady Suffolk, had likewise been led up to take their places; the four royal maidens were seated together. Yolande, the most regularly beautiful, but with an anxious look on her face, talked to Eleanor of her journey; Margaret, who had one of those very simple, innocent-looking child-faces that sometimes form the mask of immense energy of character, was more absent and inattentive to her duties as hostess; moreover, she and Jean did not understand one another's language so well as did the other two. Delicate little cakes, and tall Venice glasses, spirally ornamented, and containing light wines, were served to them on the knee by a tall, large, fair-haired youth, who was named to them as the Duke Sigismund, of Alsace and the Tyrol.

Jean had time to look about, and heartily wish that her beautiful flaxen hair was loose, and not encumbered with the rolled headgear with two projecting horns, against which Elleen had rebelled; since York and even London were evidently behind the fashion. Margaret's hair was bound with a broad band of daisies, and Yolande's with violets, both in allusion to their names, Yolande being the French corruption of Violante, her Provencal name, in allusion to the golden violet. Jean thought of the Scottish thistle, and studied the dresses, tight-fitting 'cotte hardis' of bright, deep, soft, rose colour, edged with white fur, and white skirts embroidered with their appropriate flowers. She wondered how soon this could be imitated, casting a few glances at Duke Sigismund, who stood waiting, as if desirous of attracting Yolande's attention. Eleanor, on the other hand, even while answering Yolande, had a feeling as if she had arrived at the completion of the very vision which she had imagined on the dreary tower of Dunbar. Here was the warm spring sun, shining on a scene of unequalled beauty and brilliancy, set in the spring foliage and blossom, whence, as if to rival the human performers, gushes of nightingales' song came in every interval. Hearing Eleanor's eager question whether that were the nightingale whose liquid trillings she heard, King Rene realised that the Scottish maidens knew not the note, and signed to the minstrels to cease for a time, then came and sat on a cushion beside the young lady, and enjoyed her admiration.

'Ah!' she said, 'that is the king of the minstrel birds.'

He smiled. 'The royal lady then has her orders and ranks for the birds.'

'Oh yes. If the royal eagle is the king, and the falcon is the true knight, the nightingale and mavis, merle and lark, are the minstrels. And the lovely seagull, oh, how call you it?—with the long white floating wings rising and falling, is the graceful dancer.'

'Guifette,' Rene gave the word, 'or in Provence, Rondinel della mar—hirondelle de la mer!'

'Swallow! Ah, the pilgrim birds, who visit the Holy Land.'

'Lady, you should be of our court of the troubadours,' said Rene; 'your words should be a poem.'

He was called away at the moment, and craved her licence so politely that the chivalrous minstrel king seemed to Elleen all she had dreamt of. The whole was perfect, nothing wanting save that for which her heart was all the time beating high, the presence of her beloved sister Margaret. It was as if a scene out of a romance of fairyland had suddenly taken reality, and she more than once closed her eyes and squeezed her hands to try whether she was awake.

A fanfaron of trumpets came on the wind, and all were on the alert, while Eleanor's heart throbbed so that she could hardly stand, and caught at Margaret's arm, as she murmured with a gasp, 'My sister! My sister!'

'Ah! you are happy to meet once more,' said Margaret. 'The saints only know whether Yolande and I shall ever see one another's faces again when once I am carried away to your dreary England.'

'England is not mine, lady,' said Eleanor, rather sharply. 'We reckon the English as our bitterest foes.'

'You have come with an Englishman though,' said Margaret, 'whom I am to take for my husband,' and she laughed a gay innocent laugh. A grizzled old knight, whom I am not like to mistake for my true spouse. Have you seen him? What like is he?'

'The gentlest and sweetest of kings,' returned Eleanor; 'as fond of all that is good and fair and holy as is your own royal father.'

Margaret coughed a little. 'My husband should be a gallant warlike knight,' she said, 'such as was this king's father.'

'Oh, see! cried Eleanor. 'I saw the glitter of the spears through the trees. There's another blast of the trumpets! Oh! oh! it is a gallant sight! If only Jamie, my little brother, could see it! It stirs one's blood.'

'Ah yes, Elleen,' cried Jean. 'This is something to have come for.'

'And Margaret, sweet Madge,' repeated Eleanor to herself, in her native Scotch, while King Rene's trumpets, harps, and hautbois burst forth with an answering peal, so exciting her that her yellow-brown eyes sparkled and the colour rose in her cheeks, giving her a strange beauty full of eager spirit. Duke Sigismund turned and gazed at her in surprise, and an old herald who was waiting near observed, 'Is that the daughter of the captive King of Scotland? She has his very countenance and bearing.'

The trumpeters and other attendants, bearing the blue-lilied banner of France, appeared among the trees, and dividing, formed a lane for the advance of the royal personages. King Rene went forward to meet them, foremost, so as to be ready to hold the stirrup for his sister the Queen of France. Duke Sigismund seemed about to give his hand to the Infanta Violante, as the Provencaux called Yolande, but she was beforehand with him, linking her arm into Jean's, while Margaret took Eleanor's, and said in her ear, 'The great awkward German! He is come here to pay his court to Yolande, but she will none of him. She has better hopes.'

Eleanor hardly attended, for her whole soul was bent on the party arriving. King Charles, riding on a handsome bay horse, closely followed by a conveyance such as was called in England a whirlicote, from which the Queen was handed out by her brother, and then, on a sorrel palfrey, in a blue gold-embroidered riding-suit— could that be Margaret of Scotland? The long reddish-yellow hair and the tall figure had a familiar look. King Rene was telling her something as he helped her to alight, and with one spring, regardless of all, and of all ceremony, she sprang forward. 'My wee Jeanie! My Elleen! My titties! Mine ain wee things,' she cried in her native tongue, as she embraced them by turns, as if she would have devoured them, with a gush of tears.

Though these were times of great state and ceremony, yet they were also very demonstrative times, when tears and embracings were expected of near kindred; and, indeed, the King and Queen were equally occupied with their brother and nieces; but presently Eleanor heard a low voice observe, with a sort of sarcastic twang, 'If Madame has sufficiently satiated her tenderness, perhaps she will remember the due of others.' Margaret started as if stung, and Eleanor, looking up, beheld a face, young but sharp, and with a keen, hard, set look in the narrow eyes, contracted brow, and thin lips, that made her feel as though the serpent had found his way into her paradise. Hastily turning, Margaret presented her sisters to her husband, who bowed, and kissed each with those strange thin lips, that again made Eleanor shudder, perhaps because of his compliment, 'We are graced by these ladies, in whom we have another Madame la Dauphine, as well as an errant beauty.'

Jean appropriated the last words, but Elleen felt sure that the earlier ones were ironical, both to her and to the Dauphiness, on whose cheeks they brought a flush. The two kings, however, turned to receive the sisters, and nothing could be kinder than the tone of King Charles and Queen Marie towards the sisters of their good daughter, as they termed the Dauphiness, who on her side was welcomed by Rene as the sweet niece, sharer of his tastes, who brought minstrelsy and poetry in her train.

'Trust her for that, my fair uncle,' said her husband in a cold, dry tone.

All the royal personages sat down on the cushions spread on the grass to the 'rural fare,' as King Rene called it, which he had elaborately prepared for them, while the music sounded from the trees in welcome.

All was, as the kind prince announced, without ceremony, and he placed Lord Suffolk, as the representative of Henry VI., next to the young Infanta Margaret, and contrived that the Dauphiness should sit between her two sisters, whose hands she clasped from time to time within her own in an ecstasy of delight, while inquiries came from time to time, low breathed in her native tongue, for wee Mary and Jamie and baby Annaple. 'The very sound of your tongues is music to my lugs,' she said. 'And how much mair when ye speak mine ain bonnie Scotch, sic as I never hear save by times when one archer calls to another. Jeanie, you favour our mother. 'Tis gude for ye! I am blithe one of ye is na like puir Marget!'

'Dinna say that,' cried Jean, in an access of feeling. ''Tis hame, and it's hame to see sic a sonsie Scots face—and it minds me of my blessed father.'

It was true that Margaret and Eleanor both were thorough Scotswomen, and with the expressive features, the auburn colouring, and tall figures of their father; but there was for the rest a melancholy contrast between them, for while Elleen had the eager, hopeful, lively healthfulness of early youth, giving a glow to her countenance and animation to the lithe but scarcely-formed figure, Margaret, with the same original mould, had the pallor and puffiness of ill-health in her complexion, and a largeness of growth more unsatisfactory than leanness, and though her face was lighted up and her eyes sparkled with the joy of meeting her sisters, there were lines about the brow and round the mouth ill suited to her age, which was little over twenty years.

CHAPTER 7. THE MINSTREL KING'S COURT

'Where throngs of knights and barons bold,
In weeds of peace, high triumphs hold,
With store of ladies, whose bright eyes
Rain influence, and judge the prize
Of wit or arms, while both contend
To win her grace whom all commend.'—L'Allegro.

The whole of the two Courts had to be received in the capital of Lorraine in full state under the beautiful old gateway, but as mediaeval pageants are wearisome matters this may be passed over, though it was exceptionally beautiful and poetic, owing to the influence of King Rene's taste, and it perfectly dazzled the two Scottish princesses—though, to tell the truth, they were somewhat disappointed in the personal appearance of their entertainers, who did not come up to their notion of royalty. Their father had been a stately and magnificent man; their mother a beautiful woman. Henry VI. was a tall, well-made, handsome man, with Plantagenet fairness and regularity of feature and a sweetness all his own; but both these kings were, like all the house of Valois, small men with insignificant features and sallow complexions. Rene, indeed, had a distinction about him that compensated for want of beauty, and Charles had a good-natured, easy, indolent look and gracious smile that gave him an undefinable air of royalty. Rene's daughters were both very lovely, but their beauty came from the other side of the house, with the blood of Charles the Great, through their mother, the heiress of Lorraine.

There was a curious contrast between the brothers-in-law, Charles, when dismounting at the castle gate, not disguising his weariness and relief that it was over, and Rene, eager and anxious, desirous of making all his bewildering multitude of guests as happy as possible, while the Dauphin Louis stood by, half interested and amused, half mocking. He was really fond of his uncle, though in a contemptuous superior sort of manner, despising his religious and honourable scruples as mere simplicity of mind.

Rene of Anjou has been hardly dealt with, as is often the case with princes upright, religious, and chivalrous beyond the average of their time, yet without the strength or the genius to enforce their rights and opinions, and therefore thrust aside. After his early unsuccessful wars his lands of Provence and Lorraine were islands of peace, prosperity, and progress, and withal he was an extremely able artist, musician, and poet, striving to revive the old troubadour spirit of Provence, and everywhere casting about him an atmosphere of refinement and kindliness.

The hall of his hotel at Nanci was a beautiful place, with all the gorgeous grace of the fifteenth century, and here his guests assembled for supper soon after their arrival, all being placed as much as possible according to rank. Eleanor found herself between a deaf old Church dignitary and Duke Sigismund, on whose other side was Yolande, the Infanta, as the Provencals called the daughter of Rene; while Jean found the Dauphin on one side of her and a great French Duke on the other. Louis amused himself with compliments and questions that sometimes nettled her, sometimes pleased her, giving her a sense that he might admire her beauty, but was playing on her simplicity, and trying to make her betray the destitution of her home and her purpose in coming.

Eleanor, on the other hand, found her cavalier more simple than herself. In fact, he properly belonged to the Infanta, but she paid no attention to him, nor did the Bishop try to speak to the Scottish princess. Sigismund's French was very lame, and Eleanor's not perfect, but she had a natural turn for languages, and had, in the convent, picked up some German, which in those days had many likenesses to her own broad Scotch. They made one another out, between the two languages, with signs, smiles, and laughter, and whereas the subtilties along the table represented the entire story of Sir Gawain and his Loathly Lady, she contrived to explain the story to him, greatly to his edification; and they went on to King Arthur, and he did his best to narrate the German reading of Sir Parzival. The difficulties engrossed them till the rose-water was brought in silver bowls to wash their fingers, on which Sigismund, after observing and imitating the two ladies, remarked that they had no such Schwarmerci in Deutschland, and Yolande looked as if she could well believe it, while Elleen, though ignorant of the meaning of his word, laughed and said they had as little in Scotland.

There was still an hour of daylight to come, and moon-rise would not be far off, so that the hosts proposed to adjourn to the garden, where fresh music awaited them.

King Rene was an ardent gardener. His love of flowers was viewed as one of his weaknesses, only worthy of an old Abbot, but he went his own way, and the space within the walls of his castle at Nanci was lovely with bright spring flowers, blossoming trees, and green walks, where, as Lady Suffolk said, her grandfather could have mused all day and all night long, to the sound of the nightingales.

But what the sisters valued it for was that they could ramble away together to a stone bench under the wall, and there sit at perfect ease together and pour out their hearts to one another. Margaret, indeed, touched them as they leant against her as if to convince herself of their reality, and yet she said that they knew not what they did when they put the sea between themselves and Scotland, nor how sick the heart could be for its bonnie hills.

'O gin I could see a mountain top again, I feel as though I could lay me down and die content. What garred ye come daundering to these weary flats of France?'

'Ah, sister, Scotland is not what you mind it when our blessed father lived!'

And they told her how their lives had been spent in being hurried from one prison-castle to another.

'Prison-castles be not wanting here,' replied Margaret with a sigh. Then, as Elleen held up a hand in delight at the thrill of a neighbouring nightingale, she cried, 'What is yon sing-song, seesaw, gurgling bird to our own bonnie laverock, soaring away to the sky, without making such a wark of tuning his pipes, and never thinking himself too dainty and tender for a wholesome frost or two! So Jamie sent you off to seek for husbands here, did he? Couldna ye put up with a leal Scot, like Glenuskie there?'

'There were too many of them,' said Jean.

'And not ower leal either,' said Eleanor.

'Lealty is a rare plant ony gate,' sighed Margaret, 'and where sae little is recked of our Scots royalty, mayhap ye'll find that tocherless lasses be less sought for than at hame. Didna I see thee, Elleen, clavering with that muckle Archduke that nane can talk with?'

'Ay,' said Eleanor.

'He is come here a-courting Madame Yolande, with his father's goodwill, for Alsace and Tyrol be his, mountains that might be in our ain Hielands, they tell me.'

'Methougnt,' said Eleanor, 'she scunnered from him, as Jeanie does at—shall I say whom?'

'And reason gude,' said Margaret. 'She has a joe of her ain, Count Ferry de Vaudemont, that is the heir male of the line, and a gallant laddie. At the great joust the morn methinks ye'll see what may well be sung by minstrels, and can scarce fail to touch the heart of a true troubadour, as is my good uncle Rene.'

Margaret became quite animated, and her sisters pressed her to tell them if she knew of any secret; but she playfully shook her head, and said that if she did know she would not mar the romaunt that was to be played out before them.

'Nay,' said Eleanor, 'we have a romaunt of our own. May I tell, Jeanie?'

'Who recks?' replied Jean, with a little toss of her head.

Thus Eleanor proceeded to tell her sister what—since the adventure of the goose—had gone far beyond a guess as to the tall, red-haired young man-at-arms who had ridden close behind David Drummond.

'Douglas, Douglas, tender and true,' exclaimed Margaret. 'He loves you so as to follow for weeks, nay, months, in this guise without word or look. Oh, Jeanie, Jeanie, happy lassie, did ye but ken it! Nay, put not on that scornful mou'. It sorts you not weel, my bairn. He is of degree befitting a Stewart, and even were he not, oh, sisters, sisters, better to wed with a leal loving soul in ane high peel-tower than to bear a broken heart to a throne!' and she fell into a convulsive fit of choked and bitter weeping, which terrified her sisters.

At the sound of a lute, apparently being brought nearer, accompanied with footsteps, she hastily recovered herself, and rose to her feet, while a smile broke out over her face, as the musician, a slender, graceful figure, appeared on the path in the moonlight.

'Answering the nightingales, Maitre Alain?' she said.

'This is the court of nightingales, Madame,' he replied. 'It is presumption to endeavour to rival them even though the heart be torn like that of Philomel.' Wherewith he touched his lute, and began to sing from his famous idyll—

> 'Ainsi mon coeur se guermentait
> De la grande douleur qu'il portait,
>   En ce plaisant lieu solitaire
> Ou un doux ventelet venait,
> Si seri qu'on le sentait
>   Lorsque la violette mieux flaire.'

Again, as Eleanor heard the sweet strains, and saw the long shadows of the trees and the light of the rising moon, it was like the attainment of her dreamland; and Margaret proceeded to make known to her sisters Maitre Alain Chartier, the prince of song, adding, 'Thou, too, wast a songster, sister Elleen, even while almost a babe. Dost sing as of old?'

'I have brought my father's harp,' said Eleanor.

'Ah! I must hear it,' she cried with effusion. 'The harp. It will be his voice again.'

'Madame! Madame! Madame la Dauphine. Out here! Ever reckless of dew—ay, and of waur than dew.'

These last words were added in Scotch, as a tall, dark-cloaked figure appeared on the scene from between the trees. Margaret laughed, with a little annoyance in her tone, as she said, 'Ever my shadow, good Madame, ever wearying yourself with care. Here, sisters, here is my trusty and well-beloved Dame de Ste. Petronelle, who takes such care of me that she dogs my footsteps like a messan.'

'And reason gude,' replied the lady. 'Here is the muckle hall all alight, and this King Rene, as they call him, twanging on his lute, and but that the Seigneur Dauphin is talking to the English Lord on some question of Gascon boundaries, we should have him speiring for you. I saw the eye of him roaming after you, as it was.'

'His eye seeking me!' cried Margaret, springing up from her languid attitude with a tone like exultation in her voice, such as evoked a low sigh from the old dame, as all began to move towards the castle. She was the widow of a Scotch adventurer who had won lands and honours in France; and she was now attached to the service of the Dauphiness, not as her chief lady—that post was held by an old French countess—but still close enough to her to act as her guardian and monitor whenever it was possible to deal with her.

The old lady, in great delight at meeting a compatriot, poured out her confidences to Dame Lilias of Glenuskie. Infinitely grieved and annoyed was she when, early as were the ordinary hours of the Court of Nanci, it proved that the Dauphiness had called up her sisters an hour before, and taken them across the chace which surrounded the castle to hear mass at a convent of Benedictine nuns.

It was perfectly safe, though only a tirewoman and a page followed the Dauphiness, and only Annis attended her two sisters, for the grounds were enclosed, and King Rene's domains were far better ruled and more peaceful than those of the princes who despised him. It was an exquisite spring morning, with grass silvery with dew and enamelled with flowers, birds singing ecstatically on every branch, squirrels here and there racing up a trunk. Margaret was in joyous spirits, and almost danced between her sisters. Eleanor was amazed at the luxuriant beauty of the scene, and could not admire enough. Jean, though at first a little cross at the early summons, could not but be infected with their delight, and the three laughed and frolicked together with almost childish glee in the delight of their content.

The great, gentle-eyed, long-horned kine were being driven in at the convent-yard to be milked by the lay-sisters; at another entrance, peasants, beggars, and sick were congregating; the bell from the lace-works spire rang out, and the Dauphiness led the way to the gateway, where, at her knock on the iron-studded door, a lay-sister looked through the wicket.

'Good sister, here are some early pilgrims to the shrine of St. Scolastique,' she began.

'To the other gate,' said the portress hastily. Margaret's face twinkled with fun. 'I wad fain take a turn with the beggar crew,' she said to her sisters in Scotch; 'but it might cause too great an outcry if I were kenned. Commend me to the Mere St. Antoine,' she added in French, 'and tell her that the Dauphiness would fain hear mass with her.'

The portress cast an anxious doubtful glance, but being apparently convinced, cried out for pardon, while hastily unlocking her door, and sending a message to the Abbess.

As they entered the cloistered quadrangle the nuns in black procession were on their way to mass, but turned aside to receive their visitors. Margaret knelt for a moment for the blessing and kiss of the Abbess, then greeted the nun whom she had mentioned, but begged for no further ceremony, and then was led into church.

It was a brief festival mass, and was not really over before she, with a restlessness of which her sisters began to be conscious, began to rise and make her way out. A nun followed and entreated her to stay and break her fast, but she would accept nothing save a draught of milk, swallowed hastily, and with signs of impatience as her sisters took their turn.

She walked quickly, rather as one guilty of an escapade, again surprising her sisters, who fancied the liberty of a married princess illimitable.

Jean even ventured to ask her why she went so fast, 'Would the King of France be displeased?'

'He! Poor gude sire Charles! He heeds not what one does, good or bad; no, not the murdering of his minion before his eyes,' said Margaret, half laughing.

'Thy husband, would he be angered?' pressed on Jean.

'My husband? Oh no, it is not in the depth and greatness of is thoughts to find fault with his poor worm,' said Margaret, a strange look, half of exultation, half of pain, on her face. 'Ah! Jeanie, woman, none kens in sooth how great and wise my Dauphin is, nor how far he sees beyond all around him, so that he cannot choose but scorn them and make them his tools. When he has the power, he will do more for this poor realm of France than any king before him.'

'As our father would have done for Scotland,' said Eleanor.

'Then he tells thee of his plans?'

'Me!' said Margaret, with the suffering look returning. 'How should he talk to me, the muckle uncouthie wife that I am, kenning nought but a wheen ballads and romaunts—not even able to give him the heir for whom he longs,' and she wrung her hands together, 'how can I be aught but a pain and grief to him!'

'Nay, but thou lovest him?' said Jean, over simply.

'Lassie!' exclaimed Margaret hotly, 'what thinkest thou I am made of? How should a wife not love her man, the wisest, canniest prince in Christendom, too! Love him! I worship him, as the trouveres say, with all my heart, and wad lay down my life if I could win one kind blush of his eye; and yet—and yet—such a creature am I that I am ever wittingly or unwittingly transgressing these weary laws, and garring him think me a fool, or others report me such,' clenching her hands again.

'Madame de Ste. Petronelle?' asked Jean.

'She! Oh no! She is a true loyal Lindsay, heart and soul, dour and wearisome; but she would guard me from every foe, and most of all, as she is ever telling me, from mine ain self, that is my worst enemy. Only she sets about it in such guise that, for very vexation, I am driven farther! No, it is the Countess de Craylierre, who is forever spiting me, and striving to put whatever I do in a cruel light, if I dinna walk after her will—hers, as if she could rule a king's daughter!'

And Margaret stamped her foot on the ground, while a hot flush arose in her cheeks. Her sisters, young girls as they were, could not understand her moods, either of wild mirth, eager delight in poetry and music, childish wilfulness and petulant temper or deep melancholy, all coming in turn with feverish alternation and vehemence. As the ladies approached the castle they were met by various gentlemen, among whom was Maitre Alain Chartier, and a bandying of compliments and witticisms began in such rapid French that even Eleanor could not follow it; but there was something in the ring of the Dauphiness's hard laugh that pained her, she knew not why.

At the entrance they found the chief of the party returning from the cathedral, where they had heard mass, not exactly in state, but publicly.

'Ha! ha! good daughter,' laughed the King, 'I took thee for a slug abed, but it is by thy errant fashion that thou hast cheated us.'

'I have been to mass at St Mary's,' returned Margaret, 'with my sisters. I love the early walk across the park.'

'No wonder,' came from between the thin lips of the Dauphin, as his keen little eye fell on Chartier. Margaret drew herself up and vouchsafed not to reply. Jean marvelled, but Eleanor felt with her, that she was too proud to defend herself from the insult. Madame de Ste. Petronelle, however, stepped forward and began: 'Madame la Dauphine loves not attendance. She made her journey alone with Mesdames ses soeurs with no male company, till she reached home.'

But before the first words were well out of the good lady's mouth Louis had turned away, with an air of the most careless indifference, to a courtier in a long gown, longer shoes, and a jewelled girdle, who became known to the sisters as Messire Jamet de Tillay. Eleanor felt indignant. Was he too heedless of his wife to listen to the vindication.

Madame de Ste. Petronelle took the Lady of Glenuskie aside and poured out her lamentations. That was ever the way, she said, the Dauphiness would give occasion to slanderers, by her wilful ways, and there were those who would turn all she said or did against her, poisoning the ear of the Dauphin, little as he cared.

'Is he an ill man to her?' asked Dame Lilias little prepossessed by his looks.

'He! Madame, mind you an auld tale of the Eatin wi' no heart in his body! I verily believe he and his father both were created like that giant. No that the King is sair to live with either, so that he can eat and drink and daff, and be let alone to take his ease. I have seen him; and my gude man and them we kenned have marked him this score of years; and whether his kingdom were lost or won, whether his best friends were free or bound, dead or alive, he recked as little as though it were a game of chess, so that he can sit in the ingle neuk at Bourges and toy with Madame de Beaute, shameless limmer that she is! and crack his fists with yon viper, Jamet de Tillay, and the rest of the crew. But he'll let you alone, and has a kindly word for them that don't cross him—and there be those that would go through fire and water for him. He is no that ill! But for his son, he has a sneer and a spite such as never his father had. He is never a one to sit still and let things gang their gate; but he has as little pity or compassion as his father, and if King Charles will not stir a finger to hinder a gruesome deed, Dauphin Louis will not spare to do it so that he can gain by it, and I trow verily that to give pain and sting with that bitter tongue of his is joy to him.'

'Then is there no love between him and our princess?'

'Alack, lady, there is love, but 'tis all on one side of the house. I doubt me whether Messire le Dauphin hath it in him to love any living creature. I longed, when I saw your maidens, that my poor lady had been as bonnie as her sister Joanna; but mayhap that would not have served her better. If she were as dull as the Duchess of Brittany—who they say can scarce find a word to give to a stranger at Nantes—she might even anger him less than she does with her wit and her books and her verses, sitting up half the night to read and write rondeaux, forsooth!'

'Her blessed father's own daughter!'

'That may be; but how doth it suit a wife? It might serve here, where every one is mad after poesy, as they call it; but such ways are in no good odour with the French dames, who never put eye to book, pen to paper, nor foot to ground if they can help it; and when she behoves to gang off roaming afoot, as she did this morn, there's no garring the ill-minded carlines believe that there's no ill purpose behind.'

'It is scarce wise.'

'Yet to hear her, 'tis such walking and wearing herself out that keeps the life in her and alone gives her sleep. My puir bairn, worshipping the very ground her man sets foot on, and never getting aught but a gibe or a girn from him, and, for the very wilfulness of her sair heart, ever putting herself farther from him!'

Such was the piteous account that Madame de Ste. Petronelle (otherwise Dame Elspeth Johnstone) gave, and which the Lady of Glenuskie soon perceived to be only too true during the days spent at Nanci. To the two young sisters the condition of things was less evident. To Margaret their presence was such sunshine, that they usually saw her in her highest, most flighty, and imprudent spirits, taking at times absolute delight in shocking her two duennas; and it was in this temper that, one hot noon day, coming after an evening of song and music, finding Alain Chartier asleep on a bench in the garden, she declared that she must kiss the mouth from which such sweet strains proceeded, and bending down, imprinted so light a kiss as not to waken him, then turned round, her whole face rippling with silent laughter at the amusement of Jean and Margaret of Anjou, Elleen's puzzled gravity, and the horror and dismay of her elder ladies. But Dame Lilias saw what she did not—a look of triumphant malice on the face of Jamet de Tillay. Or at other times she would sit listening, with silent tears in her eyes, to plaintive Scottish airs on Eleanor's harp, which she declared brought back her father's voice to her, and with it the scent of the heather, and the very sight of Arthur's Seat or the hills of Perth. Elleen had some sudden qualms of heart lest her sister's blitheness should be covering wounds within; but she was too young to be often haunted by such thoughts in the delightful surroundings in which that Easter week was spent—the companionship of their sister and of the two young Infantas of Anjou, as well as all the charm of King Rene's graceful attention. Eleanor had opened to her fresh stores of beauty, exquisite illuminations, books of all kinds—legend, history, romance, poetry—all freely displayed to her by her royal host, who took an elderly man's delight in an intelligent girl; nor, perhaps, was the pleasure lessened by the need of explaining to Archduke Sigismund, in German ever improving, that which he could not understand. There was a delightful freedom about the Court—not hard, rugged, always on the defence, like that of Scotland; nor stiffly ecclesiastical, as had been that of Henry of Windsor; but though there was devotion every morning, there was for the rest of the day holiday-making according to each one's taste—not hawking, for the 'bon roi René' was merciful to the birds in nesting time, for which he was grumbled and laughed at by the young nobles, and it may be feared by Jean, who wanted to exhibit Skywing's prowess; but there was riding at the ring, and jousting, or long rides in the environs, minstrelsy in the gardens, and once a graceful ballet of the King's own composition; and the evenings, sometimes in-doors, sometimes out-of-doors, were given to song and music. Altogether it was a land of enchantment to most, whether gaily or poetically inclined.

Only there were certain murmurs by the rugged Scots and fierce Gascons among the guests. George observed to David Drummond that he felt as if this was a nest of eider-ducks, all down and fluff. Davie responded that it was like a pasteboard town in a mystery play, and that he longed to strike at it with his good broadsword. The English squire who stood by, in his turn compared it to a castle of flummery and blanc-manger. A French captain of a full company declared that he wished he had the plundering of it; and a fierce-looking mountaineer of the Vosges of Alsace growled that if the harping old King of Nowhere flouted his master, Duke Sigismund, maybe they should have a taste of plunder.

There was actually to be a tournament on the Monday, the day before the wedding, and a first tournament was a prodigious event in the life of a young lady. Jean was in the utmost excitement, and never looked at her own pretty face of roses and lilies in the steel mirror without comparing it with those of the two Infantas in the hope of being chosen Queen of Beauty; but, to her great disappointment, King Rene prudently ordained that there should be no such competition, but that the prizes should be bestowed by his sister, the Queen of France.

The Marquess of Suffolk requested Sir Patrick to convey to young Douglas a free offer of fitting him out for the encounter, with armour and horse if needful, and even of conferring knighthood on him, so that he might take his place on equal terms in the lists.

'He would like to do it, the insolent loon!' was Geordie's grim comment. 'Will De la Pole dare to talk of dubbing the Red Douglas! When I bide his buffet, it shall be in another sort. When I take knighthood, it shall be from my lawful King or my father.'

'So I shall tell him,' replied Sir Patrick, 'and I deem you wise, for there be tricks of French chivalry that a man needs to know ere he can acquit himself well in the lists; and to see you fail would scarce raise you in the eyes of your lady.'

'More like they would find too much earnest in the midst of their sham?' returned Geordie. 'You had best tell your English Marquis, as he calls himself, that he had better not trust a lance in a Scotsman hand, if he wouldna have all the shams that fret me beyond my patience about their ears.'

This was not exactly what Sir Patrick told the Marquis; though he was far from disapproving of the resolution. He kept an eye on this strange follower, and was glad to see that there was no evil or licence in his conduct, but that he chiefly consorted with David and a few other young squires to whom this week, so delightful to the ladies, was inexpressibly wearisome.

Tournaments have been described, so far as the nineteenth century can describe them, so often that no one wishes to hear more of their details. These had nearly reached their culmination in the middle of the fifteenth century. Defensive armour had become highly ornamental and very cumbrous, so that it was scarcely possible for the champions to do one another much harm, except that a fall under such a weight was dangerous. Thus it was only an exercise of skill in arms and horsemanship on which the ladies gazed as they sat in the gallery around Queen Marie, the five young princesses together forming, as the minstrels declared, a perfect wreath of loveliness. The Dauphiness, with a flush on her cheek and an eager look on her face, her tall form, and dress more carefully arranged than usual, looked well and princely; Eleanor, very like her, but much developed in expression and improved in looks since she left home, and a beauty of her own; but the palm lay between the other three—Yolande, tall, grave, stately, and anxious, with darker blue eyes and brown hair than her sister, who, with her innocent childish face, showing something of the shyness of a bride, sat somewhat back, as if to conceal herself between Yolande and Jean, who was all excitement, her cheeks flushed, and her sunny hair seeming to glow with a radiance of its own. Duke Sigismund was among the defenders, in a very splendid suit of armour, made in Italy, and embossed in that new taste of the Cinquecento that was fast coming in.

The two kings began with an amicable joust, in which Rene had the best of it. Then they took their seats, and as usual there was a good deal of riding one against the other at the lists, and shivering of lances; while some knights were borne backwards, horse and all, others had their helmets carried off; but Rene, who sat in great enjoyment, with his staff in hand, between his sister and her husband, King Charles, had taken care that all the weapons should be blunted. Sigismund, a tall, large, strongly made man, was for some time the leading champion. Perhaps there was an understanding that the Lion of Hapsburg and famed Eagle of the Tyrol was to carry all before him and win, in an undoubted manner, the prize of the tourney, and the hand of the Infanta Yolande. Certainly the colour rose higher and higher in her delicate cheek, but those nearest could see that it was not with pleasure, for she bit her lip with annoyance, and her eyes wandered in search of some one.

Presently, in a pause, there came forward on a tall white horse a magnificently tall man, in plain but bright armour, three allerions or beakless eagles on his breast, and on his shield a violet plant, with the motto, Si douce est la violette. The Dauphiness leant across her sister and squeezed Yolande's hand vehemently, as the knight inclined his lance to the King, and was understood to crave permission to show his prowess. Charles turned to Rene, whose good-humoured face looked annoyed, but who could not withhold his consent. The Dauphiness, whose vehement excitement was more visible than even Yolande's, whispered to Eleanor that this was Messire Ferry de Vaudemont, her true love, come to win her at point of the lance.

History is the parent of romance, and romance now and then becomes history. It is an absolute and undoubted fact that Count Frederic or Ferry de Vaudemont, the male representative of the line of Charles the Great, did win his lady-love, Yolande of Anjou, by his good lance within the lists, and that thus the direct descent was brought eventually back to Lorraine, though this was not contemplated at the time, since Yolande had then living both a brother and a nephew, and it was simply for her own sake that Messire Ferry, in all the strength and beauty that descended to the noted house of Guise, was now bearing down all before him, touching shield after shield, only to gain the better of their owners in the encounter. Yolande sat with a deep colour in her cheeks, and her hands clasped rigidly together without a movement, while the Lorrainer spectators, with a strong suspicion who the Knight of the Violet really was, and with a leaning to their own line, loudly applauded each victory.

King Rene, long ago, had had to fight for his wife's inheritance with this young man's father, who, supported by the strength of Burgundy, had defeated and made him prisoner, so that he was naturally disinclined to the match, and would have preferred the Hapsburg Duke, whose Alsatian possessions were only divided from his own by the Vosges; but his generous and romantic spirit could not choose but be gained by the proceeding of Count Ferry, and the mute appeal in the face and attitude of his much-loved daughter.

He could not help joining in the applause at the grace and ease of the young knight, till by and by all interest became concentrated on the last critical encounter with Sigismund.

Every one watched almost breathlessly as the big heavy Austrian, mounted on a fresh horse, and the slim Lorrainer in armour less strong but less weighty, had their meeting. Two courses were run with mere splintering of lance; at the third, while Rene held his staff ready to throw if signs of fighting *a l'outrance* appeared, Ferry lifted his lance a little, and when both steeds recoiled from the clash, the azure eagle of the Tyrol was impaled on the point of his lance, and Sigismund, though not losing his saddle, was bending low on it, half stunned by the force of the blow. Down went Rene's warder. Loud were the shouts, 'Vive the Knight of the Violet! Victory to the Allerions!'

The voice of Rene was as clear and exulting as the rest, as the heralds, with blast of trumpet, proclaimed the Chevalier de la Violette the victor of the day, and then came forward to lead him to the feet of the Queen of France. His helmet was removed, and at the face of manly beauty that it revealed, the applause was renewed; but as Marie held out the prize, a splendidly hilted sword, he bowed low, and said, 'Madame, one boon alone do I ask for my guerdon.' And withal, he laid the blue eagle on his lance at the feet of Yolande.

Rene was not the father to withstand such an appeal. He leapt from his chair of state, he hurried to Yolande in her gallery, took her by the hand, and in another moment Ferry had sprung from his horse, and on the steps knight and lady, in their youthful glory and grace, stood hand in hand, all blushes and bliss, amid the ecstatic applause of the multitude, while the Dauphiness shed tears of joy. Thus brilliantly ended the first tournament witnessed by the Scottish princesses. Eleanor had been most interested on the whole in Duke Sigismund, and had exulted in his successes, and been sorry to see him defeated, but then she knew that Yolande dreaded his victory, and she suspected that he did not greatly care for Yolande, so that, since he was not hurt, and was certainly the second in the field, she could look on with complacency.

Moreover, at the evening's dance, when Margaret and Suffolk, Ferry and Yolande stood up for a stately pavise together, Sigismund came to Eleanor, and while she was thinking whether or not to condole with him, he shyly mumbled something about not regretting—being free—the Dauphin, her brother, enduring a beaten knight. It was all in a mixture of French and German, mostly of the latter, and far less comprehensible than usual, unless, indeed, maidenly shyness made her afraid to understand or to seem to do so. He kept on standing by her, both of them, mute and embarrassed, not quite unconscious that they were observed, perhaps secretly derided by some of the lookers-on. The first relief was when the Dauphiness came and sat down by her sister, and began to talk fast in French, scarce heeding whether the Duke understood or answered her.

One question he asked was, who was the red-faced young man with stubbly sunburnt hair, and a scar on his cheek, who had appeared in the lists in very gaudy but ill-fitting armour, and with a great raw-boned, snorting horse, and now stood in a corner of the hall with his eyes steadily fixed on the Lady Joanna.

'So!' said Sigismund. 'That fellow is the Baron Rudiger von Batchburg Der Schelm! How has he the face to show himself here?'

'Is he one of your Borderers—your robber Castellanes?' asked Margaret.

'Even so! His father's castle of Balchenburg is so cunningly placed on the march between Elsass and Lothringen that neither our good host nor I can fully claim it, and these rogues shelter themselves behind one or other of us till it is, what they call in Germany a Rat Castle, the refuge of all the ecorcheurs and routiers of this part of the country. They will bring us both down on them one of these days, but the place is well-nigh past scaling by any save a gemsbock or an ecorcheur!'

Jean herself had remarked the gaze of the Alsatian mountaineer. It was the chief homage that her beauty had received, and she was somewhat mortified at being only viewed as part of the constellation of royalty and beauty doing honour to the Infantas. She believed, too, that if G he could have brought her out in as effective and romantic a light as that in which Yolande had appeared, and she was in some of her moods hurt and angered with him for refraining, while in others she supposed sometimes that he was too awkward thus to venture himself, and at others she did him the justice of believing that he disdained to appear in borrowed plumes.

The wedding was by no means so splendid an affair as the tournament, as, indeed, it was merely a marriage by proxy, and Yolande and her Count of Vaudemont were too near of kin to be married before a dispensation could be procured.

The King and Queen of France would leave Nanci to see the bride partly on her way. The Dauphin and his wife were to tarry a day or two behind, and the princesses belonged to their Court. Sir Patrick had fulfilled his charge of conducting them to their sister, and he had now to avail himself of the protection of the King's party as far as possible on the way to Paris, where he would place

Malcolm at the University, and likewise meet his daughter's bridegroom and his father.

Dame Lilias did not by any means like leaving her young cousins, so long her charge, without attendants of their own; but the Dauphiness gave them a tirewoman of her own, and undertook that Madame de Ste. Petronelle should attend them in case of need, as well as that she would endeavour to have Annis, when Madame de Terreforte, at her Court as long as they were there. They also had a squire as equerry, and George Douglas was bent on continuing in that capacity till his outfit from his father arrived, as it was sure to do sooner or later.

Margaret knew who he was, and promised Sir Patrick to do all in her power for him, as truly his patience and forbearance well deserved.

It was a very sorrowful parting between the two maidens and the Lady of Glenuskie, who for more than half a year had been as a mother to them, nay, more than their own mother had ever been; and had done much to mitigate the sharp angles of their neglected girlhood by her influence. In a very few months more she would see James, and Mary, and the 'weans'; and the three sisters loaded her with gifts, letters, and messages for all. Eleanor promised never to forget her counsel, and to strive not to let the bright new world drive away all those devout feelings and hopes that Mother Clare and King Henry had inspired, and that Lady Drummond had done her best to keep up.

Duke Sigismund had communicated to Sir Patrick his intention of making a formal request to King James for the hand of the Lady Eleanor. He was to find an envoy to make his proposal in due form, who would join Sir Patrick at Terreforte after the wedding was over, so as to go with the party to Scotland.

Meantime, with many fond embraces and tears, Lady Drummond took leave of her princesses, and they owned themselves to feel as if a protecting wall had been taken away in her and her husband.

'It is folly, though, thus to speak,' said Jean, 'when we have our sister, and her husband, and his father, and all his Court to protect us.'

'We ought to be happy,' said Eleanor gravely. 'Outside here at Nanci, it is all that my fancy ever shaped, and yet—and yet there is a strange sense of fear beyond.'

'Oh, talk not that gate,' cried Jean, 'as thou wilt be having thy gruesome visions!'

'No; it is not of that sort,' returned Eleanor. 'I trow not! It may be rather the feeling of the vanity of all this world's show.'

'Oh, for mercy's sake, dinna let us have clavers of that sort, or we shall have thee in yon nunnery!' exclaimed Jean. 'See this girdle of Maggie's, which she has given me. Must I not make another hole to draw it up enough for my waist?'

'Jean herself was much disappointed when Margaret, with great regret, told her that the Dauphin had to go out of his way to visit some castles on his way to Chalons sur Marne, and that he could not encumber his hosts with so large a train as the presence of two royal ladies rendered needful. They were, therefore, to travel by another route, leading through towns where there were hostels. Madame de Ste. Petronelle was to go with them, and an escort of trusty Scots archers, and all would meet again in a fortnight's time.

All sounded simple and easy, and Margaret repeated, 'It will be a troop quite large enough to defend you from all ecorcheurs; indeed, they dare not come near our Scottish archers, whom Messire, my husband, has told off for your escort. And you will have your own squire,' she added, looking at Jean.

'That's as he lists,' said Jean scornfully.

'Ah, Jeanie, Jeanie, thou mayst have to rue it if thou turn'st lightly from a leal heart.'

'I'm not damsel-errant of romance, as thou and Elleen would fain be,' said Jean.

'Nay,' said Margaret, 'love is not mere romance. And oh, sister, credit me, a Scots lassie's heart craves better food than crowns and coronets. Hard and unco' cold be they, where there is no warmth to meet the yearning soul beneath, that would give all and ten times more for one glint of a loving eye, one word from a tender lip.' Again she had one of those hysteric bursts of tears, but she laughed herself back, crying, 'But what is the treason wifie saying of her gudeman—her Louis, that never yet said a rough word to his Meg?'

Then came another laugh, but she gathered herself up at a summons to come down and mount.

She was tenderly embraced by all, King Rene kissing her and calling her his dear niece and princess of minstrelsy, who should come to him at Toulouse and bestow the golden violet.

She rode away, looking back smiling and kissing her hand, but Eleanor's eyes grew wide and her cheeks pale.

'Jean,' she murmured, low and hoarsely, 'Margaret's shroud is up to her throat.'

'Hoots with thy clavers,' exclaimed Jeanie in return. 'I never let thee sing that fule song, but Meg's fancies have brought the megrims into thine head! Thou and she are pair.'

'That we shall be nae longer,' sighed Eleanor. 'I saw the shroud as clear as I see yon cross on the spire.'

CHAPTER 8. STINGS

'Yet one asylum is my own,
   Against the dreaded hour;
A long, a silent, and a lone,
   Where kings have little power.'—SCOTT.

At Chalons, the Sieur de Terreforte and his son Olivier, a very quiet, stiff, and well-trained youth, met Sir Patrick and the Lady of Glenuskie. Terreforte was within the province of Champagne, and as long as the Court remained at Chalons the Sieur felt bound to remain in attendance on the King—lodging at his own house, or hotel, as he called it, in the city. Dame Lilias did not regret anything which gave her a little more time with her daughter, and enabled Annis to make a little more acquaintance with her bridegroom and his family before being left alone with them. Moreover, she hoped to see something more of her cousins the princesses.

But they came not. The Dauphin and his wife arrived from their excursion and took up their abode in the Castle of Surry le Chateau, at a short distance from thence and thither went the Lady of Glenuskie with her husband to pay her respects, and present the betrothed of her daughter.

Margaret was sitting in a shady nook of the walls, under the shade of a tall, massive tower, with a page reading to her, but in that impulsive manner which the Court of France thought grossiere and sauvage; she ran down the stone stairs and threw herself on the neck of her cousin, exclaiming, however, 'But where are my sisters?'

'Are they not with your Grace? I thought to find them here!'

'Nay! They were to start two days after us, with an escort of archers, while we visited the shrine of St. Menehould. They might have been here before us,' exclaimed Margaret, in much alarm. 'My husband thought our train would be too large if they went with us.'

'If we had known that they were not to be with your Grace, we would have tarried for them,' said Dame Lilias.

'Oh, cousin, would that you had!'

'Mayhap King Rene and his daughter persuaded them to wait a few days.'

That was the best hope, but there was much uneasiness when another day passed and the Scottish princesses did not appear. Strange whispers, coming from no one knew where, began to be current that they had disappeared in company with some of those wild and gay knights who had met at the tournament at Nanci.

In extreme alarm and indignation, Margaret repaired to her husband. He was kneeling before the shrine of the Lady in the Chapel of Surry, telling his beads, and he did not stir, or look round, or relax one murmur of his Aves, while she paced about, wrung her hands, and vainly tried to control her agitation. At last he rose, and coldly said, 'I knew it could be no other who thus interrupted my devotions.'

'My sisters!' she gasped.

'Well, what of them?'

'Do you know what wicked things are said of them—the dear maids? Ah!'—as she saw his strange smile—'you have heard! You will silence the fellows, who deserve to have their tongues torn out for defaming a king's daughters.'

'Verily, ma mie,' said Louis, 'I see no such great improbability in the tale. They have been bred up to the like, no doubt a mountain kite of the Vosges is a more congenial companion than a chevalier bien courtois.'

'You speak thus simply to tease your poor Margot,' she said, pleading yet trembling; 'but I know better than to think you mean it.'

'As my lady pleases,' he said.

'Then will I send Sir Patrick with an escort to seek them at Nanci and bring them hither?'

'Where is this same troop to come from?' demanded Louis.

'Our own Scottish archers, who will see no harm befall my blessed father's daughters.'

'Ha! say you so? I had heard a different story from Buchan, from the Grahams, the Halls. Revenge is sweet—as your mother found it.'

'The murderers had only their deserts.'

Louis shrugged his shoulders, 'That is as their sons may think.'

'No one would be so dastardly as to wreak vengeance on two young helpless maids,' cried Margaret. 'Oh! sir, help me; what think you?'

'Madame knows better than I do the spirit alike of her sisters and of her own countrymen.'

'Nay, nay, Monsieur, husband, do but help me! My poor sisters in this strange land! You, who are wiser than all, tell me what can have become of them?'

'What can I say, Madame? Love—love of the minstrel kind seems to run in the family. You all have supped full thereof at Nanci. If report said true, there was a secret lover in their suite. What so likely as that the May game should have become earnest?'

'But, sir, we are accountable. My sisters were entrusted to us.'

'Not to me,' said Louis. 'If the boy, your brother, expected me to find husbands and dowers for a couple of wild, penniless, feather-pated damsels-errant, he expected far too much. I know far too well what are Scotch manners and ideas of decorum to charge myself with the like.'

'Sir, do you mean to insult me?' demanded Margaret, rising to the full height of her tall stature.

'That is as Madame may choose to fit the cap,' he said, with a bow; 'I accuse her of nothing,' but there was an ironical smile on his thin lips which almost maddened her.

'Speak out; oh, sir, tell me what you dare to mean!' she said, with a stamp of her foot, clasping her hands tightly. He only bowed again.

'I know there are evil tongues abroad,' said Margaret, with a desperate effort to command her voice; 'but I heeded them no more than the midges in the air while I knew my lord and husband heeded them not! But—oh! say you do not.'

'Have I said that I did?'

'Then for a proof—dismiss and silence that foul-slandering wretch, Jamet de Tillay.'

'A true woman's imagination that to dismiss is to silence,' he laughed.

'It would show at least that you will not brook to have your wife defamed! Oh! sir, sir,' she cried, 'I only ask what any other husband would have done long ago of his own accord and rightful anger. Smile not thus—or you will see me frenzied.'

'Smiles best befit woman's tears,' said Louis coolly. 'One moment for your sisters, the next for yourself.'

'Ah! my sisters! my sisters! Wretch that I am, to have thought of my worthless self for one moment. Ah! you are only teasing your poor Margot! You will act for your own honour and theirs in sending out to seek them!'

'My honour and theirs may be best served by their being forgotten.'

Margaret became inarticulate with dismay, indignation, disappointment, as these envenomed stings went to her very soul, further pointed by the curl of Louis's thin lips and the sinister twinkle of his little eyes. Almost choked, she stammered forth the demand what he meant, only to be answered that he did not pretend to understand the Scottish errant nature, and pointing to a priest entering the church, he bade her not make herself conspicuous, and strolled away.

Margaret's despair and agony were inexpressible. She stood for some minutes leaning against a pillar to collect her senses. Then her first thought was of consulting the Drummonds, and she impetuously dashed back to her own apartments and ordered her palfrey and suite to be ready instantly to take her to Chalons.

Madame la Dauphine's palfreys were all gone to Chalons to be shod. In fact, there were some games going on there, and trusting to the easy-going habits of their mistress, almost all her attendants had lounged off thither, even the maidens, as well as the pages, who felt Madame de Ste. Petronelle's sharp eyes no longer over them.

'Tell me,' said Margaret, to the one lame, frightened old man who alone seemed able to reply to her call, 'do you know who commanded the escort which were with my sisters, the Princesses of Scotland?'

The old man threw up his hands. How should he know? 'The escort was of the savage Scottish archers.'

'I know that; but can you not tell who they were—nor their commander?'

'Ah! Madame knows that their names are such as no Christian ears can understand, nor lips speak!'

'I had thought it was the Sire Andrew Gordon who was to go with them. He with the blue housings on the dapple grey.'

'No, Madame; I heard the Captain Mercour say Monsieur le Dauphin had other orders for him. It was the little dark one—how call they him?—ah! with a more reasonable name—Le Halle, who led the party of Mesdames. Madame! Madame! let me call some of Madame's women!'

'No, no,' gasped Margaret, knowing indeed that none whom she wished to see were within call. 'Thanks, Jean, here—now go,' and she flung him a coin.

She knew now that whatever had befallen her sisters had been by the connivance if not the contrivance of her husband, unwilling to have the charge and the portioning of the two penniless maidens imposed upon him. And what might not that fate be, betrayed into the hands of one who had so deadly a blood-feud with their parents! For Hall was the son of one of the men whose daggers had slain James I., and whose crime had been visited with such vindictive cruelty by Queen Joanna. The man's eyes had often scowled at her, as if he longed for vengeance—and thus had it been granted him.

Margaret, with understanding to appreciate Louis's extraordinary ability, had idolised him throughout in spite of his constant coldness and the satire with which he treated all her higher tastes and aspirations, continually throwing her in and back upon herself, and blighting her instincts wherever they turned. She had accepted all this as his superiority to her folly, and though the thwarted and unfostered inclinations in her strong unstained nature had occasioned those aberrations and distorted impulses which brought blame on her, she had accepted everything hitherto as her own fault, and believed in, and adored the image she had made of him throughout. Now it was as if her idol had turned suddenly into a viper in her bosom, not only stinging her by implied acquiescence in the slanders upon her discretion, if not upon her fair fame, but actually having betrayed her innocent sisters by means of the deadly enemy of their family—to what fate she knew not.

To act became an immediate need to the unhappy Dauphiness at once, as the only vent to her own misery, and because she must without loss of time do something for the succour of her young sisters, or ascertain their fate.

She did not spend a moment's thought on the censure any imprudent measure of her own might bring on her, but hastily summoning the only tirewoman within reach, she exchanged her blue and gold embroidered robe for a dark serge which she wore on days of penance, with a mantle and hood of the same, and, to Linette's horror and dismay, bade her attend her on foot to the Hotel de Terreforte, in Chalons.

Linette was in no position to remonstrate, but could only follow, as the lady, wrapped in her cloak, descended the steps, and crossed the empty hall. The porter let her pass unquestioned, but there were a few guards at the great gateway, and one shouted, 'Whither away, pretty Linette?'

Margaret raised her hood and looked full at him, and he fell back. He knew her, and knew that Madame la Dauphine did strange things. The road was stony and bare and treeless, unfrequented at first, and it was very sultry, the sun shining with a heavy melting heat on Margaret's weighty garments; but she hurried on, never feeling the heat, or hearing Linette's endeavours to draw her attention to the heavy bank of gray clouds tinged with lurid red gradually rising, and whence threatening growls of thunder were heard from time to time. She really seemed to rush forward, and poor, panting Linette toiled after her, feeling ready to drop, while the way was as yet unobstructed, as the two beautiful steeples of the Cathedral and Notre Dame de l'Epine rose before them; but after a time, as they drew nearer, the road became obstructed by carts, waggons, donkeys, crowded with country-folks and their wares, with friars and ragged beggars, all pressing into the town, and jostling one another and the two foot-passengers all the more as rain-drops began to fall, and the thunder sounded nearer.

Margaret had been used to walking, but it was all within parks and pleasances, and she was not at all used to being pushed about and jostled. Linette knew how to make her way far better, and it was well for them that their dark dresses and hoods and Linette's elderly face gave the idea of their being votaresses of some sacred order, and so secured them from actual personal insult; but as they clung together they were thrust aside and pushed about, while the throng grew thicker, the streets narrower, the storm heavier, the air more stifling and unsavoury.

A sudden rush nearly knocked them down, driving them under a gargoyle, whose spout was streaming with wet, and completed the drenching; but there was a porch and an open door of a church close behind, and into this Linette dragged her mistress. Dripping, breathless, bruised, she leant against a pillar, not going forward, for others, much more gaily dressed, had taken refuge there, and were chattering away, for little reverence was paid at that date to the sanctity of buildings.

'Will the King be there, think you?' eagerly asked a young girl, who had been anxiously wiping the wet from her pink kirtle.

'Certes—he is to give the prizes,' replied a portly dame in crimson.

'And the Lady of Beauty? I long to see her.'

'Her beauty is passing—except that which was better worth the solid castle the King gave her,' laughed the stout citizen, who seemed to be in charge of them.

'The Dauphiness, too—will she be there?'

'Ah, the Dauphiness!' said the elder woman, with a meaning sound and shake of the head.

'Scandal—evil tongues!' growled the man.

'Nay, Master Jerome, there's no denying it, for a merchant of Bourges told me. She runs about the country on foot, like no discreet woman, let alone a princess, with a good-for-nothing minstrel after her. Ah, you may grunt and make signs, but I had it from the Countess de Craylierre's own tirewoman, who came for a bit of lace, that the Dauphin is about to the Sire Jamet de Tillay caught her kissing the minstrel on a bench in the garden at Nanci.'

'I would not trust the Sire de Tillay's word. He is in debt to every merchant of the place—a smooth-tongued deceiver. Belike he is bribed to defame the poor lady, that the Dauphin may rid himself of a childless wife.'

The young girl was growing restless, declaring that the rain was over, and that they should miss the getting good places at the show. Margaret had stood all this time leaning against her pillar, with hands clenched together and teeth firm set, trying to control the shuddering of horror and indignation that went through her whole frame. She started convulsively when Linette moved after the burgher, but put a force upon herself when she perceived that it was in order to inquire how best to reach the Hotel de Terreforte.

He pointed to the opposite door of the church, and Linette, reconnoitring and finding that it led into a street entirely quiet and deserted, went back to the Dauphiness, whom she found sunk on her knees, stiff and dazed.

'Come, Madame,' she entreated, trying to raise her, 'the Hotel de Terreforte is near, these houses shelter us, and the rain is nearly over.'

Margaret did not move at first; then she looked up and said, 'What was it that they said, Linette?'

'Oh! no matter what they said, Madame; they were ignorant creatures, who knew not what they were talking about. Come, you are wet, you are exhausted. This good lady will know how to help you.'

'There is no help in man,' said Margaret, wildly stretching out her arms. 'Oh, God! help me—a desolate woman—and my sisters! Betrayed! betrayed!'

Very much alarmed, Linette at last succeeded in raising her to her feet, and guiding her, half-blinded as she seemed, to the portal of the Hotel de Terreforte—an archway leading into a courtyard. It was by great good fortune that the very first person who stood within it was old Andrew of the Cleugh, who despised all French sports in comparison with the completeness of his master's equipment, and was standing at the gate, about to issue forth in quest of leather to mend a defective strap. His eyes fell on the forlorn wanderer, who had no longer energy to keep her hood forward. 'My certie! he exclaimed, in utter amaze.

The Scottish words and voice seemed to revive Margaret, and she tottered forward, exclaiming, 'Oh! good man, help me! take me to the Lady.'

Fortunately the Lady of Glenuskie, being much busied in preparations for her journey, had sent Annis to the sports with the Lady of Terreforte, and was ready to receive the poor, drenched, exhausted being, who almost stumbled into her motherly arms, weeping bitterly, and incoherently moaning something about her sisters, and her husband, and 'betrayed.'

Old Christie was happily also at home, and dry clothing, a warm posset, and the Lady's own bed, perhaps still more her soothing caresses, brought Margaret back to the power of explaining her distress intelligibly—at least as regarded her sisters. She had discovered that their escort had been that bitter foe of their house, Robert Hall, and she verily believed that he had betrayed her sisters into the hands of some of the routiers who infested the roads.

Dame Lilias could not but think it only too likely; but she said 'the worst that could well befall the poor lassies in that case would be their detention until a ransom was paid, and if their situation was known, the King, the Dauphin, and the Duke of Brittany would be certain one or other to rescue them by force of arms, if not to raise the money.' She saw how Margaret shuddered at the name of the Dauphin.

'Oh! I have jewels—pearls—gold,' cried Margaret. 'I could pay the sum without asking any one! Only, where are they, where are they? What are they not enduring —the dear maidens! Would that I had never let them out of my sight!'

'Would that I had not!' echoed Dame Lilias. 'But cheer up, dear Lady, Madame de Ste. Petronelle is with them and will watch over them; and she knows the ways of the country, and how to deal with these robbers, whoever they may be. She will have a care of them.'

But though the Lady of Glenuskie tried to cheer the unhappy princess, she was full of consternation and misgivings as to the fate of her young cousins, whom she loved heartily, and she was relieved when, in accordance with the summons that she had sent, her husband's spurs were heard ringing on the stair.

He heard the story with alarm. He knew that Sir Andrew Gordon had been told off to lead the convoy, and had even conversed with him on the subject.

'Who exchanged him for Hall?' he inquired.

'Oh, do not ask,' cried the unhappy Margaret, covering her face with her hands, and the shrewder Scots folk began to understand, as glances passed between them, though they spared her.

She had intended throwing herself at the feet of the King, who had never been unkind to her, and imploring his succour; but Sir Patrick brought word that the King and Dauphin were going forth together to visit the Abbot of a shrine at no great distance, and as soon as she heard that the Dauphin was with his father, she shrank together, and gave up her purpose for the present. Indeed, Sir Patrick thought it advisable for him to endeavour to discover what had really become of the princesses before applying to the King, or making their loss public. Nor was the Dauphiness in a condition to repair to Court. Dame Lilias longed to keep her and nurse and comfort her that evening; but while the spiteful whispers of De Tillay were abroad, it was needful to be doubly prudent, and the morning's escapade must if possible be compensated by a public return to Chateau le Surry. So Margaret was placed on Lady Drummond's palfrey, and accompanied home by all the attendants who could be got together. She could hardly sit upright by the time the short ride was over, for pain in the side and stitch in her breath. Again Lady Drummond would have stayed with her, but the Countess de Craylierre, who had been extremely offended and scandalised by the expedition of the Dauphiness, made her understand that no one could remain there except by the invitation of the Dauphin, and showed great displeasure at any one but herself attempting the care of Madame la Dauphine, who, as all knew, was subject to megrims.

Margaret entreated her belle cousine to return in the morning and tell her what had been done, and Dame Lilias accordingly set forth with Annis immediately after mass and breakfast with the news that Sir Patrick had taken counsel with the Sieur de erreforte, and that they had got together such armed attendants as they could, and started with their sons for Nanci, where they hoped to discover some traces of the lost ladies.

Indeed, he had brought his wife on his way, and was waiting in the court in case the Princess should wish to see him before he went; but Lilias found poor Margaret far too ill for this to be of any avail. She had tossed about all night, and now was lying partly raised on a pile of embroidered, gold-edged pillows, under an enormous, stiff, heavy quilt, gorgeous with heraldic colours and devices, her pale cheeks flushed with fever, her breath catching painfully, and with a terrible short cough, murmuring strange words about her sisters, and about cruel tongues. A crowd of both sexes and all ranks filled the room, gazing and listening.

She knew her cousin at her entrance, clasped her hand tight, and seemed to welcome her native tongue, and understand her assurance that Sir Patrick was gone to seek her sisters; but she wandered off into, 'Don't let him ask Jamet. Ah, Katie Douglas, keep the door! They are coming.'

Her husband, returning from the morning mass, had way made for him as he advanced to the bed, and again her understanding partly returned, as he said in his low, dry voice, 'How now, Madame?'

She looked up at him, held out her hot hand, and gasped, 'Oh, sir, sir, where are they?'

'Be more explicit, ma mie,' he said, with an inscrutable face.

'You know, you know. Oh, husband, my Lord, you do not believe it. Say you do not believe it. Send the whispering fiend away. He has hidden my sisters.'

'She raves,' said Louis. 'Has the chirurgeon been with her?'

'He is even now about to bleed her, my Lord,' said Madame de Craylierre, 'and so I have sent for the King's own physician.'

Louis's barber-surgeon (not yet Olivier le Dain) was a little, crooked old Jew, at sight of whom Margaret screamed as if she took him for the whispering fiend. He would fain have cleared the room and relieved the air, but this was quite beyond his power; the ladies, knights, pages and all chose to remain and look on at the struggles of the poor patient, while Madame de Craylierre and Lady Drummond held her fast and forced her to submit. Her husband, who alone could have prevailed, did not or would not speak the word, but shrugged his shoulders and left the room, carrying off with him at least his own attendants.

When she saw her blood flow, Margaret exclaimed, 'Ah, traitors, take me instead of my father—only—a priest.'

Presently she fainted, and after partly reviving, seemed to doze, and this, being less interesting, caused many of the spectators to depart.

When she awoke she was quite herself, and this was well, for the King came to visit her. Margaret was fond of her father-in-law, who had always been kind to her; but she was too ill, and speech hurt her too much, to allow her to utter clearly all that oppressed her.

'My sisters! my poor sisters!' she moaned.

'Ah! ma belle fille, fear not. All will be well with them. No doubt, my good brother Rene has detained them, that Madame Eleanore may study a little more of his music and painting. We will send a courier to Nanci, who will bring good news of them,' said the King, in a caressing voice which soothed, if it did not satisfy, the sufferer.

She spoke out some thanks, and he added, 'They may come any moment, daughter, and that will cheer your little heart, and make you well. Only take courage, child, and here is my good physician, Maitre Bertrand, come to heal you.'

Margaret still held the King's hand, and sought to detain him. 'Beau pere, beau pere,' she said, 'you will not believe them! You will silence them.'

'Whom, what, ma mie?'

'The evil-speakers. Ah! Jamet.'

'I believe nothing my fair daughter tells me not to believe.'

'Ah! sire, he speaks against me. He says—'

'Hush! hush, child. Whoever vexes my daughter shall have his tongue slit for him. But here we must give place to Maitre Bertrand.'

Maitre Bertrand was a fat and stolid personage, who, nevertheless, had a true doctor's squabble with the Jew Samiel and drove him out. His treatment was to exclude all the air possible, make the patient breathe all sorts of essences, and apply freshly-killed pigeons to the painful side.

Margaret did not mend under this method. She begged for Samiel, who had several times before relieved her in slight illnesses; but she was given to understand that the Dauphin would not permit him to interfere with Maitre Bertrand.

'Ah!' she said to Dame Lilias, in their own language, 'my husband calls Bertrand an old fool! He does not wish me to recover! A childless wife is of no value. He would have me dead! And so would I—if my fame were cleared. If my sisters were found! Oh! my Lord, my Lord, I loved him so!'

Poor Margaret! Such was her cry, whether sane or delirious, hour after hour, day after day. Only when delirious she rambled into Scotch and talked of Perth; went over again her father's murder, or fancied her sisters in the hands of some of the ferocious chieftains of the North, and screamed to Sir Patrick or to Geordie Douglas to deliver them. Where was all the chivalry of the Bleeding Heart?

Or, again, she would piteously plead her own cause with her husband—not that he was present, a morning glance into her room sufficed him; but she would excuse her own eager folly—telling him not to be angered with her, who loved him wholly and entirely, and begging him to silence the wicked tongues that defamed her.

When sensible she was very weak, and capable of saying very little; but she clung fast to Lady Drummond, and, Dauphin or no Dauphin, Dame Lilias was resolved on remaining and watching her day and night, Madame de Craylierre becoming ready to leave the nursing to her when it became severe.

The King came to see his daughter-in-law almost every day, and always spoke to her in the same kindly but unmeaning vein, assuring her that her sisters must be safe, and promising to believe nothing against herself; but, as the Lady of Glenuskie knew from Olivier de Terreforte, taking no measures either to discover the fate of the princesses or to banish and silence Jamet de Tillay, though it was all over the Court that the Dauphiness was dying for love of Alain Chartier. Was it that his son prevented him from acting, or was it the strange indifference and indolence that always made Charles the Well-Served bestir himself far too late?

Any way, Margaret of Scotland was brokenhearted, utterly weary of life, and with no heart or spirit to rally from the illness caused by the chill of her hasty walk. She only wished to live long enough to know that her sisters were safe, see them again, and send them under safe care to Brittany. She exacted a promise from Dame Lilias never to leave them again till they were in safe hands, with good husbands, or back in Scotland with their brother and good Archbishop Kennedy. 'Bid Jeanie never despise a true heart; better, far better, than a crown,' she sighed.

Louis concerned himself much that all the offices of religion should be provided. He attended the mass daily celebrated in her room, and caused priests to pray in the farther end continually. Lady Drummond, who had not given up hope, and believed that good tidings of her sisters might almost be a cure, thought that he really hurried on the last offices, at which he devoutly assisted. However, the confession seemed to have given Margaret much comfort. She told Dame Lilias that the priest had shown her how to make an offering to God of her sore suffering from slander and evil report, and reminded her that to endure it patiently was treading in the steps of her Master. She was resolved, therefore, to make no further struggle nor complaint, but to trust that her silence and endurance would be accepted. She could pray for her sisters and their safety, and she would endeavour to yield up even that last earthly desire to be certified of their safety, and to see their bonnie faces once more. So there she lay, a being formed by nature and intellect to have been the inspiring helpmeet of some noble-hearted man, the stay of a kingdom, the education of all around her in all that was beautiful and refined, but cast away upon one of the most mean and selfish-hearted of mankind, who only perceived her great qualities to hate and dread their manifestation in a woman, to crush them by his contempt; and finally, though he did not originate the cruel slander that broke her heart, he envenomed it by his sneers, so as to deprive her of all power of resistance.

The lot of Margaret of Scotland was as piteous as that of any of the doomed house of Stewart. And there the Lady of Glenuskie and Annis de Terreforte watched her sinking day by day, and still there were no tidings of Jean and Eleanor from Nanci, no messenger from Sir Patrick to tell where the search was directed.

CHAPTER 9. BALCHENBURG

> 'In these wylde deserts where she now abode
> There dwelt a salvage nation, which did live
> On stealth and spoil, and making nightly rade
> Into their neighbours' borders.'—SPENSER.

A terrible legacy of the Hundred Years' War, which, indeed, was not yet entirely ended by the Peace of Tours, was the existence of bands of men trained to nothing but war and rapine, and devoid of any other means of subsistence than freebooting on the peasantry or travellers, whence they were known as routiers—highwaymen, and ecorcheurs—flayers. They were a fearful scourge to France in the early part of the reign of Charles VII., as, indeed, they had been at every interval of peace ever since the battle of Creci, and they really made a state of warfare preferable to the unhappy provinces, or at least to those where it was not actually raging. In a few years more the Dauphin contrived to delude many of them into an expedition, where he abandoned them and left them to be massacred, after which he formed the rest into the nucleus of a standing army; but at this time they were the terror of travellers, who only durst go about any of the French provinces in well-armed and large parties.

The domains of King Rene, whether in Lorraine or Provence, were, however, reckoned as fairly secure, but from the time the little troop, with the princesses among them, had started from Nanci, Madame de Ste. Petronelle became uneasy. She looked up at the sun, which was shining in her face, more than once, and presently drew the portly mule she was riding towards George Douglas.

'Sir,' she said, 'you are the ladies' squire?'

'I have that honour, Madame.'

'And a Scot?'

'Even so.'

'I ask you, which way you deem that we are riding?'

'Eastward, Madame, if the sun is to be trusted. Mayhap somewhat to the south.'

'Yea; and which side lies Chalons?'

This was beyond George's geography. He looked up with open mouth and shook his head.

'Westward!' said the lady impressively. 'And what's yon in the distance?'

'Save that this land is as flat as a bannock, I'd have said 'twas mountains.'

'Mountains they are, young man!' said Madame de Ste. Petronelle emphatically—'the hills between Lorraine and Alsace, which we should be leaving behind us.'

'Is there treachery?' asked George, reining up his horse. 'Ken ye who is the captain of this escort?'

'His name is Hall; he is thick with the Dauphin. Ha! Madame, is he sib to him that aided in the slaughter of Eastern's Eve night?'

'Just, laddie. 'Tis own son to him that Queen Jean made dae sic a fearful penance. What are ye doing?'

'I'll run the villain through, and turn back to Nanci while yet there is time,' said George, his hand on his sword.

'Hold, ye daft bodie! That would but bring all the lave on ye. There's nothing for it but to go on warily, and maybe at the next halt we might escape from them.'

But almost while Madame de Ste. Petronelle spoke there was a cry, and from a thicket there burst out a band of men in steel headpieces and buff jerkins, led by two or three horsemen. There was a confused outcry of 'St. Denys! St. Andrew!' on one side, 'Yield!' on the other. Madame's rein was seized, and though she drew her dagger, her hand was caught before she could strike, by a fellow who cried, 'None of that, you old hag, or it shall be the worse for thee!'

'St. Andrew! St. Andrew!' screamed Eleanor. 'Scots, to the rescue of your King's sisters!'

'Douglas—Douglas, help!' cried Jean. But each was surrounded by a swarm of the ruffians; and as George Douglas hastily pushed down some with his horse, and struck down one or two with his sword, he was felled by a mighty blow on the head, and the ecorcheurs thronged over him, dragging him off his horse, any resistance on the part of the Scottish archers, their escort, they could not tell; they only heard a tumult of shouts and cries, and found rude hands holding them on their horses and dragging them among the trees. Their screams for help were answered by a gruff voice from a horseman, evidently the leader of the troop. 'Hold that noise, Lady! No ill is meant to you, but you must come with us. No; screams are useless! There's none to come to you. Stop them, or I must!'

'There is none!' said Madame de Ste. Petronelle's voice in her own tongue; 'best cease to cry, and not fash the loons more.'

The sisters heard, and in her natural tone Eleanor said in French, 'Sir, know you who you are thus treating? The King's daughter—sisters of the Dauphiness!'

He laughed. 'Full well,' he answered, in very German-sounding French.

'Such usage will bring the vengeance of the King and Dauphin on you.'

He laughed yet more loudly. His face was concealed by his visor, but the ill-fitting armour and great roan horse made Jean recognise the knight whose eyes had dwelt on her so boldly at the tournament, and she added her voice.

'Your Duke of the Tirol will punish this.'

'He has enough to do to mind his own business,' was the answer.

'Come, fair one, hold your tongue! There's no help for it, and the less trouble you give us the better it will be for you.'

'But our squire!' Jean exclaimed, looking about her. 'Where is he?'

Again there was a rude laugh.

'Showed fight. Disposed of. See there!' and Jean could not but recognise the great gray horse from the Mearns that George Douglas had always ridden. Had she brought the gallant youth to this, and without word or look to reward his devotion? She gave one low cry, and bowed her head, grieved and sick at heart. While Eleanor, on her side, exclaimed,

'Felon, thou hast slain a nobleman's brave heir! Disgrace to knighthood!'

'Peace, maid, or we will find means to silence thy tongue,' growled the leader; and Madame de Ste. Petronelle interposed, 'Whisht—whisht, my bairn; dinna anger them.' For she saw that there was more disposition to harshness towards Eleanor than towards Jean, whose beauty seemed to command a sort of regard.

Eleanor took the hint. Her eyes filled with tears, and her bosom heaved at the thought of the requital of the devotion of the brave young man, lying in his blood, so far from his father and his home; but she would not have these ruffians see her weep and think it was for herself, and she proudly straightened herself in her saddle and choked down the rising sob.

On, on they went, at first through the wood by a tangled path, then over a wide moor covered with heather, those mountains, which had at first excited the old lady's alarm, growing more distinct in front of them; going faster, too, so that the men who held the reins were half running, till the ground began to rise and grow rougher, when, at an order in German from the knight, a man leapt on in front of each lady to guide her horse.

Where were they going? No one deigned to ask except Madame de Ste. Petronelle, and her guard only grunted, 'Nicht verstand,' or something equivalent.

A thick mass of wood rose before them, a stream coming down from it, and here there was a halt, the ladies were lifted down, and the party, who numbered about twelve men, refreshed themselves with the provisions that the Infanta Yolande had hospitably furnished for her guests. The knight awkwardly, but not uncivilly, offered a share to his captives, but Eleanor would have moved them off with disdain, and Jean sat with her head in her hands, and would not look up.

The old lady remonstrated. 'Eat—eat,' she said. 'We shall need all our spirit and strength, and there's no good in being weak and spent with fasting.'

Eleanor saw the prudence of this, and accepted the food and wine offered to her; but Jean seemed unable to swallow anything but a long draught of wine and water, and scarcely lifted her head from her sister's shoulder. Eleanor held her rosary, and though the words she conned over were Latin, all her heart was one silent prayer for protection and deliverance, and commendation of that brave youth's soul to his Maker.

The knight kept out of their way, evidently not wishing to be interrogated, and he seemed to be the only person who could speak French after a fashion. By and by they were remounted and led across some marshy ground, where the course of the stream was marked by tall ferns and weeds, then into a wood of beeches, where the sun lighted the delicate young foliage, while the horses trod easily among the brown fallen leaves. This gave place to another wood of firs, and though the days were fairly long, here it was rapidly growing dark under the heavy branches, so that the winding path could only have been followed by those well used to it. As it became steeper and more stony the trees became thinner, and against the eastern sky could be seen, dark and threatening, the turrets of a castle above a steep, smooth-looking, grassy slope, one of the hills, in fact, called from their shape by the French, ballons.

Just then Jean's horse, weary and unused to mountaineering, stumbled. The man at its head was perhaps not attending to it, for the sudden pull he gave the rein only precipitated the fall. The horse was up again in a moment, but Jean lay still. Her sister and the lady were at her side in a moment; but when they tried to raise her she cried out, at first inarticulately, then, 'Oh, my arm!' and on another attempt to lift her she fainted away. The knight was in the meantime swearing in German at the man who had been leading her, then asking anxiously in French how it was with the maiden, as she lay with her head on her sister's lap, Madame answered,

'Hurt—much hurt.'

'But not to the death?'

'Who knows? No thanks to you.' He tendered a flask where only a few drops of wine remained, growling something or other about the Schelm; and when Jean's lips had been moistened with it she opened her eyes, but sobbed with pain, and only entreated to be let alone. This, of course, was impossible; but with double consternation Eleanor looked up at what, in the gathering darkness, seemed a perpendicular height. The knight made them understand that all that could be done was to put the sufferer on horseback and support her there in the climb upwards, and he proceeded without further parley to lift her up, not entirely without heed to her screams and moans, for he emitted such sounds as those with which he might have soothed his favourite horse, as he placed her on the back of a stout, little, strong, mountain pony. Eleanor held her there, and he walked at its head. Madame de Ste. Petronelle would fain have kept up on the other side, but she had lost her mountain legs, and could not have got up at all without the mule on which she was replaced. Eleanor's height enabled her to hold her arm round her sister, and rest her head on her shoulder, though how she kept on in the dark, dragged along as it were blindly up and up, she never could afterwards recollect; but at last pine torches came down to meet them, there was a tumult of voices, a yawning black archway in front, a light or two flitting about. Jean lay helplessly against her, only groaning now and then; then, as the arch seemed to swallow them up, Eleanor was aware of an old man, lame and rugged, who bawled loud and seemed to be the highly displeased master; of calls for 'Barbe,' and then of an elderly, homely-looking woman, who would have assisted in taking Jean off the pony but that the knight was already in the act. However, he resigned her to her sister and Madame de Ste. Petronelle, while Barbe led the way, lamp in hand. It was just as well poor Jeanie remained unconscious or nearly so while she was conveyed up the narrow stairs to a round chamber, not worse in furnishing than that at Dunbar, though very unlike their tapestried rooms at Nanci.

It was well to be able to lay her down at all, and old Barbe was not only ready and pitying, but spoke French. She had some wine ready, and had evidently done her best in the brief warning to prepare a bed. The tone of her words convinced Madame de Ste. Petronelle that at any rate she was no enemy. So she was permitted to assist in the investigation of the injuries, which proved to be extensive bruises and a dislocated shoulder. Both had sufficient experience in rough-and-ready surgery, as well as sufficient strength, for them to be able to pull in the shoulder, while Eleanor, white and trembling, stood on one side with the lamp, and a little flaxen-haired girl of twelve years old held bandages and ran after whatever Barbe asked for.

This done, and Jean having been arranged as comfortably as might be, Barbe obeyed some peremptory summonses from without, and presently came back.

'The seigneur desires to speak with the ladies,' she said; 'but I have told him that they cannot leave la pauvrette, and are too much spent to speak with him to-night. I will bring them supper and they shall rest.'

'We thank you,' said Madame de Ste. Petronelle, 'Only, de grace, tell us where we are, and who this seigneur is, and what he wants with us poor women.'

'This is the Castle of Balchenburg,' was the reply; 'the seigneur is the Baron thereof. For the next'—she shrugged her shoulders—'it must be one of Baron Rudiger's ventures. But I must go and fetch the ladies some supper. Ah! the demoiselle surely needs it.'

'And some water!' entreated Eleanor.

'Ah yes,' she replied; 'Trudchen shall bring some.'

The little girl presently reappeared with a pitcher as heavy as she could carry. She could not understand French, but looked much interested, and very eager and curious as she brought in several of the bundles and mails of the travellers.

'Thank the saints,' cried the lady, 'they do not mean to strip us of our clothes!'

'They have stolen us, and that is enough for them,' said Eleanor.

Jean lay apparently too much exhausted to take notice of what was going on, and they hoped she might sleep, while they moved about quietly. The room seemed to be a cell in the hollow of the turret, and there were two loophole windows, to which Eleanor climbed up, but she could see nothing but the stars. 'Ah! yonder is the Plough, just as when we looked out at it at Dunbar o'er the sea!' she sighed. 'The only friendly thing I can see! Ah! but the same God and the saints are with us still!' and she clasped her rosary's cross as she returned to her sister, who was sighing out an entreaty for water.

By and by the woman returned, and with her the child. She made a low reverence as she entered, having evidently been informed of the rank of her captives. A white napkin was spread over the great chest that served for a table—a piece of civilisation such as the Dunbar captivity had not known—three beechen bowls and spoons, and a porringer containing a not unsavoury stew of a fowl in broth thickened with meal. They tried to make their patient swallow a little broth, but without much success, though Eleanor in the mountain air had become famished enough to make a hearty meal, and feel more cheered and hopeful after it. Barbe's evident sympathy and respect were an element of comfort, and when Jean revived enough to make some inquiry after poor Skywing, and it was translated into French, there was an assurance that the hawk was cared for—hopes even given of its presence. Barbe was not only compassionate, but ready to answer all the questions in her power. She was Burgundian, but her home having been harried in the wars, her husband had taken service as a man-at-arms with the Baron of Balchenburg, she herself becoming the bower-woman of the Baroness, now dead. Since the death of the good lady, whose influence had been some restraint, everything had become much rougher and wilder, and the lords of the castle, standing on the frontier as it did, had become closely connected with the feuds of Germany as well as the wars in France. The old Baron had been lamed in a raid into Burgundy, since which time he had never left home; and Barbe's husband had been killed, her sons either slain or seeking their fortune elsewhere, so that nothing was left to her but her little daughter Gertrude, for whose sake she earnestly longed to find her way down to more civilised and godly life; but she was withheld by the difficulties in the path, and the extreme improbability of finding a maintenance anywhere else, as well as by a certain affection for her two Barons, and doubts what they would do without her, since the elder was in broken health and the younger had been her nursling. In fact, she was the highest female authority in the castle, and kept up whatever semblance of decency or propriety remained since her mistress's death. All this came out in the way of grumbling or lamentation, in the satisfaction of having some woman to confide in, though her young master had made her aware of the rank of his captives. Every one, it seemed, had been taken by surprise. He was in the habit of making expeditions on his own account, and bringing home sometimes lawless comrades or followers, sometimes booty; but this time, after taking great pains to furbish up a suit of armour brought home long ago, he had set forth to the festivities at Nanci. The lands and castle were so situated, that the old Baron had done homage for the greater part to Sigismund as Duke of Elsass, and for another portion to King Rene as Duke of Lorraine, as whose vassal the young Baron had appeared. No more had been heard of him till one of his men hurried up with tidings that Herr Rudiger had taken a bevy of captives, with plenty of spoil, but that one was a lady much hurt, for whom Barbe must prepare her best.

Since this, Barbe had learnt from her young master that the injured lady was the sister of the Dauphiness, and a king's daughter, and that every care must be taken of her and her sister, for he was madly in love with her, and meant her to be his wife.

Eleanor and Madame de Ste. Petronelle cried out at this with horror, in a stifled way, as Barbe whispered it.

'Too high, too dangerous game for him, I know,' said the old woman. 'So said his father, who was not a little dismayed when he heard who these ladies were.'

'The King, my brother, the Dauphin, the Duke of Brittany—' began Eleanor.

'Alas! the poor boy would never have ventured it but for encouragement,' sighed Barbe. 'Treacherous I say it must be!'

'I knew there was treachery, 'exclaimed Madame de Ste. Petronelle, 'so soon as I found which way our faces were turned.'

'But who could or would betray us?' demanded Eleanor.

'You need not ask that, when your escort was led by Andrew Hall,' returned the elder lady. 'Poor young George of the Red Peel had only just told me so, when the caitiffs fell on him, and he came to his bloody death.'

'Hall! Then I marvel not,' said Eleanor, in a low, awe-struck voice. 'My brother the Dauphin could not have known.'

The old Scotswoman refrained from uttering her belief that he knew only too well, but by the time all this had been said Barbe was obliged to leave them, having arranged for the night that Eleanor should sleep in the big bed beside her sister, and their lady across it at their feet—a not uncommon arrangement in those days.

Sleep, however, in spite of weariness, was only to be had in snatches, for poor Jean was in much pain, and very feverish, besides being greatly terrified at their situation, and full of grief and self-reproach for the poor young Master of Angus, never dozing off for a moment without fancying she saw him dying and upbraiding her, and for the most part tossing in a restless misery that required the attendance of one or both. She had never known ailment before, and was thus all the more wretched and impatient, alarming and distressing Eleanor extremely, though Madame de Ste. Petronelle declared it was only a matter of course, and that the lassie would soon be well.

'Ah, Madame, our comforter and helper,' said Elleen.

'Call me no French names, dearies. Call me the Leddy Lindsay or Dame Elspeth, as I should be at home. We be all Scots here, in one sore stour. If I could win a word to my son, Ritchie, he would soon have us out of this place.'

'Would not Barbe help us to a messenger?'

'I doubt it. She would scarce bring trouble on her lords; but we might be worse off than with her.'

'Why does she not come? I want some more drink,' moaned Jean. Barbe did come, and, moreover, brought not only water but some tisane of herbs that was good for fever and had been brewing all night, and she was wonderfully good-humoured at the patient's fretful refusal, though between coaxing and authority 'Leddy Lindsay' managed to get it taken at last. After Margaret's experience of her as a stern duenna, her tenderness in illness and trouble was a real surprise.

No keys were turned on them, but there was little disposition to go beyond the door which opened on the stone stair in the gray wall. The view from the windows revealed that they were very high up. There was a bit of castle wall to be seen below, and beyond a sea of forest, the dark masses of pine throwing out the lighter, more delicate sweeps of beech, and pale purple distance beyond—not another building within view, giving a sense of vast solitude to Eleanor's eyes, more dreary than the sea at Dunbar, and far more changeless. An occasional bird was all the variety to be hoped for.

By and by Barbe brought a message that her masters requested the ladies' presence at the meal, a dinner, in fact, served about an hour before noon. Eleanor greatly demurred, but Barbe strongly advised consent, 'Or my young lord will be coming up here,' she said; 'they both wish to have speech of you, and would have been here before now, if my old lord were not so lame, and the young one so shy, the poor child!'

'Shy,' exclaimed Eleanor, 'after what he has dared to do to us!'

'All the more for that very reason,' said Barbe.

'True,' returned Madame; 'the savage who is most ferocious in his acts is most bashful in his breeding.'

'How should my poor boy have had any breeding up here in the forests?' demanded Barbe. 'Oh, if he had only fixed his mind on a maiden of his own degree, she might have brought the good days back; but alas, now he will be only bringing about his own destruction, which the saints avert.'

It was agreed that Eleanor had better make as royal and imposing an appearance as possible, so instead of the plain camlet riding kirtles that she and Lady Lindsay had worn, she donned a heraldic sort of garment, a tissue of white and gold thread, with the red lion ramping on back and breast, and the double tressure edging all the hems, part of the outfit furnished at her great-uncle's expense in London, but too gaudy for her taste, and she added to her already considerable height by the tall, veiled headgear that had been despised as unfashionable.

Jean from her bed cried out that she looked like Pharaoh's daughter in the tapestry, and consented to be left to the care of little Trudchen, since Madame de Ste. Petronelle must act attendant, and Barbe evidently thought her young master's good behaviour might be the better secured by her presence.

So, at the bottom of the narrow stone stair, Eleanor shook out her plumes, the attendant lady arranged her veil over her yellow hair, and drew out her short train and long hanging sleeves, a little behind the fashion, but the more dignified, as she swept into the hall, and though her heart beat desperately, holding her head stiff and high, and looking every inch a princess, the shrewd Scotch lady behind her flattered herself that the two Barons did look a little daunted by the bearing of the creature they had caught.

The father, who had somewhat the look of an old fox, limped forward with a less ungraceful bow than the son, who had more of the wolf. Some greeting was mumbled, and the old man would have taken her hand to lead her to the highest place at table, but she would not give it.

'I am no willing guest of yours, sir,' she said, perhaps alarmed at her own boldness, but drawing herself up with great dignity. 'I desire to know by what right my sister and I, king's daughters, on our way to King Charles's Court, have thus been seized and detained?'

'We do not stickle as to rights here on the borders, Lady,' said the elder Baron in bad French; 'it would be wiser to abate a little of that outre-cuidance of yours, and listen to our terms.'

'A captive has no choice save to listen,' returned Eleanor; 'but as to speaking of terms, my brothers-in-law, the Dauphin and the Duke of Brittany, may have something to say to them.'

'Exactly so,' replied the old Baron, in a tone of some irony, which she did not like. 'Now, Lady, our terms are these, but understand first that all this affair is none of my seeking, but my son here has been backed up in it by some whom'—on a grunt from Sir Rudiger—'there is no need to name. He—the more fool he—has taken a fancy to your sister, though, if all reports be true, she has nought but her royal blood, not so much as a denier for a dowry nor as ransom for either of you. However, this I will overlook, dead loss as it is to me and mine, and so your sister, so soon as she recovers from her hurt, will become my son's wife, and I will have you and your lady safely conducted without ransom to the borders of

Normandy or Brittany, as you may list.'

'And think you, sir,' returned Eleanor, quivering with indignation, 'that the daughter of a hundred kings is like to lower herself by listening to the suit of a petty robber baron of the Marches?'

'I do not think! but I know that though I am a fool for giving in to my son's madness, these are the only terms I propose; and if you, Lady, so deal with her as to make her accept them, you are free without ransom to go where you will.'

'You expect me to sell my sister,' said Eleanor disdainfully.

'Look you here,' broke in Rudiger, bursting out of his shyness. 'She is the fairest maiden, gentle or simple, I ever saw; I love her with all my heart. If she be mine, I swear to make her a thousand times more cared for than your sister the Dauphiness; and if all be true your Scottish archers tell me, you Scottish folk have no great cause to disdain an Elsass forest castle.'

An awkward recollection, of the Black Knight of Lorn came across Eleanor, but she did not lose her stately dignity.

'It is not the wealth or poverty that we heed,' she said, 'but the nobility and princeliness.'

'There is nothing to be done then, son,' said the old Baron, 'but to wait a day or two and see whether the maiden herself will be less proud and more reasonable. Otherwise, these ladies understand that there will be close imprisonment and diet according to the custom of the border till a thousand gold crowns be paid down for each of these sisters of a Scotch king, and five hundred for Madame here; and when that is like to be found, the damoiselle herself may know,' and he laughed.

'We have those who will take care of our ransom,' said Eleanor, though her heart misgave her. 'Moreover, Duke Sigismund will visit such an offence dearly!' and there was a glow on her cheeks.

'He knows better than to meddle with a vassal of Lorraine,' said the old man.

'King Rene—' began Eleanor.

'He is too wary to meddle with a vassal of Elsass,' sneered the Baron. 'No, no, Lady, ransom or wedding, there lies your choice.'

With this there appeared to be a kind of truce, perhaps in consequence of the appearance of a great pie; and Eleanor did not refuse to sit down to the table and partake of the food, though she did not choose to converse; whereas Madame de Ste. Petronelle thought it wiser to be as agreeable as she could, and this, in the opinion of the Court of the Dauphiness, was not going very far.

Long before the Barons and their retainers had finished, little Trudchen came hurrying down to say that the lady was crying and calling for her sister, and Eleanor was by no means sorry to hasten to her side, though only to receive a petulant scolding for the desertion that had lasted so very long, according to the sick girl's sensations.

Matters remained in abeyance while the illness continued; Jean had a night of fever, and when that passed, under the experienced management of Dame Elspie, as the sisters called her more and more, she was very weak and sadly depressed. Sometimes she wept and declared she should die in these dismal walls, like her mother at Dunbar, and never see Jamie and Mary again; sometimes she blamed

Elleen for having put this mad scheme into her head; sometimes she fretted for her cousins Lilias and Annis of Glenuskie, and was sure it was all Elleen's fault for having let themselves be separated from Sir Patrick; while at others she declared the Drummonds faithless and disloyal for having gone after their own affairs and left the only true and leal heart to die for her; and then came fresh floods of tears, though sometimes, as she passionately caressed Skywing, she declared the hawk to be the only faithful creature in existence.

Baron Rudiger was evidently very uneasy about her; Barbe reported how gloomy and miserable he was, and how he relieved his feelings by beating the unfortunate man who had been leading the horse, and in a wiser manner by seeking fish in the torrent and birds on the hills for her refreshment, and even helping Trudchen to gather the mountain strawberries for her. This was, however, so far from a recommendation to Jean, that after the first Barbe gave it to be understood that all were Trudchen's providing.

They suspected that Barbe nattered and soothed 'her boy,' as she termed him, with hopes, but they owed much to the species of authority with which she kept him from forcing himself upon them. Eleanor sometimes tried to soothe her sister, and while away the time with her harp. The Scotch songs were a great delight to Dame Elspie, but they made Jean weep in her weakness, and Elleen's great resource was King Rene's parting gift of the tales of Huon de Bourdeaux, with its wonderful chivalrous adventures, and the appearances of the dwarf Oberon; and she greatly enjoyed the idea of the pleasure it would give Jamie—if ever she should see Jamie again; and she wondered, too, whether the Duke of the Tirol knew the story—which even at some moments amused Jean.

There was a stair above their chamber, likewise in the thickness of the wall, which Barbe told them they might safely explore, and thence Eleanor discovered that the castle was one of the small but regularly-built fortresses not uncommon on the summit of hills. It was an octagon—as complete as the ground would permit—with a huge wall and a tower at each angle. One face, that on the most accessible side, was occupied by the keep in which they were, with a watch-tower raising its finger and banner above them, the little, squat, round towers around not lifting their heads much above the battlements of the wall. The descent on most of the sides was almost precipitous, on two entirely so, while in the rear another steep hill rose so abruptly that it seemed to frown over them though separated by a ravine.

Nothing was to be seen all round but the tops of trees—dark pines, beeches, and chestnuts in the gay, light green of spring, a hopeless and oppressive waste of verdure, where occasionally a hawk might be seen to soar, and whence the howlings of wolves might be heard at night.

Jean was, in a week, so well that there was no cause for deferring the interview any longer, and, indeed, she was persuaded that Elleen had not been half resolute or severe enough, and that she could soon show the two Barons that they detained her at their peril. Still she looked white and thin, and needed a scarf for her arm, when she caused herself to be arrayed as splendidly as her sister had been, and descended to the hall, where, like Eleanor, she took the initiative by an appeal against the wrong and injustice that held two free-born royal ladies captive.

'He who has the power may do as he wills, my pretty damsel,' replied the old Baron. 'Once for all, as I told your sister, these threats are of no avail, though they sound well to puff up your little airs. Your own kingdom is a long way off, and breeds more men than money; and as to our neighbours, they dare not embroil themselves by meddling with us borderers. You had better take what we offer, far better than aught your barbarous northern lords could give, and then your sister will be free, without ransom, to depart or to stay here till she finds another bold baron of the Marches to take her to wife. Ha, thou Rudiger! why dost stand staring like a wild pig in a pit? Canst not speak a word for thyself?'

'She shall be my queen,' said Rudiger hoarsely, bumping himself down on his knees, and trying to master her hand, but she drew it away from him.

'As if I would be queen of a mere nest of robbers and freebooters,' she said. 'You forget, Messires, that my sister is daughter-in-law to the King of France. We must long ago have been missed, and I expect every hour that my brother, the Dauphin, will be here with his troops.'

'That's what you expect. So you do not know, my proud demoiselle, that my son would scarce have been rash enough to meddle with such lofty gear, for all his folly, if he had not had a hint that maidens with royal blood but no royal portions were not wanted at Court, and might be had for the picking up!'

'It is a brutal falsehood, or else a mere invention of the traitor Hall's, our father's murderer!' said Jean, with flashing eyes. 'I would have you to know, both of you, my Lords, that were we betrayed and forsaken by every kinsman we have, I will not degrade the blood royal of Scotland by mating it with a rude and petty freebooter. You may keep us captives as you will, but you will not break our spirit.'

So saying, Jean swept back to the stairs, turning a deaf ear to the Baron's chuckle of applause and murmur, 'A gallant spirited dame she will make thee, my junker, and hold out the castle well against all foes, when once she is broken in.'

Jean and Eleanor alike disbelieved that Louis could have encouraged this audacious attempt, but they were dismayed to find that Madame de Ste. Petronelle thought it far from improbable, for she believed him capable of almost any underhand treachery. She did, however, believe that though there might be some delay, a stir would be made, if only by her own son, which would end in their situation being publicly known, and final release coming, if Jean could only be patient and resolute.

But to the poor girl it seemed as if the ground were cut from under her feet; and as her spirits drooped more and more, there were times when she said, 'Elleen, I must consent. I have been the death of the one true heart that was mine! Why should I hold out any longer, and make thee and Dame Elspie wear out your days in this dismal forest hold? Never shall I be happy again, so it matters not what becomes of me.'

'It matters to me,' said Elleen. 'Sister, thinkest thou I could go away to be happy, leaving thee bound to this rude savage in his donjon? Fie, Jean, this is not worthy of King James's daughter; he spent all those years of patience in captivity, and shall we lose heart in a few days?'

'Is it a few days? It is like years!'

'That is because thou hast been sick. See now, let us dance and sing, so that the jailers may know we are not daunted. We have been shut up ere now, God brought us out, and He will again, and we need not pine.'

'Ah, then we were children, and had seen nothing better; and—and there was not his blood on me!'

And Jean fell a-weeping.

CHAPTER 10. TENDER AND TRUE

'For I am now the Earlis son,
 And not a banished, man.'—The Nut-Brown Maid.

'O St. Andrew! St. Bride! Our Lady of Succour! St. Denys!—all the lave of you, that may be nearest in this fremd land,—come and aid him. It is the Master of Angus, ye ken—the hope of his house. He'll build you churches, gie ye siller cups and braw vestments gin ye'll bring him back. St. Andrew! St. Rule! St. Ninian!—you ken a Scots tongue! Stay his blood,—open his een,—come to help ane that ever loved you and did you honour!'

So wailed Ringan of the Raefoot, holding his master's head on his knees, and binding up as best he might an ugly thrust in the side, and a blow which had crushed the steel cap into the midst of the hair. When he saw his master fall and the ladies captured, he had, with the better part of valour, rushed aside and hid himself in the thicket of thorns and hazels, where, being manifestly only a stray horseboy, no search was made for him. He rightly concluded that, dead or alive, his master might thus be better served than by vainly struggling over his fallen body.

It seemed as though, in answer to his invocation, a tremor began to pass through Douglas's frame, and as Ringan exclaimed, 'There! there!—he lives! Sir, sir! Blessings on the saints! I was sure that a French reiver's lance could never be the end of the Master,' George opened his eyes.

'What is it?' he said faintly. 'Where are the ladies?'

'Heed not the leddies the noo, sir, but let me bind your head. That cap has crushed like an egg-shell, and has cut you worse than the sword. Bide still, sir, I say, if ye mean to do any gude another time!'

'The ladies—Ringan—'

'The loons rid aff wi' them, sir—up towards the hills yonder. Nay! but if ye winna thole to let me bind your wound, how d'ye think to win to their aid, or ever to see bonnie Scotland again?'

George submitted to this reasoning; but, as his senses returned, asked if all the troop had gone.

'Na, sir; the ane with that knight who was at the tourney—a plague light on him—went aff with the leddies—up yonder; but they, as they called the escort—the Archers of the Guard, as they behoved to call themselves—they rid aff by the way that we came by—the traitor loons!'

'Ah! it was black treachery. Follow the track of the ladies, Ringan;—heed not me.'

'Mickle gude that wad do, sir, if I left you bleeding here! Na, na; I maun see you safely bestowed first before I meet with ony other. I'm the Douglas's man, no the Stewart's.'

'Then will I after them!' cried George of Angus, starting up; but he staggered and had to catch at Ringan.

There was no water near; nothing to refresh or revive him had been left. Ringan looked about in anxiety and distress on the desolate scene—bare heath on one side, thicket, gradually rising into forest and mountain, on the other. Suddenly he gave a long whistle, and to his great joy there was a crackling among the bushes and he beheld the shaggy-faced pony on which he had ridden all the way from Yorkshire, and which had no doubt eluded the robbers. There was a bundle at the saddle-bow, and after a little coquetting the pony allowed itself to be caught, and a leathern bottle was produced from the bag, containing something exceedingly sour, but with an amount of strength in it which did something towards reviving the Master.

'I can sit the pony,' he said; 'let us after them.'

'Nae sic fulery,' said Ringan. 'I ken better what sorts a green wound like yours, sir! Sit the pony ye may, but to be safely bestowed, ere I stir a foot after the leddies.'

George broke out into fierce language and angry commands, none of which Ringan heeded in the least.

'Hist:' he cried, 'there's some one on the road. Come into shelter, sir.'

He was half dragging, half supporting his master to the concealment of the bushes, when he perceived that the new-comers were two friars, cowled, black gowned, corded, and barefooted.

'There will be help in them,' he muttered, placing his master with his back against a tree; for the late contention had produced such fresh exhaustion that it was plain the wounds were more serious than he had thought at first.

The two friars, men with homely, weather-beaten, but simple good faces, came up, startled at seeing a wounded man on the way-side, and ready to proffer assistance.

Need like George Douglas's was of all languages, and besides, Ringan had, among the exigencies of the journey, picked up something by which he could make himself moderately well understood. The brethren stooped over the wounded man and examined his wounds. One of them produced some oil from a flask in his wallet, and though poor George's own shirt was the only linen available, they contrived to bandage both hurts far more effectually than Ringan could.

They asked whether this was the effect of a quarrel or the work of robbers.

'Routiers,' Ringan said. 'The ladies—we guarded them—they carried them off—up there.'

'What ladies?—the Scottish princesses?' asked one of the friars; for they had been at Nanci, and knew who had been assembled there; besides that, the Scot was known enough all over France for the nationality of Ringan and his master to have been perceived at once.

George understood this, and answered vehemently, 'I must follow them and save them!'

'In good time, with the saints' blessing,' replied Brother Benigne soothingly, 'but healing must come first. We must have you to our poor house yonder, where you will be well tended.'

George was lifted to the pony's back, and supported in the saddle by Ringan and one of the brethren. He had been too much dazed by the cut on the head to have any clear or consecutive notion as to what they were doing with him, or what passed round him; and Ringan did his best to explain the circumstances, and thought it expedient to explain that his master was 'Grand Seigneur' in his own country, and would amply repay whatever was done for him; the which Brother Gerard gave him to understand was of no consequence to the sons of St. Francis. The brothers had no doubt that the outrage was committed by the Balchenburg Baron, the ally of the ecorcheurs and routiers, the terrors of the country, in his impregnable castle. No doubt, they said, he meant to demand a heavy ransom from the good King and Dauphin. For the honour of Scotland, Ringan, though convinced that Hall had his share in the treason, withheld that part of the story. To him, and still more to his master, the journey seemed endless, though in reality it was not more than two miles before they arrived at a little oasis of wheat and orchards growing round a vine-clad building of reddish stone, with a spire rising in the midst.

Here the porter opened the gate in welcome. The history was volubly told, the brother-infirmarer was summoned, and the Master of Angus was deposited in a much softer bed than the good friars allowed themselves. There the infirmarer tended him in broken feverish sleep all night, Ringan lying on a pallet near, and starting up at every moan or murmur. But with early dawn, when the brethren were about to sing prime, the lad rose up, and between signs and words made them understand that he must be released, pointing towards the mountains, and comporting himself much like a dog who wanted to be let out.

Perceiving that he meant to follow the track of the ladies, the friars not only opened the doors to him, but gave him a piece of black barley bread, with which he shot off, like an arrow from a bow, towards the place where the catastrophe had taken place.

George Douglas's mind wandered a good deal from the blow on his head, and it was not till two or three days had elapsed that he was able clearly to understand what his follower had discovered. Almost with the instinct of a Red Indian, Ringan had made his way. At first, indeed, the bushes had been sufficiently trampled for the track to be easy to find, but after the beech-trees with no underwood had been reached, he had often very slight indications to guide him. Where the halt had taken place, however, by the brook-side, there were signs of trampling, and even a few remnants of food; and after a long climb higher, he had come on the marks of the fall of a horse, and picked up a piece of a torn veil, which he recognised at once as belonging to the Lady Joanna. He inferred a struggle. What had they been doing to her?

Faithful Ringan had climbed on, and at length had come below the castle. He had been far too cautious to show himself while light lasted, but availing himself of the shelter of trees and of the projections, he had pretty well reconnoitred the castle as it stood on its steep slopes of turf, on the rounded summit of the hill, only scarped away on one side, whence probably the materials had been taken.

There could be no doubt that this was the prison of the princesses, and the character of the Barons of Balchenburg was only too well known to the good Franciscans.

'Soevi et feroces,' said the Prior to George, for Latin had turned out to be the most available medium of communication. Spite of Scott's averment in the mouth of George's grandson, Bell the Cat, that—

'Thanks to St Bothan, son of mine,
Save Gawain, ne'er could pen a line,'

the Douglases were far too clever to go without education, and young nobles who knew anything knew a little Latin. There was a consultation over what was to be done, and the Prior undertook to send one of his brethren into Nanci with Ringan, to explain the matter to King Rene, or, if he had left Nanci for Provence, to the governor left in charge. But a frontier baron like Balchenburg was a very serious difficulty to one so scrupulous in his relations with his neighbours as was good King Rene.

'A man of piety, peace, and learning,' said the Prior, 'and therefore despised by lawless men, like a sheep among wolves, though happy are we in living under such a prince.'

'Then what's the use of him and all his raree shows,' demanded the Scot, 'if he can neither hinder two peaceful maids from being carried off, nor will stir a finger to deliver them? Much should we heed borders and kings if it had been a Ridley or a Graeme who had laid hands on them.'

However, he consented to the Prior's proposal, and the incongruous pair set out together,—the sober-paced friar on the convent donkey, and Ringan on his shaggy pony,—both looking to civilised eyes equally rough and unkempt. At the gates they heard that King Rene had the day before set forth on his way to Aix, which boded ill for them, since more might be hoped from the impulsive chivalry of the King than from the strict scrupulosity of a responsible governor.

But they had not gone far on their way across the Place de La Carriere, where the tournament had been held, before Ringan startled his companion with a perfect howl, which had in it, however, an element of ecstasy, as he dashed towards a tall, bony figure in a blue cap, buff coat, and shepherd's plaid over one shoulder.

'Archie o' the Brake. Archie! Oh, ye're a sight for sair een! How cam' ye here?'

'Eh!' was the answer, equally astonished. 'Wha is it that cries on me here? Eh! eh! 'Tis never Ringan of the Raefoot-sae braw and grand?'

For Ringan was a wonderful step before him in civilisation.

Queries—'How cam' ye here?' and 'Whar' is the Master?'—were rapidly exchanged, while the friar looked on in amaze at the two wild-looking men, about whom other tall Scots, more or less well equipped, began to gather, coming from a hostelry near at hand.

The Earl of Angus, as they told him, had been neither to have nor to hold when first his embassy to Dunbar came back, and his son was found to be missing. He had been very near besieging the young King, until Bishop Kennedy had convinced him that no one of the Court had suspected the Master's presence, far less connived at his disappearance. The truth had been suspected before long, though there was no certainty until the letter that George Douglas had at last vouchsafed to write had, after spending a good deal of time on the road, at last reached Tantallon. Then the Earl had declared that, since his son had set out on this fool's errand, he should be suitably furnished for the heir of Angus, and should play his part as became him in their sports at Nanci, whither his letter said he was bound, instead of figuring as a mere groom of Drummond of Glenuskie, and still worse, in the train of a low-born Englishman like De la Pole.

So he had sent off ten lances, under a stout kinsman who had campaigned in France before—Sir Robert Douglas of Harside—with all their followers, and full equipment, such as might befit the heir of a branch of the great House of the Bleeding Heart. But their voyage had not been prosperous, and after riding from Flanders they had found the wedding over, and no one in the hostel having heard of the young Master of Angus, nor even having distinguished Sir Patrick Drummoud, though there was a vague idea that the Scottish king's sisters had been there.

Sir Robert Douglas had gone to have an interview with the governor left in charge. Thus the separation of the party became known to him—how the Drummonds had gone to Paris, and the Scottish ladies had set forth for Chalons; but there was nothing to show with whom the Master had gone. No sooner, then, had he come forth than half his men were round him shouting that here was Ringan of the Raefoot, that the Master had been foully betrayed, and that he was lying sair wounded at a Priory not far off.

Ringan, a perfectly happy man among those who not only had Scots tongues, but the Bleeding Heart on shield and breast, was brought up to him and told of the attack and capture of the princesses, and of the Master's wounds.

Sir Robert, after many imprecations, turned back to the governor, who heard the story in a far more complete form than if it had been related to him by Ringan and the friar.

But his hands were tied till he could communicate with King Rene, for border warfare was strictly forbidden, and unfortunately Duke Sigismund had left Nanci some days before for Luxembourg to meet the Duke of Burgundy.

However, just as George Douglas had persuaded the infirmarer to let him put on his clothes, there had been a clanging and jangling in the outer court, and the Lion and Eagle banner was visible. Duke Sigismund had drawn up there to water the horses, and to partake of any hospitality the Prior might offer him.

The first civilities were passing between them, when a tall figure, his red hair crossed by a bandage, his ruddy face paled, his steps faltering, came stumbling forward to the porch, crying, in his wonderful dialect between Latin and French,

'Sire, Domine Dux! Justitia! You loved the Lady Eleanor. Free her! They are prisoners to latroni—un routier—sceleratissimo—reiver—Balchenburg!'

Sigismund, ponderous and not very rapid, opened wide his big blue eyes, while the Prior explained in French, 'It is even so, beau sire. This poor man-at-arms was found bleeding on the way-side by our brethren, having been left for dead by the robbers of Balchenburg, who, it seems, descended on the ladies, dispersed their escort, and carried them off to the castle.'

Sigismund made some tremendously emphatic exclamation in German, and turned upon Douglas to interrogate him. They had very little of common language, but Sigismund knew French, though he hated it, and was not devoid of Latin, so that the narrative was made tolerably clear to him, and he had no doubts or scruples as to instantly calling the latrones to account, and releasing the ladies. He paced up and down the guest-chamber, his spurs clattering against the stone pavement, growling imprecations in guttural German, now and then tugging at his long fair hair as he pictured Eleanor in the miscreants' power, putting queries to George, more than could be understood or answered, and halting at door or window to shout orders to his knights to be ready at once for the attack. George was absolutely determined that, whatever his own condition, he would not be left behind, though he could only go upon Ringan's pony, and was evidently in Sigismund's opinion only a faithful groom.

It was hard to say whether he was relieved or not when there was evidently a vehement altercation in German between the Duke and a tough, grizzled old knight, the upshot of which turned out to be that the Ritter Gebhardt von Fuchstein absolutely refused to proceed through those pine and beech forests so late in the day; since it would be only too easy to lose the way, and there might be ambuscades or the like if Balchenburg and his crew were on the watch, and there was no doubt that they were allied with all the rentiers in the country.

Sigismund raged, but he was in some degree under the dominion of his prudent old Marskalk, and had to submit, while George knew that another night would further restore him, and would besides bring back his attendant.

The next hour brought more than he had expected. Again there was a clattering of hoofs, a few words with the porter, and to the utter amazement of the Prior, as well as of Duke Sigismund, who had just been served with a meal of Franciscan diet, a knight in full armour, with the crowned heart on his breast, dashed into the hall, threw a hasty bow to the Prior, and throwing his arms round the wounded man-at-arms, cried aloud, 'Geordie—the Master—ye daft callant! See what you have brought yourself to! What would the Yerl your father say?'

'I trow that I have been striving to do my devoir to my liege's sisters,' answered George. 'How does my father?—and my mother? Make your obeisance to the Duke of the Tirol, Rab. Ye can knap the French with him better than I. Now I can go with him as becomes a yerl's son, for the freedom of the lady!'

Sir Robert, a veteran Scot, who knew the French world well, was soon explaining matters to Duke Sigismund, who presently advanced to the heir of Angus, wrung his hand, and gave him to understand that he accepted him as a comrade in their doughty enterprise, and honoured his proceeding as a piece of knight-errantry. He was free from any question whether George was to be esteemed a rival by hearing it was the Lady Joanna for whose sake he thus adventured himself, whereas it was not her beauty, but her sister's intellect that had won the heart of Sigismund. Perhaps Sir Robert somewhat magnified the grandeur of the house of Douglas, for Sigismund seemed to view the young man as an equal, which he was not, as the Hapsburgs of Alsace and the Tirol were sovereign princes; but, on the other hand, George could count princesses among his ancestresses, and only Jean's personal ambition had counted his as a mesalliance.

It was determined to advance upon the Castle of Balchenburg the next morning, the ten Scottish lances being really forty men, making the Douglas's troop not much inferior to the Alsatian.

A night's rest greatly restored George, and equipments had been brought for him, which made him no longer appear only the man-at-arms, but the gallant young nobleman, though not yet entitled to the Golden Spurs.

Ringan served as their guide up the long hills, through the woods, up steep slippery slopes, where it became expedient to leave behind the big heavy war-horses under a guard, while the rest pushed forward, the Master of Angus's long legs nearly touching the ground, as, not to waste his strength, he was mounted on Ringan's sure-footed pony, which seemed at home among mountains. Sigismund himself, and the Tirolese among his followers, were chamois-hunters and used enough to climbing, and thus at length they found themselves at the foot of the green rounded slopes of the talchen or ballon, crowned by the fortress with its eight corner-turrets and the broader keep.

Were Elleen and Jean looking out—when the Alsatian trumpeter came forward in full array, and blew three sonorous blasts, echoing among the mountains, and doubtless bringing hope to the prisoners? The rugged walls of the castle had, however, an imperturbable look, and there was nothing responsive at the gateway.

A pursuivant then stood forth—for Sigismund had gone in full state to his intended wooing at Nanci—and called upon the Baron of Balchenburg to open his gates to his liege lord the Duke of Alsace.

On this a wicket was opened in the gate; but the answer, in a hoarse shout, was that the Baron of Balchenburg owned allegiance only, under the Emperor Frederick, to King Rene, Duke of Lorraine.

What hot words were thereupon spoken between Sigismund, Gebhardt, and the two Douglases it scarcely needs to tell; but, looking at the strength of the castle, it was agreed that it would be wiser to couple with the second summons an assurance that, though Duke Sigismund was the lawful lord of the mountain, and entrance was denied at the peril of the Baron, yet he would remit his first wrath, provided the royal ladies, foully and unjustly detained there in captivity, were instantly delivered up in all safety.

To this the answer came back, with a sound of derisive mockery—One was the intended wife of Baron Rudiger; the other should be delivered up to the Duke upon ransom according to her quality.

'The ransom I will pay,' roared Sigismund in German, 'shall be by the axe and cord!'

The while George Douglas gnashed his teeth with rage when the reply as to Jean had been translated to him. The Duke hurled his fierce defiance at the castle. It should be levelled with the ground, and the robbers should suffer by cord, wheel, and axe.

But what was the use of threats against men within six or eight feet every way of stone wall, with a steep slippery slope leading up to it? Heavily armed horsemen were of no avail against it. Even if there were nothing but old women inside, there was no means of making an entrance. Sigismund possessed three rusty cannon, made of bars of iron hooped together; but they were no nearer than Strasburg, and if they had been at hand, there was no getting them within distance of those walls.

There was nothing for it but to blockade the castle while sending after King Rene for assistance and authority. The worst of it was, that starving the garrison would be starving the captives; and likewise, so far up on the mountain, a troop of eighty or ninety men and horses were as liable to lack of provisions as could be the besieged garrison. Villages were distant, and transport not easy to find. Money was never abundant with Duke Sigismund, and had nearly all been spent on the entertainments at Nanci; nor could he make levies as lord of the country-folk, since the more accessible were not Alsatian, but Lorrainers, and to exasperate their masters by raids would bring fresh danger. Indeed, the two nearest castles were on Lorraine territory; their masters had not a much better reputation than the Balchenburgs, and, with the temptation of war-horses and men in their most holiday equipment, were only too likely to interpret Sigismund's attack as an invasion of their dukedom, and to fall in strength upon the party.

All this Gebhardt represented in strong colours, recommending that this untenable position should not be maintained.

Sigismund swore that nothing should induce him to abandon the unhappy ladies.

'Nay, my Lord Duke, it is only to retreat till King Rene sends his forces, and mayhap the French Dauphin.'

'To retreat would be to prolong their misery. Nay, the felons would think them deserted, and work their will. Out upon such craven counsel!'

'The captive ladies may be secured from an injury if your lordship holds a parley, demands the amount of ransom, and, without pledging yourself, undertakes to consult the Dauphin and their other kinsmen on the matter.'

'Detained here in I know not what misery, exposed to insults endless? Never, Gebhardt! I marvel that you can make such proposals to any belted knight!'

Gebhardt grumbled out, 'Rather to a demented lover! The Lord Duke will sing another tune ere long.'

Certainly it looked serious the next day when Sir Robert Douglas had had the greatest difficulty in hindering a hand-to-hand fight between the Scots and Alsatians for a strip of meadow land for pasture for their horses; when a few loaves of black bread were all that could be obtained from one village, and in another there had been a fray with the peasants, resulting in blows by way of payment for a lean cow and calf and four sheep. The Tirolese laid the blame on the Scots, the Scots upon the Tirolese; and though disputes between his Tirolese and Alsatian followers had been the constant trouble of Sigismund at Nanci, they now joined in making common cause against the Scots, so that Gebhardt strongly advised that these should be withdrawn to Nanci for the present, the which advice George Douglas hotly resented. He had as good a claim to watch the castle as the Duke. He was not going to desert his King's sisters, far less the lady he had followed from Scotland. If any one was to be ordered off, it should be the fat lazy Alsatians, who were good for nothing but to ride big Flemish horses, and were useless on a mountain.

Gebhardt and Robert Douglas, both experienced men of the world, found it one of their difficulties to keep the peace between their young lords; and each day was likely to render it more difficult. They began to represent that it could be made a condition that the leaders should be permitted to see the ladies and ascertain whether they were treated with courtesy; and there was a certain inclination on Sigismund's part, when he was driven hard by his embarrassments, to allow this to be proposed.

The very notion of coming to any terms made Geordie furious. If the craven Dutchman chose to sneak off and go in search of a ransom, forsooth, he would lie at the foot of the castle till he had burrowed through the walls or found a way over the battlements.

'Ay,' said Douglas of Harside drily, 'or till the Baron sticks you in the thrapple, or his next neighbour throws you into his dungeon.'

In the meantime the captives themselves were suffering, as may well be believed, agonies of suspense. Their loophole did not look out towards the gateway, but they heard the peals of the trumpet, started up with joy, and thought their deliverance was come. Eleanor threw herself on her knees; Lady Lindsay began to collect their properties; Jean made a rush for the stair leading to the top of the turret, but she found her way barred by one of the few men-at-arms, who held his pike towards her in a menacing manner.

She tried to gaze from the window, but it told her nothing, except that a certain murmur of voices broke upon the silence of the woods. Nothing more befell them. They eagerly interrogated Barbe.

'Ah yes, lady birds!' she said, 'there is a gay company without, all in glittering harness, asking for you, but my Lords know 'tis like a poor frog smelling at a walnut, for any knight of them all to try to make way into this castle!'

'Who are they? For pity's sake, tell us, dear Barbe,' entreated Eleanor.

'They say it is the Duke himself; but he has never durst meddle with my Lords before. All but the Hawk's tower is in Lorraine, and my Lord can bring a storm about his ears if he lifts a finger against us. A messenger would soon bring Banget and Steintour upon him. But never you fear, fair ladies, you have friends, and he will come to terms,' said good old Barbe, divided between pity for her guests and loyalty to her masters.

'If it is the Duke, he will free you, Elleen,' said Jean weeping; 'he will not care for me!'

'Jeanie, Jeanie, could you think I would be set free without you?'

'You might not be able to help yourself. 'Tis you that the German wants.'

'Never shall he have me if he be such a recreant, mansworn fellow as to leave my sister to the reiver. Never!'

'Ah! if poor Geordie were there, he would have moved heaven and earth to save me; but there is none to heed me now,' and Jean fell into a passion of weeping.

When they had to go down to supper, the younger Baron received them with the news—'So, ladies, the Duke has been shouting his threats at us, but this castle is too hard a nut for the like of him.'

'I have seen others crack their teeth against it,' said his father; and they both laughed, a hoarse derisive laugh.

The ladies vouchsafed not a word till they were allowed to retire to their chamber.

They listened in the morning for the sounds of an assault, but none came; there was absolutely nothing but an occasional hum of voices and clank of armour. When summoned to the mid-day meal, it was scanty.

'Ay,' said the elder Baron, we shall have to live hard for a day or two, but those outside will live harder.'

'Till they fall out and cut one another's throats,' said his son. 'Fasting will not mend the temper of Hans of Schlingen and Michel au Bec rouge.'

'Or till Banget descends on him for meddling on Lorraine ground,' added old Balchenburg. 'Eat, lady,' he added to Jean; 'your meals are not so large that they will make much odds to our stores. We have corn and beer enough to starve out those greedy knaves outside!'

Poor Jean was nearly out of her senses with distress and uncertainty, and being still weak, was less able to endure. She burst into violent hysterical weeping, and had to be helped up to her own room, where she sometimes lay on her bed; sometimes raged up and down the room, heaping violent words on the head of the tardy cowardly German; sometimes talking of loosing Skywing to show they were in the castle and cognisant of what was going on; but it was not certain that Skywing, with the lion rampant on his hood, would fly down to the besiegers, so that she would only be lost.

Eleanor, by the very need of soothing her sister, was enabled to be more tranquil. Besides, there was pleasure in the knowledge that Sigismund had come after her, and there was imagination enough in her nature to trust to the true knight daring any amount of dragons in his lady's cause. And the lady always had to be patient.

CHAPTER 11. FETTERS BROKEN

> Then long and loud the victor shout
> From turret and from tower rang out;
> The rugged walls replied.
> SCOTT, Lord of the Isles.

'Sir, I have something to show you.'

It was the early twilight of a summer's morning when Ringan crept up to the shelter of pine branches under which George Douglas was sleeping, after hotly opposing Gebhardt, who had nearly persuaded his master that retreat was inevitable, unless he meant to be deserted by more than half his men.

George sat up. 'Anent the ladies?' he said.

Ringan bowed his head, with an air of mystery and George doubted no longer, but let him lead the way, keeping among the brushwood to the foot of the quarry whence the castle had been built. It had once been absolutely precipitous, no doubt, but the stone was of a soft quality, on which weather told: ivy and creepers had grown on it, and Ringan pointed to what to dwellers on plains might have seemed impracticable, but to those who had bird's-nested on the crags of Tantallon had quite a different appearance. True, there was castle wall and turret above, but on this, the weather side, there had likewise been a slight crumbling, which had been neglected, perhaps from over security, perhaps on account of the extreme difficulty of repairing, where there was the merest ledge for foothold above the precipitous quarry; indeed, the condition of the place might never even have been perceived by the inhabitants, as there were no traces of the place below having been frequented.

'Tis a mere staircase as far as the foot of the walls compared with the Guillemot's crag,' observed Ringan.

'And a man with a heart and a foot could be up the wall in the corner where the ivy grows,' added George. 'It is well, Ringan, thou hast done good service. Here is the way.'

'With four or five of our own tall carles, we may win the castle, and laugh at the German pock-puddings,' added Ringan. 'Let them gang their gate, and we'll free our leddies.'

George was tempted, but he shook his head. 'That were scarce knightly towards the Duke,' he said. 'He has been gude friend to me, and I may not thus steal a march on him. Moreover, we ken na the strength of the loons within.'

'I misdoot there being mair than ten of them,' said Ringan. 'I have seen the same faces too often for there to be many. And what there be we shall take napping.'

That was true; nevertheless George Douglas felt bound in honour not to undertake the enterprise without the cognisance of his ally, though he much doubted the Germans being alert or courageous enough to take advantage of such a perilous clamber.

Sigismund had a tent under the pine-trees, and a guard before the entrance, who stood, halbert in hand, like a growling statue, when the young Scot would have entered, understanding not one word of his objurgations in mixed Scotch and French, but only barring the way, till Sigismund's own 'Wer da?' sounded from within.

'Moi—George of Angus!' shouted that individual in his awkward French. 'Let me in, Sir Duke; I have tidings!'

Sigismund was on foot in a moment. 'And from King Eene?' he asked.

'Far better, strong heart and steady foot can achieve the adventure and save the ladies unaided! Come with me, beau sire! Silently.'

George had fully expected to see the German quail at the frightful precipice and sheer wall before him, but the Hapsburg was primarily a Tirolean mountaineer, and he measured the rock with a glistening triumphant eye.

'Man can,' he said. 'That will we. Brave sire, your hand on it.'

The days were almost at their longest, and it was about five in the morning, the sun only just making his way over the screen of the higher hills to the north-east, though it had been daylight for some time.

Prudence made the two withdraw under the shelter of the woods, and there they built their plan, both young men being gratified to do so without their two advisers.

Neither of them doubted his own footing, and George was sure that three or four of the men who had come with Sir Robert were equally good cragsmen. Sigismund sighed for some Tirolese whom he had left at home, but he had at least one man with him ready to dare any height; and he thought a rope would make all things sure. Nothing could be attempted till the next night, or rather morning, and Sigismund decided on sending a messenger down to the Franciscans to borrow or purchase a rope, while George and Ringan, more used to shifts, proceeded to twist together all the horses' halters they could collect, so as to form a strong cable.

To avert suspicion, Sigismund appeared to have yielded to the murmurs of his people, and sent more than half his troop down the hill, in the expectation that he was about to follow. The others were withdrawn under one clump of wood, the Scotsmen under another, with orders to advance upon the gateway of the castle so soon as they should hear a summons from the Duke's bugle, or the cry, 'A Douglas!' Neither Sir Gebhardt nor Sir Robert was young enough or light enough to attempt the climb, each would fain have withheld his master, had it been possible, but they would have their value in dealing with the troop waiting below.

So it came to pass that when Eleanor, anxious, sorrowful, heated, and weary, awoke at daydawn and crept from the side of her sleeping sister to inhale a breath of morning breeze and murmur a morning prayer, as she gazed from her loophole over the woods with a vague, never-quenchable hope of seeing something, she became aware of something very stealthy below—the rustling of a fox, or a hare in the fern mayhap, though she could not see to the bottom of the quarry, but she clung to the bar, craned forward, and beheld far down a shaking of the ivy and white-flowered rowan; then a hand, grasping the root of a little sturdy birch, then a yellow head gradually drawn up, till a thin, bony, alert figure was for a moment astride on the birch. Reaching higher, the sunburnt, freckled face was lifted up, and Eleanor's heart gave a great throb of hope. Was it not the wild boy, Ringan Raefoot? She could not turn away her head, she durst not even utter a word to those within, lest it should be a mere fancy, or a lad from the country bird's-nesting. Higher, higher he went, lost for a moment among the leaves and branches, then attaining a crag, in some giddy manner. But, but—what was that head under a steel cap that had appeared on the tree? What was that face raised for a moment? Was it the face of the dead? Eleanor forced back a cry, and felt afraid of wakening herself from what she began to think only a blissful dream,—all the more when that length of limb had reared itself, and attained to the dizzy crag above. A fairer but more solid face, with a long upper lip, appeared, mounting in its turn. She durst not believe her eyes, and she was not conscious of making any sound, unless it was the vehement beating of her own heart; but perhaps it was the power of her own excitement that communicated itself to her sleeping sister, for Jean's voice was heard, 'What is it, Elleen; what is it?'

She signed back with her hand to enjoin silence, for her sense began to tell her that this must be reality, and that castles had before now been thus surprised by brave Scotsmen. Jean was out of bed and at the loophole in a moment. There was room for only one, and Eleanor yielded the place, the less reluctantly that the fair head had reached the part veiled by the tree, and Jean's eyes would be an evidence that she herself might trust her own sight.

Jean's glance first fell on the backs of the ascending figures, now above the crag. 'Ah! ah!' she cried, under her breath, 'a surprise—a rescue! Oh! the lad— stretching, spreading! The man below is holding his foot. Oh! that tuft of grass won't bear him. His knees are up. Yes—yes! he is even with the top of the wall now. Elleen! Hope! Brave laddie! Why—'tis—yes—'tis Ringan. Now the other, the muckle carle—Ah!' and then a sudden breathless silence came over her.

Eleanor knew she had recognised that figure!

Madame de Ste. Petronelle was awake now, asking what this meant.

'Deliverance!' whispered Eleanor. 'They are scaling the wall. Oh, Jean, one moment—'

'I canna, I canna,' cried Jean, grasping the iron bar with all her might: 'I see his face; he is there on the ledge, at fit of the wall, in life and strength. Ringan—yes, Ringan is going up the wall like a cat!'

'Where is he? Is he safe—the Duke, I would say?' gasped Eleanor. 'Oh, let me see, Jeanie.'

'The Duke, is it? Ah! Geordie is giving a hand to help him on the ground. Tak' tent, tak' tent, Geordie. Dinna coup ower. Ah! they are baith there, and one—two —three muckle fellows are coming after them.'

'Climbing up there!' exclaimed the Dame, bustling up. 'God speed them. Those are joes worth having, leddies!'

'There! there—Geordie is climbing now. St. Bride speed him, and hide them. Well done, Duke! He hoisted him so far. Now his hand is on that broken stone.

Up! up! His foot is in the cleft now! His hand—oh!—clasps the ivy! God help him! Ah, he feels about. Yes, he has it. Now—now the top of the battlement. I see no more. They are letting down a rope. Your Duke disna climb like my Geordie, Elleen!'

'Oh, for mercy's sake, to your prayers, dinna wrangle about your joes, bairns,' cried Madame de Ste. Petronelle. 'The castle's no won yet!'

'But is as good as won,' said Eleanor. 'There are barely twelve fighting men in it, and sorry loons are the maist. How many are up yet, Jeanie?'

'There's a fifth since the Duke yet to come up,' answered Jean, 'eight altogether, counting the gallant Ringan. There!'

"Tis the warder's horn. They have been seen!' and the poor women clasped their hands in fervent prayer, with ears intent; but Jean suddenly darted towards her clothes, and they hastily attired themselves, then cautiously peeped out at their door, since neither sight nor sound came to them from either window. The guard who had hindered their passage was no longer there, and Jean led the way down the spiral stairs. At the slit looking into the court they heard cries and the clash of arms, but it was too high above their heads for anything to be seen, and they hastened on.

There also in the narrow court was a fight going on—but nearly ended. Geordie Douglas knelt over the prostrate form of Rudiger von Balchenburg, calling on him to yield, but meeting no answer. One or two other men lay overthrown, three or four more were pressed up against a wall, howling for mercy. Sigismund was shouting to them in German—Ringan and the other assailants standing guard over them; but evidently hardly withheld from slaughtering them. The maidens stood for a moment, then Jean's scream of welcome died on her lips, for as he looked up from his prostrate foe, and though he had not yet either spoken or risen, Sigismund had stepped to his side, and laid his sword on his shoulder.

'Victor!' said he, 'in the name of God and St. Mary, I make thee Chevalier. Rise, Sire George of Douglas!'

'True knight!' cried Jean, leaping to his side. 'Oh, Geordie, Geordie, thou hast saved us! Thou noblest knight!'

'Ah! Lady, it canna be helpit,' said the new knight. "Tis no treason to your brother to be dubbed after a fair fight, though 'tis by a Dutch prince.'

'Thy King's sister shall mend that, and bind your spurs,' said Jean. 'Is the reiver dead, Geordie?'

'Even so,' was the reply. 'My sword has spared his craig from the halter.'

Such were the times, and such Jean's breeding, that she looked at the fallen enemy much as a modern lady may look at a slain tiger.

Eleanor had meantime met Sigismund with, 'Ah! well I knew that you would come to our aid. So true a knight must achieve the adventure!'

'Safe, safe, I am blessed and thankful,' said the Duke, falling on one knee to kiss her hand. 'How have these robbers treated my Lady?'

'Well, as well as they know how. That good woman has been very kind to us,' said Eleanor, as she saw Barbe peeping from the stair. 'Come hither, Barbe and Trudchen, to the Lord Duke's mercy.'

They were entering the hall, and, at the same moment, the gates were thrown open, and the men waiting with Gebhardt and Robert Douglas began to pour in. It was well for Barbe and her daughter that they could take shelter behind the ladies, for the men were ravenous for some prize, or something to wreak their excitement upon, besides the bare walls of the castle, and its rude stores of meal and beer. The old Baron was hauled down from his bed by half-a-dozen men, and placed before the Duke with bound hands.

'Hola, Siege!' said he in German, all unabashed. 'You have got me at last—by a trick! I always bade Rudiger look to that quarry; but young men think they know best.'

'The old traitor!' said George in French. 'Hang him from his tower for a warning to his like, as we should do in Scotland.'

'What cause have you to show why we should not do as saith the knight?' said Sigismund.

'I care little how it goes with my old carcase now,' returned Balchenburg, in the spirit of the Amalekite of old. 'I only mourn that I shall not be there to see the strife you will breed with the lute-twanger or his fellows at Nanci.'

Gebhardt here gave his opinion that it would be wise to reserve the old man for King Rene's justice, so as to obviate all peril of dissension. The small garrison, to be left in the castle under the most prudent knight whom Gebhardt could select, were instructed only to profess to hold it till the Lords of Alsace and Lorraine should jointly have determined what was to be done with it.

It was not expedient to tarry there long. A hurried meal was made, and then the victors set out on the descent. George had found his good steed in the stables, together with the ladies' palfreys, and there had been great joy in the mutual recognition; but Jean's horse was found to show traces of its fall, and her arm was not yet entirely recovered, so that she was seated on Ringan's sure-footed pony, with the new-made knight walking by her side to secure its every step, though Ringan grumbled that Sheltie would be far safer if left to his own wits.

Sigismund was proposing to make for Sarrebourg, when the glittering of lances was seen in the distance, and the troop was drawn closely together, for the chance that, as had been already thought probable, some of the Lorrainers had risen as to war and invasion. However, the banner soon became distinguishable, with the many quarterings, showing that King Rene was there in person; and Sigismund rode forward to greet him and explain.

The chivalrous King was delighted with the adventure, only wishing he had shared in the rescue of the captive princesses. 'Young blood,' he said. 'Youth has all the guerdons reserved for it, while age is lagging behind.'

Yet so soon as Sir Patrick Drummond had overtaken him at Epinal, he had turned back to Nanci, and it was in consequence of what he there heard that he had set forth to bring the robbers of Balchenburg to reason. To him there was no difficulty in accepting thankfully what some would have regarded as an aggression on the part of the Duke of Alsace, and though old Balchenburg, when led up before him, seemed bent upon aggravating him. 'Ha! Sir King, so a young German and a wild Scot have done what you, with all your kingdoms, have never had the wit to do.'

'The poor old man is distraught,' said the King, while Sigismund put in—

'Mayhap because you never ventured on such audacious villainy and outrecuidance before.'

'Young blood will have its way,' repeated the old man. 'Nay, I told the lad no good would come of it, but he would have it that he had his backers, and in sooth that escort played into his hands. Ha! ha! much will the fair damsels' royal beaufrere thank you for overthrowing his plan for disposing of them.'

'Hark you, foul-mouthed fellow,' said King Rene; 'did I not pity you for your bereavement and ruin, I should requite that slander of a noble prince by hanging you on the nearest tree.'

'Your Grace is kindly welcome,' was the answer.

Rene and Sigismund, however, took counsel together, and agreed that the old man should, instead of this fate, be relegated to an abbey, where he might at least have the chance of repenting of his crimes, and be kept in safe custody.

'That's your mercy,' muttered the old mountain wolf when he heard their decision.

All this was settled as they rode back along the way where Madame de Ste. Petronelle had first become alarmed. She had now quite resumed her authority and position, and promised protection and employment to Barbe and Trudchen. The former had tears for 'her boy,' thus cut off in his sins; but it was what she always foreboded for him, and if her old master was not thankful for the grace offered him, she was for him.

King Rene, who believed not a word against his nephew, intended himself to conduct the ladies to the Court of his sister, and see them in safety there. Jean, however, after the first excitement, so drooped as she rode, and was so entirely unable to make answer to all the kindness around her, that it was plain that she must rest as soon as possible, and thus hospitality was asked at a little country castle, around which the suite encamped. A pursuivant was, however, despatched by Rene to the French Court to announce the deliverance of the princesses, and Sir Patrick sent his son David with the party, that his wife and the poor Dauphiness might be fully reassured.

There was a strange stillness over Chateau le Surry when David rode in triumphantly at the gate. A Scottish archer, who stood on guard, looked up at him anxiously with the words, 'Is it weel with the lassies?' and on his reply, 'They are sain and safe, thanks, under Heaven, to Geordie Douglas of Angus!' the man exclaimed, 'On, on, sir squire, the saints grant ye may not be too late for the puir Dolfine! Ah! but she has been sair misguided.'

'Is my mother here?' asked David.

'Ay, sir, and with the puir lady. Ye may gang in without question. A' the doors be open, that ilka loon may win in to see a princess die.'

The pursuivant, hearing that the King and Dauphin were no longer in the castle, rode on to Chalons, but David dismounted, and followed a stream of persons, chiefly monks, friars, and women of the burgher class, up the steps, and on into the vaulted room, the lower part shut off by a rail, against which crowded the curious and only half-awed multitude, who whispered to each other, while above, at a temporary altar, bright with rows of candles, priests intoned prayers. The atmosphere was insufferably hot, and David could hardly push forward; but as he exclaimed in his imperfect French that he came with tidings of Madame's sisters, way was made, and he heard his mother's voice. 'Is it? Is it my son? Bring him. Oh, quickly!'

He heard a little, faint, gasping cry, and as a lane was opened for him, struggled onwards. In poor Margaret's case the etiquette that banished the nearest kin from Royalty in articulo mortis was not much to be regretted. David saw her—white, save for the death-flush called up by the labouring breath, as she lay upheld in his mother's arms, a priest holding a crucifix before her, a few ladies kneeling by the bed.

'Good tidings, I see, my son,' said Lady Drummond.

'Are—they—here?' gasped Margaret.

'Alack, not yet, Madame; they will come in a few days' time.' She gave a piteous sigh, and David could not hear her words.

'Tell her how and where you found them,' said his mother.

David told his story briefly. There was little but a quivering of the heavy eyelids and a clasping of the hands to show whether the dying woman marked him, but when he had finished, she said, so low that only his mother heard, 'Safe! Thank God! Nunc dimittis. Who was it—young Angus?'

'Even so,' said David, when the question had been repeated to him by his mother.

'So best!' sighed Margaret. 'Bid the good father give thanks.'

Dame Lilias dismissed her son with a sign. Margaret lay far more serene. For a few minutes there was a sort of hope that the good news might inspire fresh life, and yet, after the revelation of what her condition was in this strange, frivolous, hard-hearted Court, how could life be desired for her weary spirit? She did not seem to wish—far less to struggle to wish—to live to see them again; perhaps there was an instinctive feeling that, in her weariness, there was no power of rousing herself, and she would rather sink undisturbed than hear of the terror and suffering that she knew but too well her husband had caused.

Only, when it was very near the last, she said, 'Safe! safe in leal hands. Oh, tell my Jeanie to be content with them—never seek earthly crowns—ashes—ashes—Elleen—Jeanie—all of them—my love-oh! safe, safe. Now, indeed, I can pardon—'

'Pardon!' said the French priest, catching the word. 'Whom, Madame, the Sieur de Tillay?'

Even on the gasping lips there was a semi-smile. 'Tillay—I had forgotten! Tillay, yes, and another.'

If no one else understood, Lady Drummond did, that the forgiveness was for him who had caused the waste and blight of a life that might have been so noble and so sweet, and who had treacherously prepared a terrible fate for her young innocent sisters.

It was all ended now; there was no more but to hear the priest commend the parting Christian soul, while, with a few more faint breaths, the soul of Margaret of Scotland passed beyond the world of sneers, treachery, and calumny, to the land 'where the wicked cease from troubling, and where the weary are at rest.'

CHAPTER 12. SORROW ENDED

'Done to death by slanderous tongues
   Was the Hero that here lies:
Death, avenger of wrongs,
   Gives her fame which never dies.'
                Much Ado About Nothing.

A day's rest revived Jean enough to make her eager to push on to Chalons, and enough likewise to revive her coquettish and petulant temper.

Sigismund and Eleanor might ride on together in a species of paradise, as having not only won each other's love, but acted out a bit of the romance that did not come to full realisation much more often in those days than in modern ones. They were quite content to let King Rene glory in them almost as much as he had arrived at doing in his own daughter and her Ferry, and they could be fully secure; Sigismund had no one's consent to ask, save a formal licence from his cousin, the Emperor Frederick III., who would pronounce him a fool for wedding a penniless princess, but had no real power over him; while Eleanor was certain that all her kindred would feel that she was fulfilling her destiny, and high sweet thoughts of thankfulness and longing to be a blessing to him who loved her, and to those whom he ruled, filled her spirit as she rode through the shady woods and breezy glades, bright with early summer.

Jean, however, was galled by the thought that every one at home would smile and say that she might have spared her journey, and that, in spite of all her beauty, she had just ended by wedding the Scottish laddie whom she had scorned. True, her heart knew that she loved him and none other, and that he truly merited her; but her pride was not willing that he should feel that he had earned her as a matter of course, and she was quite as ungracious to Sir George Douglas, the Master of Angus, as ever she had been to Geordie of the Red Peel, and she showed all the petulance of a semi-convalescent. She would not let him ride beside her, his horse made her palfrey restless, she said; and when King Rene talked about her true knight, she pretended not to understand.

'Ah!' he said, 'be consoled, brave sire; we all know it is the part of the fair lady to be cruel and merciless. Let me sing you a roman both sad and true!'

Which good-natured speech simply irritated George beyond bearing. 'The daft old carle,' muttered he to Sir Patrick, 'why cannot he let me gang my ain gate, instead of bringing all their prying eyes on me? If Jean casts me off the noo, it will be all his fault.'

These small vexations, however, soon faded out of sight when the drooping, half-hoisted banner was seen on the turrets of Chateau le Surry, and the clang of a knell came slow and solemn on the wind.

No one was at first visible, but probably a warder had announced their approach, for various figures issued from the gateway, some coming up to Rene, and David Drummond seeking his father. The tidings were in one moment made known to the two poor girls—a most sudden shock, for they had parted with their sister in full health, as they thought, and Sir Patrick had only supposed her to have been chilled by the thunderstorm. Yet Eleanor's first thought was, 'Ah! I knew it! Would that I had clung closer to her and never been parted.' But the next moment she was startled by a cry—Jean had slid from her horse, fainting away in George Douglas's arms.

Madame de Ste. Petronelle was at hand, and the Lady of Glenuskie quickly on the spot; and they carried her into the hall, where she revived, and soon was in floods of tears. These were the days when violent demonstration was unchecked and admired as the due of the deceased, and all stood round, weeping with her. King Charles himself leaning forward to wring her hands, and cry, 'My daughter, my good daughter!' As soon as the first tempest had subsided, the King supported Eleanor to the chapel, where, in the midst of rows of huge wax candles, Margaret lay with placid face, and hands clasped over a crucifix, as if on a tomb, the pall that covered all except her face embellished at the sides with the blazonry of France and Scotland. Her husband, with his thin hands clasped, knelt by her head, and requiems were being sung around by relays of priests. There was fresh weeping and wailing as the sisters cast sprinklings of holy water on her, and then Jean, sinking down quite exhausted, was supported away to a chamber where the sisters could hear the story of these last sad days from Lady Drummond.

The solemnities of Margaret's funeral took their due course—a lengthy one, and then, or rather throughout, there was the consideration what was to come next. Too late, all the Court seemed to have wakened to regret for Margaret. She had been open-handed and kindly, and the attendants had loved her, while the ladies who had gossiped about her habits now found occupation for their tongues in indignation against whosoever had aspersed her discretion. The King himself, who had always been lazily fond of the belle fille who could amuse him, was stirred, perhaps by Rene, into an inquiry into the scandalous reports, the result of which was that Jamet de Tillay was ignominiously banished from the Court, and Margaret's fair fame vindicated, all too late to save her heart from breaking. The displeasure that Charles expressed to his son in private on the score of poor Margaret's wrongs, is, in fact, believed to have been the beginning of the breach which widened continually, till finally the unhappy father starved himself to death in a morbid dread of being poisoned by his son.

However, for the present, the two Scottish princesses reaped the full benefit of all the feeling for their sister. The King and Queen called them their dearest daughters, and made all sorts of promises of marrying and endowing them, and Louis himself went outwardly through all the forms of mourning and devotion, and treated his two fair sisters with extreme civility, such as they privately declared they could hardly bear, when they recollected how he had behaved before Margaret.

Jean in especial flouted him with all the sharpness and pertness of which she was capable; but do what she would, he received it all with a smiling indifference and civility which exasperated her all the more.

The Laird and Lady of Glenuskie were in some difficulty. They could not well be much longer absent from Scotland, and yet Lilias had promised the poor Dauphiness not to leave her sisters except in some security. Eleanor's fate was plain enough, Sigismund followed her about as her betrothed, and the only question was whether, during the period of mourning, he should go back to his dominions to collect a train worthy of his marriage with a king's daughter; but this he was plainly reluctant to do. Besides the unwillingness of a lover to lose sight of his lady, the catastrophe that had befallen the sisters might well leave a sense that they needed protection. Perhaps, too, he might expect murmurs at his choice of a dowerless princess from his vassals of the Tirol.

At any rate, he lingered and accompanied the Court to Tours, where in the noble old castle the winter was to be spent.

There Sir Patrick and his wife were holding a consultation. Their means were well-nigh exhausted. What they had collected for their journey was nearly spent, and so was the sum with which Cardinal Beaufort had furnished his nieces. It was true that Eleanor and Jean were reckoned as guests of the French King, and the knight and lady and attendants as part of their suite; but the high proud Scottish spirits could not be easy in this condition, and they longed to depart, while still by selling the merely ornamental horses and some jewels they could pay their journey. But then Jean remained a difficulty. To take her back to Scotland was the most obvious measure, where she could marry George of Angus as soon as the mourning was ended.

'Even if she will have him,' said Dame Lilias, 'I doubt me whether her proud spirit will brook to go home unwedded.'

'Dost deem the lassie is busking herself for higher game? That were an evil requital for his faithful service and gallant daring.'

'I cannot tell,' said Lilias. 'The maid has always been kittle to deal with. I trow she loves Geordie in her inmost heart, but she canna thole to feel herself bound to him, and it irks her that when her sisters are wedded to sovereign princes, she should gang hame to be gudewife to a mere Scots Earl's son.'

'The proud unthankful peat! Leave her to gang her ain gate, Lily. And yet she is a bonny winsome maid, that I canna cast off.'

'Nor I, Patie, and I have gi'en my word to her sister. Yet gin some prince cam' in her way, I'd scarce give much for Geordie's chance.'

'The auld king spake once to me of his younger son, the Duke of Berry, as they call him,' said Sir Patrick; 'but the Constable told me that was all froth, the young duke must wed a princess with a tocher.'

'I trust none will put it in our Jeanie's light brain,' sighed Lily, 'or she will be neither to have nor to hold.'

The consultation was interrupted by the sudden bursting in of Jean herself. She flew up to her friends with outstretched hands, and hid her face in Lilias's lap.

'Oh, cousins, cousins! tak' me away out of his reach. He has been the death of poor Meg, now he wants to be mine.'

They could not understand her at first, and indeed shame as well as dismay made her incoherent—for what had been proposed to her was at that time unprecedented. It is hard to believe it, yet French historians aver that the Dauphin Louis actually thought of obtaining a dispensation for marrying her. In the unsettled condition of the Church, when it was divided by the last splinterings, as it were, of the great schism, perhaps the astute Louis deemed that any prince might obtain anything from whichever rival Pope he chose to acknowledge, though it was reserved for Alexander Borgia to grant the first licence of this kind. To Jean the idea was simply abhorrent, alike as regarded her instincts and for the sake of the man himself. His sneering manner towards her sister had filled her with disgust and indignation, and he had, in those days, been equally contemptuous towards herself—besides which she was aware of his share in her capture by Balchenburg, and whispers had not respected the manner in which his silence had fostered the slanders that had broken Margaret's heart.

'I would sooner wed a viper!' she said.

What was Louis's motive it is very hard to guess. Perhaps there was some real admiration of Jean's beauty, and it seems to have been his desire that his wife should be a nonentity, as was shown in his subsequent choice of Charlotte of Savoy. Now Jean was in feature very like her sister Isabel, Duchess of Brittany, who was a very beautiful woman, but not far from being imbecile, and Louis had never seen Jean display any superiority of intellect or taste like Margaret or Eleanor, but rather impatience of their pursuits, and he therefore might expect her to be equally simple with the other sister. However that might be, Sir Patrick was utterly incredulous; but when his wife asked Madame Ste. Petronelle's opinion, she shook her head, and said the Sire Dauphin was a strange ower cannie chiel, and advised that Maitre Jaques Coeur should be consulted.

'Who may he be?'

'Ken ye not Jaques Coeur? The great merchant of Bourges—the man to whom, above all others, France owes it that we be not under the English yoke. The man, I say, for it was the poor Pucelle that gave the first move, and ill enough was her reward, poor blessed maiden as she was. A saint must needs die a martyr's death, and they will own one of these days that such she was! But it was Maitre Coeur that stirred the King and gave him the wherewithal to raise his men—lending, they called it, but it was out of the free heart of a true Frenchman who never looked to see it back again, nor even thanks for it!'

'A merchant?' asked Sir Patrick.

'Ay, the mightiest merchant in the realm. You would marvel to see his house at Bourges. It would fit a prince! He has ships going to Egypt and Africa, and stores of silk enough to array all the dames and demoiselles in France! Jewels fit for an emperor, perfumes like a very grove of camphire. Then he has mines of silver and copper, and the King has given him the care of the coinage. Everything prospers that he sets his hand to, and he well deserves it, for he is an honest man where honest men are few.'

'Is he here?'

'Yea; I saw his green hood crossing the court of the castle this very noon. The

King can never go on long without him, though there are those that so bate him that I fear he may have a fall one of these days. Methinks I heard that he ay hears his morning mass when here at the little chapel of St. James, close to the great shrine of St. Martin, at six of the clock in the morning, so as to be private. You might find him there, and whatever he saith to you will be sooth, whether it be as you would have it, or no.'

On consideration Sir Patrick decided to adopt the lady's advice, and on her side she reflected that it might be well to take care that the interview did not fail for want of recognition.

The glorious Cathedral of Tours was standing up dark, but with glittering windows, from the light within deepening the stained glass, and throwing out the beauty of the tracery, while the sky, brightening in the autumn morning, threw the towers into relief, when, little recking of all this beauty, only caring to find the way, Sir Patrick on the one hand, the old Scots French lady on the other, went their way to the noble west front, each wrapped in a long cloak, and not knowing one another, till their eyes met as they gave each other holy water at the door, after the habit of strangers entering at the same time.

Then Madame de Ste. Petronelle showed the way to the little side chapel, close to the noble apse. There, beneath the six altar-candles, a priest was hurrying through a mass in a rapid ill-pronounced manner, while, besides his acolyte, worshippers were very few. Only the light fell on the edges of a dark-green velvet cloak and silvered a grizzled head bowed in reverence, and Madame de Ste. Petronelle touched Sir Patrick and made him a significant sign.

Daylight was beginning to reveal itself by the time the brief service was over. Sir Patrick, stimulated by the lady, ventured a few steps forward, and accosted Maitre Coeur as he rose, and drawing forward his hood was about to leave the church.

'Beau Sire, a word with you. I am the kinsman and attendant of the Scottish King's sisters.'

'Ah! one of them is to be married. My steward is with me. It is to him you should speak of her wardrobe,' said Jaques Coeur, an impatient look stealing over his keen but honest visage.

'It is not of Duke Sigismund's betrothed that I would speak,' returned the Scottish knight; 'it is of her sister.'

Jaques Coeur's dark eyes cast a rapid glance, as of one who knew not who might lurk in the recesses of a twilight cathedral.

'Not here,' he said, and he led Sir Patrick away with him down the aisle, out into the air, where a number of odd little buildings clustered round the walls of the cathedral, even leaning against it, heedless of the beauty they marred.

'By your leave, Father,' he said, after exchanging salutations with a priest, who was just going out to say his morning's mass, and leaving his tiny bare cell empty. Here Sir Patrick could incredulously tell his story, and the merchant could only sigh and own that he feared that there was every reason to believe that the intention was real. Jaques Coeur, religiously, was shocked at the idea, and, politically, wished the Dauphin to make a more profitable alliance. He whispered that the sooner the lady was out of reach the better, and even offered to advance a loan to facilitate the journey.

There followed a consultation in the securest place that could be devised, namely, in the antechamber where Sir Patrick and Lady Drummond slept to guard their young princesses, in the palace at Tours, Jean, Eleanor, and Madame de Ste. Petronelle having a bedroom within.

Sir Patrick's view was that Jean might take her leave in full state and honour, leaving Eleanor to marry her Duke in due time; but the girl shuddered at this. 'Oh no, no; he would call himself my brother for the nonce and throw me into some convent! There is nothing for it but to make it impossible. Sir Patie, fetch Geordie, and tell him, an' he loves me, to wed me on the spot, and bear me awa' to bonnie Scotland. Would that I had never been beguiled into quitting it.'

'Geordie Douglas! You were all for flouting him a while ago,' said Eleanor, puzzled.

'Dinna be sae daft like, Elleen, that was but sport, and—and a maid may not hold herself too cheap! Geordie that followed me all the way from home, and was sair hurt for me, and freed me from yon awsome castle. Oh, could ye trow that I could love ony but he?'

It was not too easy to refrain from saying, 'So that's the end of all your airs,' but the fear of making her fly off again withheld Lady Drummond, and even Eleanor.

George did not lodge in the castle, and Sir Patrick could not sound him till the morning; but for a long space after the two sisters had laid their heads on the pillow Jean was tossing, sometimes sobbing; and to her sister's consolations she replied, 'Oh, Elleen, he can never forgive me! Why did my hard, dour, ungrateful nature so sport with his leal loving heart? Will he spurn me the now? Geordie, Geordie, I shall never see your like! It would but be my desert if I were left behind to that treacherous spiteful prince,—I wad as soon be a mouse in a cat's claw!'

But George of Angus made no doubt. He had won his ladylove at last, and the only further doubt remained as to how the matter was to be carried out. Jaques Coeur was consulted again. No priest at Tours would, he thought, dare to perform the ceremony, for fear of after-vengeance of the Dauphin; and Sir Patrick then suggested Father Romuald, who had been lingering in his train waiting to cross the Alps till his Scotch friends should have departed and winter be over; but the deed would hardly be safely done within the city.

The merchant's advice was this: Sir Patrick, his Lady, and the Master of Angus had better openly take leave of the Court and start on the way to Brittany. No opposition would be made, though if Louis suspected Lady Jean's presence in their party, he might close the gates and detain her; Jaques Coeur therefore thought she had better travel separately at first. For Eleanor, as the betrothed bride of Sigismund, there was no might therefore remain at Court with the Queen. Jaques Coeur, the greatest merchant of his day, had just received a large train of waggons loaded with stuffs and other wares from Bourges, on the way to Nantes, and he proposed that the Lady Jean should travel with one attendant female in one of these, passing as the wife and daughter of the foreman. These two personages had actually travelled to Tours, and were content to remain there, while their places were taken by Madame de Ste. Petronelle and Jean.

We must not describe the parting of the sisters, nor the many messages sent by Elleen to bonny Scotland, and the brothers and sisters she was willing to see no more for the sake of her Austrian Duke. Of her all that needs to be said is that she lived and died happy and honoured, delighting him by her flow of wit and poetry, and only regretting that she was a childless wife.

Barbe and Trudchen were to remain in her suite, Barbe still grieving for 'her boy,' and hoping to devote all she could obtain as wage or largesse to masses for his soul, and Trudchen, very happy in the new world, though being broken in with some difficulty to civilised life.

Having been conveyed by by-streets to the great factory or shop of Maltre Coeur at Tours, a wonder in itself, though far inferior to his main establishment at Bourges, Madame de Ste. Petronelle and Jean, with her faithful Skywing nestled under her cloak, were handed by Jaques himself to seats in a covered wain, containing provisions for them and also some more delicate wares, destined for the Duchess of Brittany. He was himself in riding gear, and a troop of armed servants awaited him on horseback.

'Was he going with them?' Jean asked.

'Not all the way,' he said; but he would not part with the lady till he had resigned her to the charge of the Sire de Glenuskie. The state of should accompany any valuable convoy, that his going with the party would excite no suspicion.

So they journeyed on in the wain at the head of a quarter of a mile of waggons and pack-horses, slowly indeed, but so steadily that they were sure of a good start before the princess's departure was known to the Court.

It was at the evening halt at a conventual grange that they came up with the rest of the party, and George Douglas spurred forward to meet them, and hold out his eager arms as Jean sprang from the waggon. Wisdom as well as love held that it would be better that Jean should enter Brittany as a wife, so that the Duke might not be bribed or intimidated into yielding her to Louis. It was in the little village church, very early the next morning, that George Douglas received the reward of his long patience in the hand of Joanna Stewart, a wiser, less petulant, and more womanly being than the vain and capricious lassie whom he had followed from Scotland two years previously.

Printed in Great Britain
by Amazon